D1580882

CATCH THE FALLEN SPARROW

Priscilla Masters

Joanna Piercy
Mystery Series No 2

Published in 2014 by Telos Moonrise: Criminal Pursuits
(An imprint of Telos Publishing Ltd)
17 Pendre Avenue, Prestatyn, LL19 9SH

Catch the Fallen Sparrow © 1996, 2014 Priscilla Masters

Cover Design: David J Howe
Cover Art: Iain Robertson

ISBN: 978-1-84583-884-3

The moral right of the author has been asserted.

British Library Cataloguing in Publication Data. A
catalogue record for this book is available from the
British Library.

This book is sold subject to the condition that it shall not
by way of trade or otherwise, be lent, resold, hired out or
otherwise circulated without the publisher's prior
written consent in any form of binding or cover other
than that in which it is published and without a similar
condition including this condition being imposed on the
subsequent purchaser.

1

The man's head had been carved out of rock. The distinctive shape black against the violent pink of the dawn sky: large domed forehead, crooked broken nose, granite chin pointing down towards the foot of the mountain. It had been naturally carved, by wind, by rain, by season's weathering, by frost that had split deep fissures into the crags. Bitter cold and unprotected from miles and miles of moorland, high soft ground with no guiding path and one solitary road that crossed it. It was no place to be on this chill morning that heralded the first frost of the winter. Here – so high – wind blasted the granite man, but he never moved except to wink at people passing along the road. This wink was a trick of nature – rock behind a hole – that made the eye appear to close and open again as the traveller passed.

Normally at this time of the morning there was no sign of human habitation – a few skylarks, a kestrel, rabbits, stoats, weasels, but no sign of man.

This morning was different.

As pink was glazed with gold, a wisp of smoke heavy with the scent of burning meat touched the damp air. A small blue spiral wound upwards across the ridge, wafting the unfamiliar scent across the cave entrance.

Four o'clock on a chill September morning?

A strange time and place to be cooking meat.

In the truck they bumped across the solitary stripe of moorland road, shining black slicing through dull grey scrub, laughing and chucking the tube of camouflage paint to one another.

'How do I look?' Gary grinned, smeared a wide streak across his face, another, wider one underneath his eyes, gripped his rifle, pulled on his balaclava and looked across at the others. They all seemed different now, aggressive, threatening. He made an animal noise deep in his throat, the sound of a young, adult male, predatory and ready to hunt ... to hurt. He felt better now, much better, and dug his companion sharply in the ribs.

'Ready for action then, Tom-boy?' He laughed, exposing a gap in his top front teeth – an incisor lost to one of the wardens.

Gary leaned forward in his seat, looked out of the back of the truck and watched the narrow moorland road disappear. Already he felt the familiar buzz. He got a kick out of these exercises, A team and B team. Hunting the enemy set the juices running. And the others were in the truck behind, just approaching the brow of the hill. Today they were the enemy. And Private Gary Swinton needed an enemy much more than he needed a friend. Object of this exercise: to reach the Winking Man first – unseen. So they would crawl on their bellies up one side of the crag. And B team would be on the other side. With a yell and a sharp dig in the Man's ribs with his bayonet they would announce victory.

The truck jolted to a stop. The sergeant leapt out and stood aggressively in front of them, legs apart, hands gripping his rifle butt.

'*Listen to me, you ignorant buggers.*'

He was bellowing. He always bellowed. It was his only voice. Never a whisper or a coax. He had no dulcet tone in his voice. He bellowed to his children when he saw them. He bellowed to his wife when he wanted to leap on her.

'Two companies – right? One of you get to the west of the rocks. B team to the east.'

He looked around dubiously. '*Have you got that?*'

They grunted assent, sat tensely coiled like springs, ready for action.

'Whoever gets to the nose first gets free beer tonight. Right?'

'Right.'

The sergeant's eyes wandered slowly round the company, memorising every man until his glance fell on Swinton. 'And if I catch you so much as tickling anyone with your rifle butt or your fists, you're in the can for a month. Understand, Swinton?'

Gary glowered, looked past the sergeant to the sharp, black crags and beyond to the Winking Man's profile.

The sergeant dealt him a blow on his shoulder.

'Understand, do you, Swinton? You touch anyone and I'll bloody thrash you to within an inch of your miserable life.'

Gary's breath came fast and hard but he nodded.

'Right, any trouble ...' His eyes swept the whole company and his hand tightened on the rifle butt. He had no need to say more. Not one of the watching soldiers doubted he would still use it, hard and on the back of the head with a practised blow that made you dizzy and sick for days.

The ground was soggy and wet, the wind biting and the soil black, soft peat that stuck to your boots, as you sank up to your ankles. The whole scene was lit with the dull, grey glow of yet another dismal day. The brief glimpse of sun at dawn had gone. It had hidden behind thick, dark cumuli. Swinton stared up the mountain and began to plan. To reach the summit they should have to crawl on their bellies up the gullies.

Tom-boy was staring at the crag too. 'It's these bloody rifles that make it difficult.'

Swinton turned around. 'Don't start your moaning, Tom,' he said through his teeth. 'Just get on with it and keep your bloody head down. If you don't want to carry your rifle you can leave it behind.'

'Ha bloody ha.'

Swinton faced forwards, towards the pinnacle of the crag. 'Well, don't moan then. We're soldiers. We have to have guns. If you don't like carrying them be a bloody cook and carry a spoon.'

Tom-boy seemed to shrink inside his pale skin, striped with dark camouflage paint that somehow failed to offer the macho look he so craved.

Swinton glanced at him and felt like lashing out – folding his fists into the soft, white flesh. Instead he thought about conquering the mountain.

The sergeant barked an order to B team and they melted away behind the rocks, invisible now in khaki and face paint, leaves stuck to their helmets. But Swinton knew they were there.

'Right, you bloody bastards. Get down.'

The sergeant kicked Tom-boy on the rump and

the soldier fell on his face with a soft moan.

In unison the others dropped. Rifles clattered to the ground.

The sergeant bent down and put his face close to Swinton's. 'Now get to the fucking top, bastard.'

Swinton wriggled forward, using his elbows, his knees, his belly. Puddles and streams had chosen the same, easy route in the low contours of the hill and the water seeped in, reaching his knees first. But if they kept their heads down in their khaki and camouflage paint they were invisible. And one day – in Northern Ireland or some other troubled spot – being invisible might save their lives.

Swinton crawled a few feet further up the gully, his eyes trained on the hook nose of granite and the black ridge beyond, watching for signs of movement against the dull sky. He inched forwards, ignoring the creeping wet and Tom-boy's noisy panting behind him. He crawled through sheep pellets, keeping low, his gun banging against his back. He never looked to the side or behind but could hear the others rasping through the heather, squelching through the mud as he concentrated on the ridge and the first sign of B team reaching the top. But the silhouette remained unbroken as they crept towards the summit.

It was when he was three-quarters of the way up the hill that he stopped, sniffed, caught the burning scent on the wind. He froze, sniffed again, turned around.

'Tom-boy,' he said urgently, 'can you smell something?'

Tom took a deep breath in. 'Smells like meat,' he said, 'cookin'.' He frowned and gave one of his nervous giggles. 'Gary,' he said tentatively, 'it's just after five in the morning. It's been raining half the night. It's absolutely freezing up here.' He paused, unwilling to say more. When he spoke again, his words were said softly, and he paused between each word:

'Fancy – having – a – barbecue – now.' The last word came out in a rush.

Swinton's eyes narrowed. He had smelt this scent before. He breathed in quickly. 'Barbecue?' His eyes looked strangely disturbed in the tiger stripes of camouflage paint. His head shot up. His mouth dropped open. To cover his uneasiness he sneered at his friend. 'Who'd have a barbecue up here at this time of the day, Tom?' he said in a strangled voice.

Tom, never quick, missed his meaning. 'I can definitely smell it,' he insisted. 'Meat – cooking.'

Swinton's eyes scanned the rocky outcrop, black and angular against the sky now streaked with heavy rain clouds, then slowly his gaze dropped along the valley until they found the origin of the scent – a spiral of smoke, a little to the right, where a deep fissure in the rock swept downwards towards the road. It was from here that the scent of meat cooking was wafting up the gully, wrapped in faint blue smoke. At the bottom of the gully there was definitely something burning. Through the gloom, Swinton peered, his eyes shaded with his hand, his head craning forwards, as though to take his bulging eyes nearer. At first he could pick out only huddled, charred rags ...

The next instant, ignoring all his training to keep low, quiet and invisible, Private Gary Swinton stood upright and hurled away his rifle with a high-pitched scream that seemed to last from the top of the hill all the way down until he reached the pile of rags.

A confused and muddled Tom-boy ran with him,

not understanding anything until they got to the bottom and flung their flak jackets on the burning body of a boy.

Detective Inspector Joanna Piercy locked the door, then peeled down her cycling shorts and threw off her T-shirt. She stepped out of her trainers, sluiced her face and arms in the sink, patted herself dry with a balding towel. From a shelf she took a tin of deodorant and sprayed liberally. Next she folded the clothes carefully and placed them in the top drawer of the filing cabinet. The shoes she threw in the bottom of the cupboard. Then from a coat hanger behind the door she took a short, black skirt and a cream blouse. A pair of tights from her bag and some high-heeled black shoes. Nearly ready. Damn – she jumped. Someone was banging on the door.

'Hang on a minute.'

They did this every morning, knowing she had to change before she was ready for work. Perhaps one morning she would forget to lock the door and then they could barge in and pretend it was all a mistake, catch her in knickers and bra. Honestly, she thought, coppers' schoolboy humour.

The banging came again. She flicked a comb through her thick, dark hair, let the water out of the sink and stared at her reflection. What the hell was she going to do?

There were so many parts to this story ... Matthew a lover, Matthew a loved colleague ... Matthew a married man – unattainable. These were all the Matthews she knew ... familiar, comfortable people – someone who weaved in and out of her life with an undemanding casualness. She had somehow imagined it would always be like that.

The letter had come as a shock. It had sounded so very decisive. He would give his marriage one last, committed try. If it failed, he had to leave. 'You do understand, don't you, Jo? Eloise is only ten. For her sake I must try.'

She took a deep breath in and was unsure that she wanted her equilibrium rocked so fundamentally.

The hammering on the door became more insistent. She grimaced. No time to ponder now.

Another bang. 'It's Mike.'

'Well, come in,' she said, irritated.

'The bloody door's locked.'

She opened it and faced him in the doorway. 'Well?'

'Body found on the moors.'

Mike's voice was quick and excited. This was a small, safe town. Bodies weren't common. She stared at him.

'Accident? Someone slip while climbing?'

He shook his head. 'Not unless they tried to cook themselves after they fell. When it was found it was still burning.'

'Burning?'

He nodded. 'Soldiers found it. Saw the smoke.' Mike's voice held the same creeping horror she felt. 'Someone had tried to burn it.'

'Steady on, Mike,' she said. 'It doesn't necessarily mean it's homicide.'

Mike looked at her pityingly and Joanna found herself wishing Matthew was around.

'What were the soldiers doing up there?'

'They were on exercises at the Winking Man,'

Mike said. 'They saw the smoke. One of them said he recognised the smell.'

Joanna looked at him.

'I thought it was funny.'

'Did he say more?'

Mike shook his head, and she nodded and rubbed her face.

'We can talk to him later about that. Anything else?'

'Not much yet.'

'The deceased?' She met his eyes and he frowned.

'They said it was just a kid.'

She sighed. There was revulsion for any murder. But the killing of a child, and then to try to destroy the body with fire ... Even hardened, toughened police officers, both men and women, were sickened.

She moved back into the room, frowned, glanced down at the wire tray on her desk. 'There haven't been any kids reported missing, have there?'

He shook his head.

'Get someone onto it,' she said, 'now. Any kids reported missing within ...' She paused. 'We'll start with a 50-mile radius. Description?'

'Vague so far,' Mike said. 'Nine or ten ... fair hair ... trainers, baggy jeans. No coat.'

She nodded. 'It must have been freezing up there last night.'

'It was freezing,' Mike said. 'That's official. Black ice warning on local radio this morning. I heard it.'

Joanna stood still for a moment. 'Poor kid,' she said softly, then looked up. 'Who's up there now?'

'Timmis and McBrine – on moorland patrol. They weren't far away.'

'Get them to seal the area off,' she instructed. 'No-one ... no-one is to approach the area.' She paused. 'I don't want the usual forensic nightmare. What evidence is up there I want neatly bagged and labelled. Pathologist?'

'I rang the emergency number,' he said. 'Dr Levin's away.'

She felt irritated. What right had Matthew to be away when she needed him? 'I knew that,' she said, and found she couldn't look at him. She felt Mike expected further explanation. 'He's gone away – on holiday with his wife and Eloise.'

Mike's eyebrows lifted. 'Cosy,' he said, his dark eyes resting on her thoughtfully.

'Yes,' she said. 'Cosy.' She busied herself slipping her jacket on. 'I believe a locum is covering. Get her up there, Mike.'

'Her?'

'Someone up from Birmingham,' she said, 'on loan for a fortnight. Also please get hold of the photographer. Then ...' she smiled at him, 'do you think you could give me a lift?'

His eyes were mocking. 'And I was thinking you would ride your bike up there.'

'By the time I got there,' she said drily, 'you'd have solved the darned thing. It's hills all the way.'

He smiled then. 'You'll need a coat,' he said gruffly. 'It's cold on those moors.'

She held the door open for him. 'So shall we go?'

2

It was the scent of charred meat that had drawn Alice to the mouth of the cave. Sitting still, like a Neolithic woman, she had watched the body slung over the shoulders, the heavy hike up the side of the moor through the fading darkness. As she sat she had seen the small body doused in petrol then the quick flame as it burned. She had given the smouldering body a wreath, laid the flowers at the child's feet. She would have stayed there but the noise of the vans disturbed and frightened her. As the soldiers jumped from the wagons she melted back into the cave from where she watched, motionless.

She saw the grotesque pantomime, the soldiers creeping on their bellies and the noisy run with flailing arms. And then, as the sun rose, the scene came to life.

She scuffed to the back of the cave, waiting for Jonathan to wake, cold now and shivering, clasping her arms around her in an attempt to get warm. She dare not light the fire. The smoke would be spotted. But it was cold. She glanced at Jonathan. How could he sleep so long? He lay in the dim, sharp light, small puffs of breath smoking from his open mouth. His fingers in black, woollen mittens sometimes clenched then relaxed as he dreamed.

'A kingdom needs a king,' he muttered, clutching his filthy coat around his skinny body. 'A kingdom needs a king.'

She touched him with her foot. 'Wake, Jonathan,' she said. 'Wake.'

At last he grunted and rolled over, snapped his mouth shut and sat up, a wild expression in his eyes when he saw her bending over him. 'What is it?' He saw the blackened embers in the cave. 'Why aren't the fires lit?'

'Someone took a body up 'ere,' she said slowly. 'And they burned it.'

He frowned. 'What for?'

'I don't know, do I?' She was silent for a minute. 'Jonathan,' she said slowly, 'it were a child.'

His glance moved to the mouth of the cave. 'There's police outside,' she said, 'lots of them, poking around. Looks like they're staying.'

He looked enquiringly at her. 'Not army again?' he asked.

'No. The army, they was here earlier, like they are sometimes, creeping on the 'ill. These be different. P'lice.' She stared at him hard, squatted down on her huge haunches by the dead embers of a recent fire. 'Somethin' 'appened,' she said earnestly. 'This morning, afore dawn ... The soldiers,' she began, ''twas them found it.' She cackled a dry laugh. 'Screamin' like they was possessed.'

Jonathan Rutter scratched his head. 'Found what?'

'The child's body,' she said patiently.

Jonathan jerked to his feet and accused her. 'You been dreamin' – or drinkin'?'

'Look for yourself.' She pursed her lips and sat, Buddha-like, her eyes watching him as he moved low and with monkey agility on his haunches, to the mouth of the cave. There he lay, furtively peeping out, down the grey-green moorside to the navy figures dotted at the bottom, near the road. It did not do to be seen. Others mocked their status and their home, failed to understand their reasons for living apart from the rest of their race, high up here in the cave, watched only by the Winking Man. People persecuted those they did not understand, so they had let them believe they had left their cave. But they hadn't. They had remained here and were still here in their rightful home. What did they care for such unnecessary things as taps for water and switches for electricity? Water came from the sky. Warmth and light from the sun when it chose to shine. All they needed was here, in this one dark but dry room, hollowed out of rock.

Jonathan watched the movement of the police far below, then half-turned, silhouetted against the hazy light that shone into the cave. 'What happened, Alice?' he asked.

'The soldiers must have seen it,' she said, still staring out across the landscape – high peaks, wide valleys, pale sunshine streaking down in broad stripes, lemon and black. 'Or else they smelled it. They started running and screaming.'

'They always does that.'

'There was smoke comin' from him,' she said.

He stared at her then from beneath thick, tangled eyebrows. 'Why burn a child?' he asked.

She looked at him pityingly. 'There's reasons you

burns bodies,' she said. 'Eatin' or gettin' rid of, or sacrifice maybe.'

He pursed his lips. 'So which were it?'

She shot another look at him.

'Who was the child?' he asked. 'How did he get there?'

'He was brought,' she said, 'on someone's shoulders.'

'Poor child,' he said. 'Poor child.'

'You haven't worked it out, have you, Jonathan,' she said quietly. 'Don't you know? It'll mean people. There'll be more people 'ere in the next few days than all the ones what came in the last year. And for folks like us what's different, people means trouble. They'll come,' she said softly, nodding her head so that long straggles of iron-grey hair escaped and hung like thin ropes each side of her face. 'They'll come,' she said confidently, 'and they'll cause us trouble. You watch, Jonathan.'

But Jonathan was the optimist. 'They'll not bother us,' he said slowly, still peering down the slope. 'Why should they care about us?'

She gave him another almost pitying look. 'They'll come because they'll either think we done it or we know who done it.'

'But we don't.'

Alice tightened her lips.

The couple looked at one another, their eyes anticipating the threat of intrusion to this wild and lonely place. They stared down to the bottom of the crag and watched the small red car that moved quickly up the moors road, drawing to a halt in the lay-by. They watched the woman with black, gypsy hair blowing around her face and the tall man. They watched as the two began to climb towards the clump of policemen guarding the small mound underneath the blanket.

It was a stiff climb to the gully and the scent of charred meat still clung to the damp morning air – a faint scent but unmistakable. It turned Joanna Piercy's stomach. The two scene-of-crimes officers were already there, together with a slim woman with pale hair. She stared unsmilingly at Joanna and held out her hand.

'Cathy,' she said. 'Cathy Parker, pathologist. I'm covering for Matthew while he's away.' She gave another of her disconcerting stares. 'I've heard a lot about you.'

Joanna felt at a disadvantage. What had she heard? What did Matthew say about her? How did he describe her? Friend, girlfriend, surreptitious mistress? And now how? Future wife? She felt confused and uncertain. She shook her head, not knowing how to fend off the remark, then glared across the damp moor.

'Have you had a look?'

Cathy Parker nodded. 'Just a very preliminary one,' she said. 'I can't tell you much. It's a boy – not very old – rather small, probably ten, 11.' She grimaced. 'Skinny. He's been strangled – almost certainly manually. I can see definite finger marks on the throat. Then it looks as though someone tried to destroy the evidence.' She glanced down at the hump beneath the police blanket. 'There's a strong smell of petrol.'

Joanna too looked at the sheeted figure. 'How long has he been dead?'

The pathologist shrugged her shoulders. 'Very hard to say exactly – the burning, the bleak weather up here. The army said it was freezing around dawn.' She sighed.

'I can only think it was some time last night. Right off the cuff, between nine and midnight – at the latest, one. He'd been dead for at least three hours before I got here. And that was at eight. By the way ...' she glanced around, 'he didn't die here. He was brought here already dead.' She looked apologetically at Joanna. 'Lividity,' she said. 'You can see it on the face and here.' She touched the tiny gold sleeper in the child's ear.

All that Joanna could feel was some relief that the boy had not lain there alive, dying through the night.

'He was found by the army at five,' Cathy continued. 'By then lividity had already appeared. He was stored somewhere – on his side – then dumped here. We'll know a lot more, of course, when I do the PM. Parts of the body are very, very cold but the lower limbs and most of the clothing were well alight.' She looked at Joanna. 'I'm sorry, Inspector. I shall have to speak to the fire people, but superficially it looks as though he had been burning for less than an hour – two at the absolute most. Wind can either fan flames or put them out. It's rather difficult and the ground was very damp. There are some unusual circumstances and I shall have to do more research, but if the body had been burning for about an hour before five a.m. and he had lain somewhere for a time after death, you can see midnight is around the latest he could have died.'

Joanna had to ask the obvious. 'Had he been molested?'

Cathy Parker shook her head. 'I don't think so. His clothing isn't torn. Of course I'll have to take swabs and things back at the mortuary.' She bit her lip. 'I'm sorry,' she added, 'I don't think even Matthew could have been more precise. We'll have to wait for the PM.'

Again the mention of Matthew's name made Joanna

feel uneasy. She closed her eyes for a moment and gave an irritated cough. Then she crossed the couple of yards to the body and lifted the sheet. Waxen face, eyes closed, fair hair, short stepped haircut, gold sleeper in one ear, ominous dark marks around the throat. The clothes had been old, scruffy, far too big, probably had never fitted him. Now they were charred. He looked a neglected boy.

She frowned. 'He doesn't look strangled,' she said.

Cathy gave a sad smile. 'Most people think strangling makes the face blacken, the tongue protrude, petechiae around the eyes,' she said. 'It usually does. Nevertheless, this child was strangled and I think he actually died of a vasovagal attack – shock, if you like, rather than slow throttling. He would have died very quickly, lost consciousness almost immediately.' She stopped for a moment, then said softly, 'He was dead before he was burned.'

'I see,' Joanna said, and was glad. At least the boy had not suffered, had not lain out on the moor, freezing slowly, alone with his murderer, frightened in the dark.

So his face was calm. She looked further.

'Any ideas where his body was stored?'

Cathy peeled her gloves off. 'Not so far,' she said, 'but it's usually a car boot.' She stopped and glanced around at the grey moor. 'How else would he have got the kid up here?'

Joanna stared then at the hands and remembered Matthew's pet theory ... In 90 percent of murder cases the answers can be found in the hands. She studied the boy's hands, already encased in plastic bags. Dirty hands with bitten nails, amateur tattoos on the knuckles. L-O-V-E on the right; H-A-T-E on the left. And on the second finger of the left hand – the one with the T – a ring. Careful not to touch it she bent over and stared at the monogram –

entwined initials watched by an eye. The ring looked expensive and fine, solid gold and very out of place. It belonged on the fat finger of a wealthy businessman. Not on the small dirty hand of this scruffy, dead child.

She looked further down. Charred black baggy jeans too big for this small, thin boy. And where the jeans had been burned away, white stick legs badly burned. The scent of charred human flesh mixed with the peculiar dead smell made Joanna feel sick. It was so strong she could almost see it in the air, a yellowish tinge.

She glanced at the shoes; a pair of Reebok trainers. They, too, were big for the boy's thin feet. Also partly destroyed by the splashed petrol but quite new. And expensive. Underneath, the soles were surprisingly clean considering the black mud that clung to her own shoes.

She replaced the sheet and spoke to the two scene-of-crimes officers. 'You'd better get to work,' she said. 'Bag him up. Leave the ring on. We'll remove it at the mortuary.' She hesitated. 'Make sure you bag the shoes too,' she added, wondering if both they and the ring had been stolen. Or was there in the background a doting mother, an indulgent father? She looked back at the waxen face and shook her head. For this child there had been neither. If her initial instinct was correct there was no-one in this boy's life who was either doting or indulgent. And he had not been reported missing. She glanced down and knew this was a type of child the police were becoming far too familiar with – the drifters ... the shirtless ones ... street children ... the untouchables. All over the world there were children like this one – problems. In God's name, she thought, where were their parents?

She turned back to Mike. 'We need the uniformed men to scour the area all around here,' she said, 'especially between here and the road. You know the procedure. I'll brief them back at the nick in half an hour. Who found the body?'

Detective Sergeant Mike Korpanski glanced at the two soldiers seated on the back of the army lorry, still with their camouflaged faces. 'Couple of soldier boys,' he said, 'from the army camp.' He gave a wry smile. 'They look young, not much more than kids themselves. It gave them a bit of a shock. At first they thought it was a barbecue.'

Joanna nodded. 'I'll speak to them back at the nick,' she said. 'Have the photography boys finished yet?'

One of them held up his camera and shouted back, 'Yes.'

'I'll want a good picture of the hands,' she told him. 'I want the tattoos – and the ring, too. Perhaps you'll get a better picture of that when it's removed by the SOCOs at PM.'

The cameraman nodded. 'Fine,' he said. 'Better light there too. I'll come along.'

She turned to Cathy Parker. 'Have you finished here?'

Cathy gave another of her strange smiles. 'Yes. I'll ring the coroner when I get back, then do the PM. Two o'clock suit you, Inspector?'

Joanna thought quickly. She nodded. 'Fine. Seal the area off.'

Mike was speaking to one of the uniformed officers.

He called over to her. 'Inspector, they found this near the boy's body.' He handed her a tiny bunch of heather, neatly knotted with the strong grasses that grew on the moors.

Joanna studied it. It was expertly done, intricately knotted. Who on earth would have taken the time to plait a wreath for the dead child?

'Who did it, Mike?' she asked. 'Who put it there? A remorseful murderer?' She answered her own question. 'I don't think so,' she said, but all the same she felt as much of a cold, uneasy feeling at the sight of this tiny bunch of heather and grasses as she had at the sight of the body. She handed it to the SOC officer. 'Bag it up too,' she said.

She met Mike's eyes and voiced an outlandish thought. 'Witchcraft...? You could believe anything up here,' she said quietly, gazing around the bleak panorama. 'I can't think of any logical explanation.'

'Well, it *isn't* witchcraft. We know that. This is the 1990s.'

'So what do you think?'

He simply shook his head.

The SOC officer dropped the heather into his plastic bag as Joanna returned her attention to the boy and watched as they slid the body into the body bag and placed it in the van. A phrase pushed into her mind. Was it from *The History of Mr Polly*? 'Once someone had kissed his toenails.' Had anyone ever adored his little pink toes? Or had the neglect started from birth? A feeling of utter hopelessness washed over her. A child should have a better bite of life than this.

From her eyrie in the mouth of the cave Alice watched the slim figure hesitate, look around her, then follow the procession down the mountain to the waiting navy van. She watched as the policewoman and the policeman climbed into the small red car and wound their way from the valley, back towards the town. She turned to Jonathan. 'They've gone.'

He was at the back of the cave, huddled in a pile of

rags. 'All of them?'

She shook her head. 'They left some 'ere. They'll be back – more of them. That woman with the dark hair. She will bring them back. 'Er's the one bossin' them around.' She paused for a moment then commented, 'They 'ave took 'im now, the child.'

'Better 'e go.'

'We can't have a fire, Jonathan. Not till they've gone.'

He nodded.

Jason had again noticed the empty bed the minute he'd woken up. God, Dean would cop it if he'd damned well absconded again. It was only a week since the last time and they'd been bloody furious then – threatened him with all sorts of things. The boy frowned and sat up in bed, thinking. They couldn't do anything – not really. They had no real powers. There was nothing to worry about. It was just that he hadn't thought Dean would take off again so soon. He was usually back for at least a week. And how long would he be gone for this time? A day – a week – a month? For a kid who looked like a goody-goody choirboy he was bloody clever at keeping out of the noseys' sight.

Where the hell did he get to? Jason's lip curled. Dean was a quiet one – good at keeping secrets. Perhaps his 'family' were looking after him. And then maybe this time he wouldn't come back at all. And who would want to, to this dump? The Nest, he thought disgustedly. What a stupid name for a children's home. If there was anywhere else in the bloody wide world he could go, he'd go there. Even the streets had to be better than this ... But at that thought Jason's heart began to race. The streets ... that was what he feared more than anything – that underworld of penniless vagrants who would all claw at him. Here was not heaven but at least he was safe. Out there – who knew who might get him? So here he was – stuck.

He frowned. Was Dean on the streets? No, he thought, Dean was off having adventures, like last time.

The shadow across the doorway put a stop to his daydreaming.

'Right, Jason, time to get up now. We have school today, don't we?'

It was said in a pleasant enough voice. Patronising but pleasant. The trouble was, Jason couldn't stand him.

'*We* haven't got school,' he said sarcastically. 'Just I have.'

'I think you forgot the "sir".' Mr Riversdale's plump face was unfriendly. As much as Jason Fogg didn't like him; he, Mark Riversdale, hated Jason. 'You have got school today, and what's more I expect you to break the habit of a lifetime and actually go – unlike last week. You weren't at school last Friday, were you? Mack phoned me.'

Jason stared at the ceiling 'What's the bloody point?' he asked. 'I'm going to get no bloody exams, and even if I did there's no job at the end of it. There's people been to university out there on the dole,' he jeered. 'What chance is there for me?'

Mark Riversdale pushed his heavy glasses up the bridge of his nose. 'Unfortunately, part of my job, Jason, is that I'm expected to send you to school. Part of your job is to go. *I* get black marks if you don't. *You* get black marks if you don't. Understand?'

Jason rolled over onto his stomach. 'I don't have to go to school to follow me chosen career,' he said.

'And what is your chosen career?' Riversdale snorted. 'Burglary, shoplifting, car theft, beating up the over-seventies for five quid?'

'No – a drugs pusher. More money.' Jason grinned. He loved to push Mr Reasonable right to the point where he snapped.

Riversdale felt his patience begin to fray. 'Oh – just get up for once without this stupid performance,' he said, and glanced at the hump in the other bed. 'And get Dumbo up over there.'

Now Jason thought quickly. He shot out of bed. 'Yes, sir,' he said, standing smartly to attention.

The warden flushed. 'Get some clothes on. Haven't you ever heard of pyjamas, Jason?'

Jason grinned and Mark Riversdale walked out. Jason crossed to the bed and patted the pillow. 'I've just bought you one day, little Dean, by flashing myself to old Rivers. No more. One day – that's all you got. Then they'll find out and you'll have to fend for yourself. Friends can only go so far.' He knew Kirsty would agree. He'd tell her later – give her a laugh.

There were five people in the mortuary – the two SOC officers ready to receive the clothes, the ring, the swabs to be sent to forensics; Cathy Parker, the pathologist; and the mortician to assist; as well as Joanna. Joanna stood back and listened to Cathy's clear voice dictating ...

'Length 140 centimetres. Weight ... Head circumference ... Bruising around the cricoid cartilage, signs of manual strangulation. Measurements of distances between thumbprints.' She looked up at Joanna. 'Here, look.' Joanna peered at the opened neck and Cathy pointed at a tiny bone. 'The hyoid,' she explained. 'It's broken. It was definitely manual strangulation. A medium-sized hand.' She frowned. 'Doesn't exactly narrow the field.'

'Nails?' Joanna asked, and Cathy Parker looked at her with respect.

'I see Matthew has taught you something. They were not long talons but definitely not bitten.' She spoke into the Dictaphone. 'Some nail marks. Right ...' she turned to one of the SOC officers, 'we'll cut the clothes off.'

There was something infinitely pathetic about the removal of clothing from the thin body ... clothes the boy had probably scrabbled into hastily – as boys do. The threadbare sweatshirt advertising a brand of cola, the baggy jeans that hid such thin legs, a pair of holed, grubby, white sports socks, underwear and a huge T-shirt, all dropped into plastic bags, labelled and piled up ready for forensics. The only odd note was the new Reeboks. Joanna picked them up, safely encased in their plastic bags. They were cross-laced. Joanna looked at one of the SOC officers.

'How much?' she asked, holding out the shoe. 'Eighty, 90 quid,' he said. 'They don't come cheap.'

She nodded. 'I thought as much.'

Cathy was still dictating. 'White Caucasian male ... age about ten ...'

An hour later she spoke to Joanna. 'I'll have the report typed up by tomorrow but, off the cuff, manual strangulation – as you know,' she said in a voice purposely matter-of-fact. For all of them the post-mortem of a murdered child was a distressing event. 'He was physically small – not terribly well nourished but not emaciated.' She looked at Joanna. 'His disappearance hasn't been reported?'

Joanna shook her head. 'No.'

'Then we have to consider the possibility that he is an absconder, perhaps from a children's home or from a family where he was not missed. Don't people sometimes wait a while with a kid who's done a "runner" before ...?'

She paused, then picked up one of the child's hands. 'The tattoos ...' She ran one of her fingers along the knuckles of the right hand. 'Love,' she read. 'These are quite interesting, Inspector, aren't they? Amateurishly done a few years ago. I've only ever seen them on a child so young who was in care ... Still,' she smiled, 'I expect you've noticed them too. There are a few other unsavoury aspects to this boy. He'd tried a noxious mix a few times of intravenous drugs.' She pointed to the ugly, pitted scars that spotted both arms. 'Usually caused by Harpic, talcum powder, sodium bicarbonate or even flour. It ekes out the drugs and causes the ulcers. He'd had a go a time or two but I don't really think he was an habitual user – at least I can see no evidence of regular use; one or two scars, that's all. He was rather undernourished and had slightly prominent ears. Left ear pierced – by an amateur. The holes aren't straight. Teeth not too decayed – one or two properly-done fillings, which I've recorded. Teeth nicotine-stained, as were his fingers.'

She looked at Joanna. 'If it's any consolation there's no trace of carbon monoxide or soot in the lungs. I am perfectly satisfied that he was dead before being set on fire. He put up no fight.' She touched Joanna's shoulder. 'He died a quick and humane death – lost consciousness swiftly. He did not struggle. He probably never knew what happened. But as there is one side – here is another. He had been sexually abused over a long period

– possibly a number of years. I think it started when he was quite young. There's intense scarring around the anus. He might have been five or six when first abused, possibly even younger.'

'The motive was sexual?'

Cathy Parker shook her head. 'No,' she said. 'I doubt it. I'll have to wait for the results of the swabs, of course, but I don't think there was a sexual motive for this boy's death. He had not been abused recently – possibly not for a year or more. There was no new scarring. The old scars had healed up. However ...' she showed Joanna tiny round marks on the thin, bony chest with its prominent ribs and stick-like upper arms. 'You know what these are?' she asked, and Joanna nodded. 'Someone burned him on numerous occasions with a cigarette. Again ...' she touched the marks, 'not recently. I think the last one was done not less than six months ago.'

Joanna blinked. 'Was there no-one to act as advocate for this poor sod?' she asked. 'And the thousands like him? No-one he could turn to? Damn it,' she said angrily, 'where is this caring society we're all supposed to be part of?'

'Try social services,' Cathy said drily.

'Well, his mother then?'

'Come on ...' Cathy's eyes met hers. She turned to the trolley and picked up the ring. 'What do you make of this?'

'Either a present,' Joanna said, 'maybe from a friend – or else he nicked it.'

Cathy peered at it. 'It's got initials on it. And it's fairly distinctive. It should be a good lead.'

'It's a start,' Joanna agreed.

Cathy crossed to the sink and began washing her

hands as the mortician sewed up the body, then she turned back and stared for a while at the boy's face, still calm and waxen.

'He must have been a very pretty child, you know,' she said, 'with his blond hair and blue eyes and, I dare say, a cocky, confident manner, fashionable clothes and a swagger. Under other circumstances he might have been a choirboy, or a teacher's pet, a Little Lord Fauntleroy, or had doting parents.'

'Unfortunately,' Joanna said, 'he had none of that. Accident of birth and he ends up like this, on the slab aged ten.'

Cathy Parker replaced the sheet, covering the boy's face, and the mortician's assistant wheeled the trolley back into the refrigerated temporary grave.

'So where do I look?' Joanna muttered more to herself than out loud. 'And where do I begin?'

Cathy was drying her hands on the towel. 'Have you heard anything from Matthew?' she asked casually.

Joanna flushed. 'A letter,' she said, 'before he went.'

Cathy Parker gave her a hard stare. 'Jane Levin and I have been friends for many years.'

Joanna closed her ears to it.

She returned to the station and met Mike Korpanski coming out of her office. 'So you're back?' he said. 'How did the PM go?'

'As we thought – manual strangulation. We've informed the coroner's office. They've set the inquest for next week. There doesn't seem much doubt about the verdict. Homicide.'

He nodded.

'There were a few important facts brought to light that you should know about, Mike.' She looked at the tall

DS with his black hair and muscular frame – the result of many hours spent at the local gym – and she thought how much she had grown to depend on him in the six months they had worked together. How very different was the easy, friendly relationship that had sprung up recently from the early weeks of resentment and hostility.

'The boy was the victim of repeated abuse – from an early age, five or six, both physical and probably mental. Cathy Parker found unmistakable evidence of repeated sexual abuse. But none recently and the motive for his murder was probably not sexual. He had also been burned with a cigarette on more than one occasion and was a drug abuser.'

Mike gave a quick snort. 'A typical teenager then?'

'Hardly,' she said.

Mike frowned. 'So it wasn't a sexual assault?'

'No – it didn't look like it. No clothes torn, no recent scarring. He'd been left alone for a number of months – Cathy guessed a year. The abuse had stopped. Was there anything you particularly wanted?' she asked, nodding towards her office door.

'Yes.' He grinned. 'The soldier boys – the pair who found the body. They're here waiting to make a statement.'

She looked at him. 'Anything I should pick up on?'

He shook his head. 'Not really.' Then he added, 'I suppose you noticed the one with the red hair had tattoos? Love and Hate.'

'They're common enough.'

His eyes met hers. 'They really do look the same. But you've seen the boy's tattoos closer than I have. See for yourself.'

She nodded, then hesitated. 'I think I'll see the

other one first. His name?'

'Thomas Jones. Taffy was a Welshman ...'

Tom-boy shuffled in awkwardly, still in bulky camouflage fatigues and heavy boots.

Joanna sat down behind her desk, switched on the tape recorder, recorded the date, time, two officers present.

'Private Jones,' she said, 'take your time and tell me what happened.'

He swallowed. 'We was doin' exercises on the moors ...'

'Roughly what time was it?'

'About five.' He looked wary. 'We thought it was some meat cooking, you see.'

'Why don't you start at the beginning,' she suggested helpfully.

'We was doing exercises up on the Roaches,' he said again, rubbing his chin and smearing the camouflage paint messily across his face. 'They was just comin' up over the back of the hill.' His enthusiasm was growing. 'It made it easier for us.'

She gave him a questioning look.

'We was divided up into two teams,' he explained. 'A and B team. They was shown up against the light, you see, quite clearly.'

She did see. An image of stealthy, moving camouflage, that strange illusion of seething ground. She had noticed it herself once when up on the moors, had watched the ground itself seem to boil before she had realised it was the soldiers, on their bellies, stealing through heather and scrub, splashing along puddles and streams, invisible to the eye, creeping up towards the Winking Man. 'Go on,' she said.

'I didn't notice nothing at first,' he said, 'but I could smell something – like meat cooking. I said to Gary, "Fancy someone having a barbecue now."' He blinked, rubbed his eyes, looked at the black smears on the back of his hands. He giggled. 'I bet I look a sight,' he said. Then he stared at her hard for a moment, his eyes a light contrast against the blackened face. 'The next minute, Gary was chargin' down the hill like the bloody Light Brigade, screamin' and holdin' his gun out like the enemy was at the bottom.'

'And what did you do?'

The soldier's shoulders dropped. 'I ran after 'im. And then when I got to the bottom I saw the little heap of rags.' He looked at Joanna then swivelled around to stare at Detective Sergeant Korpanski. 'I'll never forget the sight of that kid burnin',' he said, 'for as long as I live – or that smell either. It was enough to make me sick.'

'But you weren't sick?'

'No,' he said, 'I wasn't.'

'Then what did you do?'

'We pulled our jackets off, put the fire out, covered him up.' He blinked tightly against the suspicion of a tear. 'By then the sergeant was wonderin' what the hell we were up to. It was him what rung the police.' He slumped forward in his chair, his face still tight with shock. 'That's about it,' he said, and Joanna nodded.

'I thought it was probably like that,' she said. 'Did you notice any cars when you first arrived at the lay-by?'

Private Thomas Jones shook his head. 'Not a bloody livin' thing.'

Joanna licked her lips. 'Tell me, Private Jones,' she spoke softly, 'this is very important. Did you touch anything?'

He looked worried. 'No,' he said, 'on my honour I did not. Apart from puttin' our jackets over him to put the fire out we didn't touch anything.

Taking the tiny bunch of grasses out of her top drawer, Joanna asked, 'Did you notice these?'

He looked genuinely puzzled and shook his head. 'No,' he said. 'I didn't see them.'

When the soldier had shuffled out, Joanna turned to Mike. 'As simple as he seems, Mike?'

He nodded. 'I think that held the ring of truth.'

She jerked her head towards the door. 'And the other one?'

'I'm not so sure about him, Jo,' he said.

She stood up and opened the door. 'Let's see, shall we?'

Private Gary Swinton walked in, his short ginger hair looking pale against the blackened face. It made it difficult to judge his expression but they both knew it would be truculent, aggressive. Years in the police force had taught them both to sniff out various attitudes – however hard the wearer might try to conceal them. To coin a phrase, Joanna thought she would not like to meet him alone on a dark night.

The usual formalities over, she met the pale eyes. 'We understand it was a little after five a.m. that you began to ascend the crag known as the Winking Man?'

Gary Swinton nodded. 'Yeah,' he said carelessly, perched on the edge of his seat.

'You were about halfway up the hill when Tom caught the scent of charred flesh.' She knew she was questioning him with a particular care. The tattoos had already alerted her to one tiny link. But it was something else that was making her skin tingle. She felt sure that the dead boy, when alive, would have worn this same air – keep away, stay out. Repel all boarders – no-one too close, especially not the police. She met it increasingly now. In the last two years it had touched epidemic proportions.

'Then what happened, Private Swinton?'

Gary stared at the floor. 'I smelt it first,' he said gruffly. 'Tom thought it was a bloody barbecue.'

'But you didn't?'

'Different smell.'

Joanna and Mike exchanged quick glances. 'Not the smell of beef burgers, soldier?'

He looked pityingly at her, then the steel curtain of wariness dropped down heavily. 'Dunno,' he said.

She let it pass. 'Then what, Gary?'

'I saw the clothes,' he said. 'Knew there was something wrong.'

'But you were a long way off.'

'Good eyesight,' he grunted.

She left that one too for another day.

'Witnesses say you were screaming as you ran,' she said.

'Instinct. They teach us to do that in the army.'

She leaned across the desk. 'I thought,' she said softly, 'that in the army they taught you to be quiet?'

He looked concerned. 'Not when you're charging.'

'Charging?'

He seemed even more uncomfortable. 'You know what I mean.'

'Then what?' The brevity of the question sounded brutal but she had a feeling Private Gary Swinton would respond better to that tone than to any other.

To her surprise his voice, when he replied, was husky with emotion.

'I saw the kid,' he said, and smothered his face with his hands.

She waited.

'I saw his legs first.'

She knew. They had been worst attacked by the fire. Thin legs, the jeans scorched and blackened, flesh charred, bone visible.

'Then his body ...' The soldier was shaking. He glared at the floor. 'I saw his face last.'

'And?' she said.

'We put the fire out. The way we were taught – with our jackets.'

'Had you ever seen the boy before?' He shook his head. 'Course not.'

She glanced at the L-O-V-E, H-A-T-E on his hands but didn't speak.

When the soldier left the room Mike looked at her. 'You didn't ask him about the tattoos,' he said accusingly.

'No,' she replied, 'I decided to leave that – for the time being.' She met his eyes. 'I want their jackets to go to forensics.'

'Both of them?'

She nodded. 'Both of them.'

'What are you looking for?'

'Petrol,' she said, 'splashed.'

Mike shook his head but she defended her action. 'There's no harm in checking a statement.' She paused, then asked, 'What do you think?'

He frowned. 'Difficult to tell, isn't it, what's going on under all that war paint.'

'No harm in checking them both out,' she repeated.

Joanna had been allocated a team of four POs and two DCs with a promise of more when she needed them. On top of this the whole of the Leek force would carry out the necessary checking of statements and house-to-house questioning. First priority was to find out who the boy was. So a police artist had visited the mortuary and spent an hour sketching the child as he would have looked – alive, eyes open, lips parted, hair tousled and wearing the unburnt clothes. And they had held the front page of the late edition of the evening newspaper with a blank panel.

At the briefing, some of the force copied down details faithfully, word for word. Others sat and watched with rapt attention. Each person present had his or her own way of dealing with the case of a young boy found murdered, his body then mutilated. But in the end they would all have to dovetail and produce a finished case – if it was possible. And this was their uniting hope – that they would bring the killer to the courts.

'First of all,' Joanna said, turning to face them, 'let me tell you the way I mean to work – with you. Butt in if you have a comment or question. Try all your ideas out here – in this room. Please do not hesitate – however far-fetched you think it might be. I do not intend to aim for haste but for a watertight conviction of the guilty party. In other words, we want the person who did this found guilty and locked away so other children are safe. But I also want it handled so properly they could film it and use it as a police training video. I want no assumptions made – no corners cut. Now ... We have a white

Caucasian male. Age uncertain but roughly ten.' She indicated the police picture of the dead boy's waxen face. 'The boy had blond hair, blue eyes, was 140 centimetres tall.' She paused. 'Distinguishing marks – left ear pierced and tattoos.'

She held up the pictures of the dead child's hands. 'Love, Hate ... Amateurishly done.' She looked around the room. 'We've all seen this sort of thing. Kids get together – usually do it themselves or a mate does it. But you and I know the sort of background this child probably came from. Only children who feel they would not get a beating from their mother or father would have dared come home with tattoos like these on their knuckles. I am not being classist but I am being a realist.' She paused, expecting at the least muttering, at the most an objection. None came so she continued. 'There is also a drugs connection – some nasty, scarred needle marks on both arms, the kind of scarring that comes from mixing drugs with talc, Harpic, flour.' She looked around the room. 'You know the sort of thing. Drugs mixed with something. He was a slim child — bordering on being undernourished. However, I am bound to say the pathologist's opinion was that the child was not a frequent or habitual drugs user – just that he did have access to drugs and did use them on a number of occasions.'

She hesitated before continuing. 'The boy had been the subject of repeated physical and sexual abuse in the past but – again quoting the pathologist – not in the last year or more. It does not look as though there was a sexual motive to the crime we are investigating, although I hardly need impress on you, it may well have a bearing.

'So – we are looking at a child who had contact

with the underclasses. It is unlikely that he came from a privileged background. However hard the voices scream, this is fact. As police we know it.' She watched the blond rookie at the back of the room scribbling furiously and recalled her first ever murder briefing – an old woman, clubbed to death in her own sitting room, blood everywhere ... Murders were all different and yet all basically the same – ugly.

'Any comments so far?'

There weren't and she frowned. 'I want to draw your attention to two things. First his shoes.' She pinned up the picture of the new Reeboks. 'They are, as you can see, practically new. The soles are clean and show no sign of wear. These are expensive shoes. Possibly they were shoplifted. I hardly need to point out that if they were bought, someone must have been either very fond of him or was bribing him. Also if they were bought, the person didn't know his size.

'The shoes may prove a vital lead and I'd like a couple of you to try the shoe shops, please. Find out if they were bought or stolen. Please try locally first. If we have no luck there we'll have to take the rest of the Potteries. If they were bought, we need to know by whom – and if payment was in cash or by cheque. You know the routine.'

The young rookie was still scribbling furiously. Joanna felt almost annoyed – would he ever look up?

'The other thing is this ring ...'

Again the picture on the board – a drawing this time. 'It was found on the dead boy's finger. It's distinctive and expensive ... Initials, I think "AL", although we may be wrong.' She smiled. 'They are rather entwined. Also the watching eye. Please find out anything you can about this ring. It seems as though it too could be stolen. But if it was given, then by whom ... to whom, when and why?

'This boy,' she continued, looking at the mortuary picture of the now-peaceful face, 'was manually strangled. Bear in mind it was a swift death. There is a possibility that it happened accidentally. The abuser is possibly not the killer. The killer is not absolutely necessarily the person or persons who tried to fire the body. I impress on you: make no assumptions. I don't need to tell you we must apprehend the person responsible for the death of this child and he or she must be brought to justice without prejudice.' Her voice became steely. 'Is this clear?'

They all nodded, and she was satisfied and glad she had made this point at the beginning of the investigation. She turned to Mike. 'Detective Sergeant Korpanski?'

'Children's homes,' he said. 'I think they are our best bet.' He cleared his throat. 'We also need to speak to anyone who might have seen a car drive across the moors early this morning – before five. I'll draw up a team for the fingertip search. And don't forget soil samples. The soil up there is distinctive – dark and peaty. It holds tyre marks and footprints reasonably well. Get some of it to the lab for filing. Smith, King, Farthing, Scott ...' He proceeded to draw up lists and allocations – some to the moors, some to the children's homes. A few to cover sports-shoe shops, others to cover jewellers.

Joanna left the room abruptly and the officers stood up, dividing themselves into their groups under Mike Korpanski's supervision. Only then did the young, blond rookie, PC Phil Scott, finish his scribbling and trail past the board. He stopped in front of the picture of the ring and frowned. Then he caught up with the others.

'Hey,' he said. 'The ring. You know the ring ... The one on the boy ...'

The others looked uninterested. 'I think you're on the moors for the afternoon, Phil.'

'But–'

'No buts.' DC Alan King gave him a playful punch. 'And it's bloody pouring, so take your mac.'

3

Matthew Levin scuffed along the beach, holding his daughter's hand. He felt irritated at the whole pace of this holiday, the child, the wife. He felt overwhelmed with frustrated energy and annoyed with himself for coming on this doomed endeavour. He'd known he would be stifled by them both, but he had never guessed to such an extent. His powerful shoulders dropped with guilt and unhappiness. He felt swamped by fripperies, constant dress changes and the endless shopping expeditions to which he had submitted. He ran his fingers through his short, blond hair. He had tried. God, he really had tried. But it was no use. With his family he had absolutely nothing in common. The feminine in them was too strong. Perhaps the masculine in him was also too dominant.

Even the sailing had had to be toned down for Jane, who was a nervous sailor, a poor swimmer and hated boats. She feared them – felt insecure on the heaving deck. So the only possible exhilaration – an afternoon's sailing in stormy weather - would have to be forfeited. Instead they would have to wait for another calm day when the sea would reflect like a millpond and they would sit and bake underneath the hot, Greek sun.

Matthew Levin stared out across the swaying sea. God, what he would give to be out there, battling against the wind – reining it in to take him where he would go. And it would have been heaven to have had Joanna there with him, at his side, both of them working together. A swift vision of strong brown legs, smooth and firm, and that quick laugh she would give, triumphantly, at the challenge of pitting their skills together against the elements.

But here he was ... on a golden beach, stood on hot sand, beneath a cloudless blue sky, watching the waves slap against the boat. And he knew. He could not possibly feel more miserable. And now Eloise had lost her bracelet somewhere on this beach and Jane expected him to spend all afternoon searching for it.

'I know it's here somewhere.' Eloise pouted a little and watched her father through her eyelashes. She tugged his arm. 'Please look for it, Daddy. Please.

Matthew was exasperated. 'No,' he said. 'No. We'll never find it.' He glanced along the expanse of sand. 'It'll be buried by now. You'll never find it. We'll just have to claim off the insurance.'

Eloise began to howl, flicked one pale plait back over her shoulder and stuck her thumb in her mouth, noisily sucking it.

Jane intervened. 'Don't be hard on her, Matthew,' she said. 'Don't be angry. It was carelessness – that's all. Nothing more.' She looked at her daughter. 'Wasn't it, darling? Don't suck your thumb.'

Eloise ignored the censure but took the proffered excuse and seized it eagerly. 'That's right, Mummy,' she said. 'Carelessness.' She slipped her arm through her father's. 'Just carelessness. I wasn't being purposely bad,

Daddy. I didn't mean to. I wasn't being quite careful enough.' She frowned, looking anxiously from her father to her mother and back to her father again. 'And Granny would be so upset if I had lost it. Daddy ...' she added firmly, 'we must find it.' She screwed her face up. 'Come on,' she said, dropping to her knees on the hot sand. 'Help me look.'

Matthew gave her a glance of exasperation. 'No,' he said. 'It's a waste of time.'

The child attacked his Achilles' heel and began to howl again.

'Someone else will find it!' Tears splashed down her cheeks. 'What'll Granny say when she knows I've lost it? She'll be furious and horrible,' she wailed. 'She'll say I've been careless.' She sniffed loudly, ignoring the blob of mucus that bubbled from her nose.

Matthew stood by helplessly.

'I'll never see it again and it's worth ever such a lot of money.' Her tears were accompanied by spasmodic sobs.

'Darling, don't cry,' Matthew pleaded uncomfortably. 'Please don't cry.'

The child sobbed louder.

Matthew glanced at her anxiously. Her tears had always moved him to a feeling of helpless frustration. It made him feel sick and responsible. He simply wanted her to stop crying. 'Darling ...' he said, 'darling ...'

Eloise only howled louder. 'Granny will hate me.'

'No she won't.' Jane put her arm around the girl's shoulders and drew her towards her, kissing the top of her head as though calming a baby. She looked up at Matthew. 'She's inconsolable,' she said accusingly. Then she clutched his arm. 'Help us look,' she hissed. Her face was hard and unforgiving and still pale. 'Or do you mean you can simply sit here on the beach and watch your own daughter break her heart. But yes,' she added softly, 'I can believe that.'

Eloise looked out from beneath her mother's shoulder and glimpsed her father's face, pink with anger, flushed and sweating – for all the cool breeze that was blowing hard in from the sea.

Her mother's voice was shrill. 'Is that how little you really care about us?'

Matthew struggled to gain control, to explain, but he was now so furious he had lost his powers of reasoned argument. The other couples sitting on the beach heard only him shouting, saw him furiously arguing with his wife and daughter. They nudged one another.

Matthew was breathing hard now. Temper and reason tussled.

Jane squeezed his arm. 'Look at me,' she said. 'Look at me.'

He could barely prevent his lip from curling with dislike.

Her eyes were hard as ice as she spoke. 'Don't think I'll *ever* let you go to her.'

Police Constable Phil Scott was allocated to the search of the moors, combing the area in a straight line between the lay-by on the main road and the spot where the child's body had been found. A preliminary search had been made of a narrow 'corridor' that was clear of forensic evidence and taped off. But the person who had dropped the boy's body into the small hollow might not have taken the direct route. So the police were combing the area directly to the right and left of the forensic corridor. However, by lunchtime nothing had been found – at least nothing of importance – just an eclectic assortment of chewing-gum wrappers and crisp packets, some old used toilet paper, a couple of deflated Durexes. All were put in a black plastic bin liner. But none of the police officers religiously picking up everything that was not the strong, coarse, moorlands grass believed this garbage of the human race would lead to a murderer.

Farthing looked at Scottie gloomily. 'Sometimes,' he said, 'this whole thing's a bleedin' waste of time. There's bugger all up here.' He scanned the wide sweep of moorland topped with fierce-looking storm clouds. 'And it's going to soddin' well rain.'

Someone had had the consideration to fetch fish and chips from the local shop and they sat on the ridge, near the police van. After a hearty meal, washed down with flasks of tea, they were ready to begin the afternoon. But Scottie held back. He found Mike Korpanski sitting in the front of the van and rapped on the window.

'Excuse me, sir. Can I have a word?'

Mike wound the window down, still chewing chips.

'I think I've seen that ring before. The one that was on the boy. I've been thinking about it, sir.'

'Where?' Mike was excited – this was how investigations began, one tiny droplet of knowledge, then a succession, dripping quickly. And then a trickle that eventually gushed with information that led to a conviction. But it all started like this – one person saying they 'thought' ... they 'might' ...

'I'm not absolutely certain,' Scottie said, 'but I think it was one of the pieces reported stolen from a house break-in a year or two ago.'

'In Leek?'

PC Phil Scott nodded.

Mike grinned. 'Jump in, Scottie,' he said. 'And if you're right there's a pint for you later at the local.'

Joanna was spending the morning on the telephone and writing reports. At lunchtime she rang the lab and asked to speak to Cathy Parker.

After a pause, Cathy came on the line. She read out the results of the other forensic tests carried out on the body. 'The boy had eaten about two hours before he died. Some chips and a meat pie.'

Joanna nodded. 'The chip shops are open till midnight. He could have got them from there. I suppose it's another avenue to explore. What about the results of the semen tests?'

'Negative. As I thought,' Cathy said. 'The motive was not sexual – or if it was, the boy's sudden death killed the urge. Of course the lack of semen proves no penetration but it might be present on the clothes.' She paused for a minute. 'How long before you get the tests on the clothing?'

'A day or two. Shouldn't be longer. The press interest in a child murder means that we get priority at the lab. The outcry is always deafening.'

Joanna put a few of the uniformed men on to cover the fish and chip shops, which were just opening to serve lunch. Mike arrived as she was wondering about her own lunch, toying with the idea of some sandwiches and a yoghurt, but she could tell from the excitement in his eyes that something had surfaced and suddenly lunch didn't seem quite so important. Behind him trailed the young, blond rookie she had noticed scribbling furiously throughout the briefing.

'Come in.' She smiled. 'PC Scott, isn't it?'

'I hope I'm not wasting your time,' he said awkwardly.

'Don't worry,' she reassured him. 'Much better to waste a few minutes now than perhaps days while you decide whether to speak or not.'

He felt heartened. 'May I have another look at the ring?'

She stared at him for a moment and he opened his notebook and tilted the page towards her to show her a drawing he had made. He noticed she studied it for a very long time without saying a word, frowned, held the notebook herself. She scrutinised the crude pencil drawing then looked up.

'It does look the same,' she agreed. 'What was it made of?'

'Solid gold,' he said.

She stood up. 'There's only one way to find out.'

It was bagged up in the interview room and they went together. Joanna picked out the ring and handed it to him.

'Is this it?' she asked.

Phil Scott was learning from her methods. He too said nothing until he had studied the ring carefully and then he handed it back to her, 'Yes, I thought it was the same one,' he said. 'It was stolen ... house break-in, about a year ago. It was on the list of things stolen and there was a photograph of it.'

She looked at him. 'Which house break-in?' she said. 'Where?'

'Rock House,' he said. 'The big house on the moorland road. The big grey place.' He grinned. 'I don't think I'll ever forget it. It was my first day in the force.

About a year ago.'

She was impressed. 'And you remembered it all this time?'

He nodded, clear blue eyes fixing on hers. 'I'm a bit slow,' he said, 'often have to write everything down – otherwise I forget things.' He grimaced. 'Spend all my time making notes. That's why I was fairly sure. Had to check – but I'd drawn a diagram in my notebook.'

'And whose house was it?'

'Ashford Leech,' he said. 'He's the MP for Staffs Moorlands – or he was. He died a few months ago.'

'A car accident?'

'No. He was ill. He died in hospital.'

Joanna stared at him. 'And the ring was amongst the items stolen? You're sure.'

The young constable nodded. 'Yes, ma'am.'

'Did we get the burglar?'

He shook his head. 'No. We thought it might be kids.' He looked uneasy, shuffled uncomfortably on his feet. 'There was something funny about it. Something not quite right.'

'Get me the file. Bring it to my office.' She smiled. 'Then you can go back on the moors.'

She turned the lamp on over her desk, sat back and began reading the file. From the first page it was interesting. Not only because it was one of the many thousands of unsolved burglaries that filled their lists. But there were things here that were not quite right – anomalies. As she read the list of items taken she was puzzled. 'No,' she muttered. 'No – not like this. Mike,' she said, 'what do you think of this? First of all they decided to break in on a Monday lunchtime when the cleaner was there and her old jalopy parked right out the front to announce the fact. Then they were supposed to have climbed a glass roof to get in through a bedroom window when the conservatory door was open all the time.'

'So where was the cleaner?'

'According to this ...' she glanced down at the file, 'she was, quite by chance, in the back doing some ironing. They took such funny things too – a photograph album that had been in a cupboard in the sitting room; forced a lock to get it. But they left the television and the video, a pretty little clock – even money lying around.'

He sat up. 'Strange burglars,' he said.

'Also they took the ring from a bedroom where it was hidden in a box in a drawer full of lingerie, but left other more valuable and less distinctive pieces.' She glanced at Mike. 'So what do you make of that?' She slammed the file shut.

'Well ...,' he thought for a minute, 'they're either very clever burglars or extremely stupid burglars.'

'Or else,' she prompted.

'Or else the Leeches were lying.'

'Exactly. But why would a respected MP lie and claim his house was broken into? Why call the police at all? And just where does the dead boy fit into all this?'

She picked up the telephone directory, thumbed down the list of Ls until she came to A. Leech, Rock House ... But when she dialled the number, she was greeted only with a curt message in a female voice to say that Gilly Leech was not in, at present, but would return the call as soon as was convenient.

Joanna made a face at Mike. 'Answerphone,' she said, then glanced at her watch. 'Now for the bit I hate. Press conference.'

But it went better than she had hoped. The questions were predictable and easy. She found herself relieved that her one-time neighbour Caroline Penn was safely in London, working for a national newspaper. When she had worked locally she had always had an uncomfortable knack of asking the most awkward questions – the type of penetrating missiles that were the most difficult to evade. Without her the assembled press were well behaved and confined their questions to the more routine. Who was the boy? How had he died? Did they have a description – of the boy, of the assailant? What did they know so far?

And it was very little. But, as Joanna said to Mike later, 24 hours earlier that boy had still been alive.

She asked the two detective constables to question the owners of the eight fish and chip shops in Leek. If the boy had got food from one of them the previous night it would establish he had been in Leek, probably came from Leek. She would find him soon. The lunchtime edition of the *Evening Sentinel* reached Leek just after two. She had arranged for a photo-fit picture of the dead boy to fill the front page.

Why had no-one reported him missing yet?

The *Evening Sentinel* was delivered to her office just before three and Joanna looked at it eagerly. This had to bring someone forward who had known the boy. She scoured the front page. The artist's impression was excellent. This was how the boy must have looked when he was alive. There was a detailed description of his clothes. She ran her finger down the list. Yes, it was all there. She blessed the local reporters. This would find an identity. She grinned at Mike. 'Are we betting?' she asked. 'Twenty-four hours and we'll have a name.'

He shook his head. 'You'll find no takers. We'll have his name all right.' His face clouded. 'Trouble is,' he said, 'we'll have people who knew him – relatives.'

She glanced back at the artist's impression. 'If he was loved,' she said slowly, 'why hasn't anyone come forward? It's struck me this case is all the wrong way round. Usually with children we are informed they are missing. We hunt and find a body – or not. It's rare to find a child's body without hunting for it.'

Mike agreed.

'So where are his parents?'

'I suppose you think it's funny – or clever.' Mark Riversdale was confronting Jason and Kirsty in the kitchen of The Nest. 'Not telling me he'd gone – again,' he said in disgust. 'How infantile can you get.'

Neither of the teenagers said a word, but they glanced at each other. After a pause Mark carried on. 'I suppose he's gone off again.' He wagged an index finger at them. 'Where does he get to when he sets off like this?'

Again, neither of them spoke.

Mark sighed. 'Well, at least tell me this – and I expect the truth. When did you last see him?'

Jason heaved a long sigh. Wherever he was, Dean would be safe now. He, Jason, had bought him 24 hours to get where he was going. Covering for him wouldn't help. He gave a quick glance at Mark Riversdale and saw the warden was furious. 'Yesterday morning, sir,' he said.

'So he could have been gone a day and a half. Thirty-six bloody hours. Where?'

'I don't know.'

The warden looked sceptical. 'You know,' he growled. 'You're just not telling. Where is he?'

The boy shrugged his shoulders. 'Don't know, sir,' he repeated mechanically.

Mark gave a loud sigh and a groan. 'More damned paperwork,' he said. 'I really thought he'd stop absconding. I gave him a talking to last week. I thought we'd connected. He's disappeared less in the last year. I was a fool to imagine he'd settle down. Kirsty,' he appealed, 'where is he?'

As the girl stared at the floor he coaxed her.

'Come on, love – you can tell me.' Then his patience snapped. 'Kirsty, when did you last see Dean?'

'Yesterday morning,' the girl said. 'Early. I think he left early – before I was up anyway.' She shrugged her shoulders and blinked. 'I didn't actually see him go.'

'Why didn't you tell me? You know Dean has been in trouble for absconding.' He bit his lip. 'And I suppose he wasn't at school today?'

Both teenagers shook their heads. There was no point trying to cover for him. Rivers would soon ring the school and find out he had skipped it.

Mark Riversdale paused before leaving the kitchen. 'What I'd like to know is where does he get to on these jaunts? Who looks after him? Someone does ... Someone gives him things. They can't all be nicked ...'

As the door closed after him, Jason looked at Kirsty. 'Sue Whalley told me they found a body on the moors early this morning. It was a boy. Her dad told her. He's a copper.' His eyes grew round and frightened. 'What if it's Dean?'

'Hah.' Kirsty gave an explosive, disdainful sound. 'It won't be 'im. It won't be the nipper. I never knew a kid what could look after 'imself better than Dean –'e always lands on 'is feet. Bloody clever – for a little un.'

Kirsty had a small, heart-shaped face, pale with freckles, but her prettiness was marred by a thin, mean mouth with an ugly twist to it. It twisted even more now.

'Yeah,' she said, 'lands on 'is feet – every time. Lucky little bleeder.'

Jason kicked the leg of the table thoughtfully. 'Do you know what I fancy doin'?' he asked.

'What?' The girl looked only mildly interested.

'Tattoin' little Timmy.'

'Old Man Rivers'll kill you.'

The boy kicked the leg of the table even harder. 'Two more bloody years in this dump,' he muttered. 'Treat us like kids they do.'

'And then what?' the girl asked scornfully. 'Two years – then what?'

'A place of my own ... somewhere where no-one'll interfere.'

It was the list of objects stolen that intrigued her. Why take a photograph album? Easily traced, valueless ... It was the same with the ring. She stared at it, the looped A that ran into an equally flourishing L, watched by an almost Masonic eye. Why leave money and the easily sold things – television, video, cameras ... a clock? Damn, she thought. It didn't make sense. But if the house had not been burgled, why would a family call the police and report a burglary? Could they have been mistaken? Forgotten? She leafed through the report again. Then there was the broken glass.

And now the ring had turned up on a murdered boy ...

She rolled her pen between her fingers.

Mike wandered in and perched on the desk and she looked up at him. 'There's something funny about this.' She indicated the report. 'I can't quite see the connection but I bet a pie and a pint that there is one.'

He picked up the folder and nodded, then asked in a casual voice that didn't fool her for a minute, 'Where is Levin anyway?'

'Cephalonia,' she said sharply. 'And he's probably having a wonderful time.' She met his eyes. 'So can we drop the subject now?'

4

Joanna fingered the folder but Mike's question had conjured up an unwelcome image – Matthew on a family holiday with his daughter and his wife. She had met Jane Levin twice. The first time had been at a restaurant. She had burst in on them, her guilty husband and his mistress, vengeful, furious, mad with jealousy. Matthew had followed Jane home, a penitent sheep, leaving Joanna to pay the bill and abandon the restaurant under the curious gaze of the other diners.

The second time she had met Jane she had been under control, investigating the murder of a nurse. Matthew had been involved – more involved than he had at first admitted. She had had to question him further – and to save him embarrassment and suspicion, and herself from an unenviable 'bringing him in for questioning', she had driven to his farmhouse at the foot of the moors. There she had met Jane again ... Thin and unhappy-looking with a sharp edge to the clean and Nordic beauty that encased her like ice – and a child who mirrored her insecurity and clung to her like bindweed.

Matthew's wife she may have been but Joanna had never quite learned to hate her ...

Mike was still watching her. 'Thirteen hours,' he said. 'Thirteen hours since we found his body. And no-one's come forward. Why not?'

'Maybe he hasn't been missed,' she ventured. 'Parents away on holidays ... think he's elsewhere – with a friend? I don't know.' She ran her fingers through her hair and frowned. 'I don't feel we can get anywhere in this investigation, Mike, until we know who he is. Somebody will come forward soon. Let's clock off now,' she suggested, 'and have an early start in the morning. Maybe tomorrow will bring us an identity.'

But that night, as she neared home, she couldn't face spending another evening alone. So instead of entering her own home she knocked on the next door, a stout old-panelled thing with a wrought-iron knocker.

Tom Fairway opened it, still in his navy solicitor's suit. He gave a broad grin when he saw her. 'Jo,' he said delightedly. 'My prayers have been answered. A beauty has arrived to share my evening. Brilliant. Come in – have a drink.'

Tom's cottage was hazy with a warm smell of wood-smoke, and there was a deep armchair either side of the fire. He poured two tall glasses of red wine and raised his glass to her with a grin.

'What brilliant luck,' he said. 'I was just wishing for company. The night is young; I've a fresh salmon in the fridge, given by a grateful client impressed by my skills as a defence counsel.' He glanced at her severely. 'You know you lot really can be quite cruel to elderly gentlemen with clean licences ... You ought to pick on someone your own age and size ...'

She let him rattle on, watching his thin, intelligent face, the gold-rimmed glasses that caught the light of the fire, his restless, fidgety hands that displayed his nervous quick personality. They had lived next door to one another for more than four years, had slept together just once and immediately realised they would remain friends for life but never make love again. It had intruded on a deep, close friendship. They had witnessed each other's disastrous affairs, watched each other break hearts and have their own broken in turn. Tom's particular Achilles' heel was Caroline, recently removed to the London tabloid, with whom he had lived in uneasy turbulence for four years. Joanna's had been Matthew Levin. While Tom had moved up the legal ladder to a senior position in Manchester she had taken the right exams, kissed the right hands and been rewarded with the title of Detective Inspector. And they had remained living with a thin wall separating their homes.

It was not until their second glass of wine that Joanna broached the subject that had brought her there. Tom listened while she related all the details of the boy found on the moors.

'I need your cleverness,' she said.

Immediately Tom set his glass down on the small occasional table to his side and settled back in his chair in what Joanna laughingly called his 'legal position'. His thin face almost quivered with alertness and intelligence.

'What is it?' He studied her carefully. 'Is it something to do with the case?'

She nodded. 'Why would someone fake a burglary?' she asked.

'That one's easy, Jo,' he said quickly. 'People fake burglaries for financial gain.' He stopped. 'To claim off the insurance.'

'But if they didn't claim off the insurance? If the pieces were intrinsically valueless?'

'I think,' he said, then laughed, 'this one's more tricky. I would venture to suggest that there are one or two possible reasons. Either to explain the absence or presence of an object.'

She looked at him. 'Translate,' she said, laughing.

'Well, either ... Either to explain the fact that something was missing,' he said, 'or to explain away the fact that it was in the possession of someone in whose possession it should not have been.' He grinned. 'Do I make myself clear?'

She nodded. 'I think so.'

But her mind was still pondering that strange mix of objects.

'And why hasn't anyone come forward to claim the boy?'

'Possibly,' Tom said, 'because no-one knows he's missing.'

It was late in the day when Mike took the car out on the moor. He pulled up at the lay-by and stared out. Miles and miles of nothing. No houses or trees. Nowhere for anyone to hide – just the dark, menacing moor guarded by the craggy outcrop. And already, late on this gloomy September afternoon, the scene looked grey and menacing. A fitting setting for a violent crime, a graveyard of nature's making. He shivered. Though it was warm in the town he knew the minute he swung open the car door the wind would almost tear it off its hinges and the damp chill rising from ground that never dried out, summer and winter alike, would seem to penetrate his bones. This scene had been his own private nightmare, uncharted ground, unexplored and remote. He had always visualised undiscovered bodies on this high ground.

He got out of the car and immediately the elements beat around him. He walked slowly towards the navy van and found the uniformed police sergeant with his hands cupped round a beaker of steaming soup. He grinned and accepted one himself.

The sergeant winked. 'Courtesy of the publican,' he said. 'Reckon he has a guilty conscience?'

Mike shook his head. 'Probably nothing worse than serving after hours. Up here they seem to think the law doesn't apply.'

The sergeant peered through the windscreen of the van at the bleak surroundings. 'You can see what they mean, can't you? It seems a lawless sort of place.'

Mike tightened his lips. 'Nowhere is outside the law. The DI wants to know – have you found anything?'

The sergeant shook his head. 'Hardly anything, sir. A couple of burnt-out matches, a plastic bottle that smelt of petrol. That's been bagged. Those plastic bottles can be quite good at holding prints. That is, if he didn't wear gloves.' He gave a wry smile. 'Plenty of used Durexes. We didn't find any recent tyre marks near here – and that is puzzling us. Am I right in thinking he was murdered elsewhere?'

Mike frowned. 'We can't be absolutely sure. I'll have to talk to DI Piercy about it. I do know from observation that the soles of his shoes looked clean. We don't think he walked here. As soon as we get the forensic report in writing we'll let you have it.'

'Did you get a lead on the shoes yet, sir?'

Mike shook his head. 'Haven't had a chance to speak to anyone about that yet,' he said. 'I was anxious to see if you'd found anything.'

The sergeant gave him a quick look. 'We'd feel a lot happier if we knew who he was and how the hell he got up here.' He sighed. 'We haven't found any tyre tracks that look recent and the ground's soft. You'd have thought a car would have skidded ... maybe got stuck. We've got the soil samples. But ...' he paused, 'we could almost think he was dropped from above. We can't see how he got here. It doesn't make sense, sir. It's nearly half a mile from the road. Carrying a dead body would have weighed the perpetrator down.'

Mike frowned and scratched his head. Then together the two policemen climbed the hill towards the point where pink plastic tape was marking an area. Mike looked down at the scorched, flattened grass, a short length, not much more than four feet. In a long line, stretching right across the hillside, the police were hunting for something – anything that would lead them to the ... he voiced the word 'Bastard'... who had done this to the kid he had seen lying with a pale face in the damp heather. Mike had a healthy, policeman's dislike of the criminal, and as though in answer, a sheet of heavy, grey rain suddenly blotted out the sky and thundered onto the moor.

5

Alice sat at the edge of the cave early that morning, watching the figures in their clean white overalls as they combed the moist heather and scrub. She wrapped her topcoat around her and fastened it with the piece of string. The moors would yield little to their unpractised eyes. Only she and Jonathan were able to read the signs. She shifted a little; the wind was biting this morning. She pulled the scarf over her face. In the gloom of the dull day she looked like a huge, immobile scarecrow. The boy had already been dead when he was brought to his torching. Alice, Queen of the Roaches, held her hand over her eyes to shield a sudden glare – a hole in the low clouds and a silver streak of sunshine as though the Lord was offering a silver pathway for the boy's soul to climb heavenwards. She turned to Jonathan. 'I never seen so many people up here,' she said. 'It's been a bad thing, the child being put here.' Her voice took on a grumbling, self-pitying tone. 'It's took our privacy.'

Jonathan too was crouched in the entrance to the cave. 'They'll be gone,' he said, but Alice was not to be consoled.

'And then the trippers will start,' she said.

'Lookin' to see where the boy lay.'

Jonathan also watched the men in their white suits hunt the ground. 'Maybe you should tell them,' he said gruffly.

Alice turned on him fiercely. 'Tell them what?' she challenged.

'What you saw.'

She gave a sudden low laugh. 'You don't know what I saw, Jonathan. You was sleepin'.'

'But I do know,' he insisted, and he looked at her sideways, scratching the side of his mouth. 'You saw it all, didn't you?'

She shrugged her shoulders. 'What business is it of yours, Jonathan Rutter? Or of theirs either?' She jerked her head towards the slope of the mountain and wiped her nose on her filthy sleeve. 'And do you think, Jonathan, that they will leave us alone if I tells them? Do you think that will be an end to it all? No. No, I tell you, I would have to go to the court – like when they had a go at evicting us from here. I would have to testify and identify and the newspaper people would be taking pictures and then they would all know we was livin' 'ere.'

He grunted. 'And why shouldn't we stay? We don't do no harm.'

She gave him a quick look. 'You don't understand, do you, Jonathan? They don't like us up 'ere.'

'Why ever not?'

'Because most people don't live in caves no more.'

'More fools them,' Jonathan sneered. 'Avin' mortgages for places when there's good, dry caves for the takin'.'

'They don't like us bein' 'ere because we is

different. People only trusts what is the same as themselves. We is different, so because we is, they don't like it. That's why they wants us to live in one of the council places in the town. Conformin', the social workers calls it.'

'Well, I don't want to live in one of them council places,' he said, flinging another stiff brown blanket around his shoulders. 'I is perfectly comfortable livin' ere. These moors 'ave provided an 'ome for me all o' my life, 'ceptin the years I spent in the war. I won't never leave now.' His voice was low. 'Perhaps you're right. We should leave well alone. Then maybe they'll leave us alone.'

'Huh.' She grunted and sat back on her haunches, a motionless figure watching the search.

'It might already be too late,' Alice said quietly, an hour later. 'Look.'

A red car was winding along the road, furiously swinging round the corners. At the foot of the crag the car screeched to a halt. A slim woman with yellow hair climbed out, with a man holding bulky camera equipment, and another man dressed in a thick, white sweater and Wellington boots. The woman glanced upwards and Alice and Jonathan moved back inside the cave, hidden from view by the tall rock that stuck out into the skyline like a dark, granite tombstone.

The three put their heads together, then one of them returned to the car and pulled out a large floodlight lamp.

The two in the cave watched fearfully. Alice spoke first. She was crying now. 'Why did they have to bring the child here? Why did they have to come to our part? We don't want you here.' She stood up. 'Go back.'

The camera crew clumped around the car seemed to be in deep discussion. A decision was reached and slowly the man with the huge camera began aiming it at the wide sweep of moors and moving it slowly around ... the granite crag of the Winking Man, the jutting rocks, down the smooth hillside and finally into the massive dish of the valley far down below as though viewed from an aeroplane. He seemed to keep the camera trained, for a while, on the distant town of Leek. Then he removed the bulky equipment from his shoulders, and the woman stood in front of the camera and, lit by the white lamp, spoke into it.

Jonathan shook his fist from the mouth of the cave. 'Leave us be!' he shouted. 'Leave us be. Go back!' His words were lost in the wide sweep of the moors, dotted by the men in white and the strange trio clustered around their massive equipment.

Jonathan was flailing his hands around in panic. Alice folded him into her arms and held him to her, rocking him like a child.

'This is it,' she said. 'The end. We'll not be left in peace now.'

Joanna was sitting opposite Mike in her office, a large notepad in front of her. 'Right,' she said. 'The preliminary forensic report on the shoes is that they were brand new. Had been worn for six or so hours at the most. Probably along a street... traces of dog faeces, dust and a small amount of mud. A few dark fibres, probably from a carpet, and some longer ones that just could be from the inside of a car. Apparently these particular sports shoes retail at about £60. Compared with the rest of the boy's clothes they would seem expensive. He could definitely not have walked a single step on those moors. He was killed elsewhere, Mike, and then brought to the Roaches. We have to assume he was taken there by car with the sole purpose of burning the body. I think it's reasonable to assume that the killer was hoping to destroy the body completely. It's just possible that the arrival of the army diverted him from finishing the task. He might have still been there when the army arrived.'

Mike objected. 'We asked them, Jo. No-one noticed a car there.'

Joanna crossed the room to a huge map of the area. 'There is a back road,' she said. 'Look ... The army drove up here, approaching from this side.' She ran her finger along the main Leek to Buxton road.

'But the killer, carrying the body of the boy plus petrol, would have had to cross the top of the Roaches,' Mike objected again. 'Why should he do that?'

'I've thought of a reason,' Joanna replied. 'He might have known that the army would be arriving later for exercises and wanted to conceal his car from the main road.'

'Then why take the body back towards the road to burn it?'

'We have to go out there,' Joanna said. 'And we need to speak to the army – find out if they always do their exercises in the same place. Also ...' she jabbed her finger at the end of the small track that led to Flash 'I think there's a farm here. It might be a good thing to speak to the farmer and to the landlord of the Winking Man.'

'If he wasn't disturbed by the army it is also possible that he left the body burning, assuming it would be completely destroyed,' she continued. 'I've spoken to the fire people, and they are sure that the body would not have been destroyed, but in another half an hour the boy would have been unrecognisable by his clothes or his features – even his fingerprints – or by anything other than dental records.' She looked at Mike. 'That would still have been before 6.30 am.'

'I want to see Private Swinton again,' she said suddenly. 'I still believe that the body was burned to destroy forensic evidence. And one sure piece of evidence was the tattoos on his fingers. It could be an embarrassing link for Private Swinton. But there was not quite enough petrol, the clothes were not saturated and the ground was very damp. So luckily we have a body only partially destroyed.'

'But we still don't have a name for Burning Boy,' Mike said.

She glanced at him, startled. 'Is that what you've called him?'

He looked apologetic. 'It was Scottie who called him that, said it reminded him of Moses and the Burning Bush – you know, the mountain in the Ten Commandments ... It looked sort of bleak and very high ...'

She stared at him. 'Have the boys found out anything about the source of the shoes?'

'Not so far.' He grimaced, glad to leave an uncomfortable subject. 'It would have been half-day closing yesterday afternoon, wouldn't it?'

'And the children's homes?'

'They've covered a couple – going to some more this morning. Nothing so far.'

'At what time have we scheduled our briefing?'
'Ten.'

She stopped for a minute then sighed. 'That poor child. I hate to think what he must have gone through – for all of his short, sordid, horrible little life.' She looked at Mike. 'Don't you get a feeling in the pit of your stomach when you see these kids on the streets?'

Mike grinned. 'Yeah,' he said. 'I feel I want to lock them up now – before they start on their life of crime.'

'We're failing them,' she said, 'these kids. They don't set off from the same starting line. Some of them never get across the line. They don't even run the same bloody race. Life is different for them right from the word go.' She leaned back in her chair, sighed, closed her eyes. 'They never discover the meaning of words like love and trust, truth, honesty, kindness ...'

Mike cleared his throat noisily. 'Don't take this the wrong way, Joanna, but I don't think it's a good idea for us to be too idealistic.'

'Perhaps we'd be better coppers if we were a bit more idealistic,' she said.

Mike crossed the room. 'We start off being idealistic. A couple of years later we get cynical. Guess who makes us that way?'

'But we don't do anything to help them.'

'Because it isn't our job, Joanna – that's why.'

'But there isn't really anyone.'

'There's plenty of people,' Mike said. 'They just ignore their chances.'

She looked quizzically at him. 'You really think so?'

'Parents,' he said.

'But if they had parents surely all this wouldn't happen to them.'

'Sometimes,' he said darkly, 'it's the parents who are doing it to them.'

She nodded. 'Yes,' she replied, 'sometimes, and sometimes it isn't.'

Eloise scuffed through hot, dry sand along the steep path that led to the sea while her parents watched.

Jane spoke first. 'You can't do it, Matthew,' she said. 'You can't leave.'

He frowned at her. 'Jane,' he said. 'Please. Don't make it hard.'

Jane Levin's face tightened as she watched her daughter wade into the sea, up to her waist. 'I won't make it easy, Matthew,' she said softly. 'There is nothing – absolutely *nothing* – I won't do to keep you.' She drew in a long, deep breath. 'I will rake up every single speck of dirt that I can think of.' She stopped and looked at him. 'I will embarrass you in any way I can.' She turned and glared at him. 'I will make any life you might try to build together miserable. I am warning you now, Matthew. You – are – my – husband and you will *stay* my husband.' She stared out over the sparkling sea. 'I like the life I lead, Matthew. I'm comfortable at the farmhouse and I intend staying there.'

'It's all right,' Matthew said. 'I've arranged a flat.'

Jane stared at him. 'And what about Eloise?'

Matthew looked at her taut face, at the thin, mean lips, and wondered. Had he ever kissed them and found them soft and yielding? No – at least not that he remembered. He buried his face in his hands and groaned.

Jane watched Eloise, decked out in her scarlet bikini, snorkel mask and rubber fins, slip her breathing tube into her mouth. Then with a splash she was gone, and Jane followed the pipe and the chain of bubbles as the child inspected the rock bottom to the bay.

Matthew also watched as the flippers kicked with a loud splash and the little pipe moved along the ripples like the periscope of a diminutive submarine. Eloise's blond hair floated like beautiful, pale seaweed. And Matthew wondered when would be the best time to speak to the child.

Jason Fogg was lying on his bed.

'I heard it on the radio ...' He frowned at Kirsty. 'What if it's Dean?'

She gave a snort. 'Don't be bloody daft,' she said. 'Why should it be? There's thousands of kids his age out there ...' She paused. 'What exactly did they say on Radio Stoke?'

Jason stared at the carpet, concentrating. 'A boy, about ten, blond hair ... Oh yeah, they said he was wearing black jeans.' He glanced at Kirsty. 'My jeans are gone. He was always takin' them. They was too big for him,' he complained.

Kirsty tugged at a piece of her dark, tangled hair. 'That don't mean much. Loads of kids wear black jeans. Oh come on, Jason,' she said, 'he'll turn up.' She looked confident. 'I know he will.'

At 13 and a half, Kirsty always resorted to a blind, determined optimism, doggedly convincing herself nothing was wrong – all would turn out all right in the end. The truth was that for her it never had turned out all right in the end, but she would have tagged the phrase 'so far' onto any statement about her future life.

It was different for Jason. He had had one stroke of luck but failed to recognise it until the last year, three years too late. At 11 he had been fostered with a possibility of adoption. However, the huge dose of smother love, together with a cheerful and determined father – two parents who had felt they had a right to delve into all four corners of his life – had been too much for him. The extreme claustrophobia of the relationship had ended with a screaming, shouting, throwing episode at three o'clock in the morning after his foster mother had found him with his hand down his pyjama trousers and woken him from sleep. The on-call social worker had been called there and then. And, amid allegations of 'not being nice,' Jason had been returned, confused, to the small children's home, the social worker telling him all the way back that he had done nothing wrong. His child's mind had formed the question: 'So why are they kicking me out?'

'Back to The Nest,' he had said with a large slice of bravado. But inside he had been crying and deeply puzzled. 'If that's parents,' he had said to Dean that night, 'you can stick 'em.'

And Dean had agreed. He had understood. He knew about 'happy families' ... He'd once been placed with a couple of religious fanatics who had had the idea of saving a child. Pretty little Dean, with his choirboy looks and innocent eyes, had seemed ideal. But in the first 24 hours he had used dirty words so many times they had stuck their fingers in their ears to block them out. And when Dean had used the 'F' word to the vicar after church on Sunday morning they had felt they'd bitten off more than they could chew and marched him back to the children's home with marks on his bottom from where they had tried to beat some 'decency' into him.

Dean's second home experience had been, for him, easier to understand. The woman had been a hatchet-faced tyrant who worked in a local slaughterhouse. All the affection the boy had received had been from her husband, who had kissed him, given him sweets, shared his bed.

His next experience had been the one that remained to haunt him. Because he had been happy, fostered by a dirty, fat creature, blessed with 13 other foster children. The dirt hadn't mattered. The poverty and meagre food hadn't mattered either. The fact that he had shared the bedroom with five other boys had never mattered. But the social worker had believed that all these things did matter, and Dean had been returned to the children's home. After that he had simply refused to go with anyone else and had run away every single time they suggested it. As he told Jason and Kirsty, 'If I can't stop with Mrs Swires they can stick it.' And when the home had finally suggested the humiliation of putting his photograph in the newspaper together with an appeal for a 'family', he had known that something drastic would have to be done.

'But,' Jason muttered to himself very softly, 'Dean was all right in the end.'

The sports shop had a sale on of expensive trainers. *Half-price*, the vivid pink signs said, and PC Roger Farthing looked at the prices and wondered who the hell could afford these sorts of shoes – even at 'half-price'. Outside in a basket were some odd pairs, tied together by the laces. With a policeman's awareness of crime he thought it was a bloody silly place to leave expensive shoes.

He picked up a pair, white with purple and gold flashes on the sides, huge tongues lolling out, and marched straight into the shop. It was fluorescent bright and sparkling white everywhere, with a lime green carpet on the floor. There were racks of T-shirts and baggy jogging pants, tennis rackets, golf balls.

A thin man in a short-sleeved white T-shirt looked up.

'Are you the owner of this shop?' the PC asked.

The man nodded.

PC Farthing took out his pencil. 'Your name?'

'Keithy,' he said. 'Keithy Latos.'

Farthing wrote it down. 'We're making some enquiries about a pair of shoes,' he said, and dropped the trainers on the counter 'Like these.'

The man's eyes flickered, dropped quickly to the shoes then looked up. 'Where did you get them from?'

'The basket outside.'

The man picked them up. 'Like these, you say?'

PC Farthing nodded, watching the man carefully. He had a slight tremor and the laces tapped against the shoes. They were parallel-laced – unlike the child's.

'Have you sold a pair of these, size sevens, in the last couple of days?'

The man had small eyes, like a pig's. He avoided Farthing's gaze as though desperate to conceal something. 'Why do you want to know?' he asked carelessly.

'In connection with a serious crime.' Farthing had learned this phrase at police training college.

Latos licked his lips. 'Serious crime?'

His eyes were darting all over the place. And Farthing knew instinctively he had both bought and read the morning's newspaper.

Keithy gulped for air. 'Sold – no.' He gave a short laugh. 'In fact, nobody's bought any like this for a couple of weeks.' He eyed the policeman anxiously as though it was important he was believed. 'Gone out of fashion,' he said. 'Why do you think I've stuck them out the front half-price? No-one wants those sort any more – old hat. They all have to have Nikes now. Even half-price no-one wants them.'

Roger Farthing thought quickly. 'You haven't had a pair nicked, have you?'

'Don't know,' Keithy said carelessly. 'How many's in the basket?'

They both went outside the shop and PC Farthing waited while Keithy picked out the shoes, heaping them up into his arms.

'Yeah,' he said uncertainly. 'There could be a pair missing.' He looked at Roger Farthing. 'What size did you say?'

'Sevens.'

'Could be,' he said.

'Don't you know for sure?'

'Not till I stock-take.'

Roger Farthing could have cheerfully strangled the man. He drew out the photograph then of the dead boy and watched Keithy's face blanch.

'My God,' he said, looking shocked at the policeman. 'This kid's dead, isn't he?' He looked again at the picture. 'Isn't this the kid they found up on the Roaches?'

'Yes,' Roger Farthing replied, 'wearing a pair of trainers exactly like these.' He indicated the shoes.

Keithy stared at them, his Adam's apple suddenly bobbing up and down.

'I'd be grateful if you'd do a stock-take immediately. It's important we know where the boy got the shoes from.'

Keithy swallowed noisily. 'Course,' he said.

Roger stuck the picture of the dead boy in front of his face. 'Know him, do you?'

Keithy looked at the picture, quickly at the policeman, then back to the picture again. 'I don't think so,' he said.

'You're sure?'

'I might do ...' He was flustered now. 'They all look the same ... same jeans and anoraks, hairdos ...'

'Sports shoes.' Roger put in gently.

Keithy's eyes flickered. 'Those too,' he muttered.

Roger Farthing handed him one of the posters they had had printed. The usual thing – 'Do You Know This Boy?' and the artist's impression below. 'Would you mind putting one of these up in your shop?'

He looked irritated. 'Yes I would,' he said shortly. 'I don't want a picture of a dead kid up in here. This is a sports shop – not *Crimewatch*.'

'Even if it helped find his killer?'

Keithy bit his lip. 'All right then,' he said reluctantly, cornered into acquiescence. He grabbed the poster, tearing the corner.

'And by the way,' Farthing said, 'if I was you, I wouldn't leave the shoes outside. It's inviting theft.'

Keithy too readily agreed with him, and PC Farthing found himself disliking him with his slicked hair, tight T-shirt over a bony chest, the affected bounce in his step as though he was wearing some of his own 'Air step' shoes.

'You know, you ought to keep a record of what's gone missing.' Farthing suggested. 'If people don't report crime it cocks up our figures. We think Leek's more law-abiding than it really is.'

'Quite,' said Keithy, and Farthing got the distinct

impression he was dying to get rid of him. 'So you'll stock-take?'

'Right away, officer.'

'And you'll let us know at the nick?'

'Yeah ... yeah.'

'You'll ring us up – ask for me?'

'Yeah.'

'Well, thank you.' Roger Farthing turned to go. 'By the way, Mr Latos, where were you on Sunday night?'

Keithy looked confident. 'I went to the Buxton Opera House,' he said. 'To see the D'Oyly Carte singers.'

'And what were they singing?'

'*The Mikado*.' He grinned.

'And did anyone see you?'

'Lots of people. I've got lots of friends in Buxton. People who like the opera.'

Farthing found himself shrinking from the man's tone. 'Who did you go with?'

'With a – friend.'

'I see,' Roger Farthing said. 'Of course we'll need his name.'

Keithy giggled. 'It might have been a lady.'

'His or her name then.'

'Martin,' Keithy said coyly, 'Martin Shane. He lives in Cheddleton, in a little cottage in the High Street. He'll vouch for me. We were together all evening.'

'What time did you part?'

Keithy fiddled with the neck of his T-shirt. 'Well, we didn't – exactly,' he said. 'He'd had a lot to drink. He stayed the night here. There's no law about it.'

'No.' Farthing shook his head. He wrote the name down in his black notebook. 'Please,' he said, 'look at the picture again. Are you sure you have never seen this boy before?'

Keithy put his head to one side, like a thin, scraggy-necked bird. 'I don't think so.'

'So you aren't one hundred percent sure?'

Keithy looked up then. 'I meet a lot of people working in this line of business,' he said plaintively. 'I can't possibly remember absolutely everyone, you know, officer.' He fingered the photograph. 'Pretty little thing, isn't he?'

'Wasn't he.' Farthing found it difficult to keep the sarcasm out of his voice. 'He was – before someone killed him.'

6

According to their details only six children were housed at 51 Greystoke Road, a large, terraced Victorian house, almost in the centre of the town. PC Cheryl Smith and DC Alan King had been assigned to make the enquiries here, to try to connect the dead boy with a living home, to find a name, friends, someone who cared.

Cheryl Smith stared up at the tall house with its wide bay windows and two small gables at the very top and made a wry face. 'The Nest.' She read the sign at the side of the door. 'Hardly seems appropriate, does it?'

Alan shook his head. 'Well, I'd hardly call the kids that come from these places little birds,' he said, 'but it's a home.'

She looked at him. 'You believe they think of these institutions as a home?' She queried. 'I rather think they consider them nearer to a prison.'

'Maybe that's more to do with their attitude,' he said. 'The places I know do a bloody good job of making them homely. Besides, perhaps a nest might be right for little birds, but these are something else. More like fierce little rats with sharp teeth, erratic tempers, unpredictable and aggressive behaviour. Perhaps a prison is more appropriate.'

'Now, now,' she said. 'Doesn't do to have these preconceived ideas. They're just children – like all the others.'

He made a face. 'Who are you trying to fool?' he said. 'Come on. The trouble is they aren't anything like the other children, are they? They stick out. From their clothes to their hair to their behaviour. And that's what makes them even more different.'

She glared at him as he banged on the door. 'There's no need to act the dawn raid, policeman-on-duty bit. Can't you understand this is half the trouble? You have certain preconceptions about young institutionalised kids and you barge into their home. No wonder they learn to hate us.'

He turned to her then. 'Whose side are you on, Constable?'

'There you go again,' she said. 'Get it into your thick skull. There *aren't* any sides.'

Alan King opened his mouth to speak but before he could do so the door was opened by a thin girl of about 13 still in her check school summer dress and a navy cardigan that had dropped down off her shoulders. Her hostility was thick from the moment her eyes brushed the black and silver uniforms.

'Who've you come to moan about now?' she asked, her green eyes flashing. 'Can't you lot leave us alone? What is it now? Someone lost a penny in the supermarket?'

Cheryl stepped forward. 'Can we speak to the warden, love?'

'Tell me what it's about first.' The girl held her ground, blocked the doorway. 'He's out anyway.'

DC Alan King let out a quiet expletive and Cheryl

moved in front of him. 'Who's in then, love?'

The girl glowered at them. 'Don't call me love,' she said waspishly. 'I'm not your love or bleedin' anybody else's love. He's here. I suppose you'll have to come in, make your trouble.'

'Just let us have a word with the warden.'

Reluctantly the girl stepped back and opened the door halfway. 'All right.'

Cheryl smiled. 'We haven't come to get anyone into trouble,' she said pleasantly.

The girl shrugged and said nothing.

She could have been a pretty girl, blessed with tangled dark hair and a heart-shaped face and the green intelligent eyes of a clever cat. But already her mouth had hardened with all that life had mercilessly hurled at her and it was a thin, mean line that would always find it a struggle to laugh or smile. And her bony shoulders drooped with a faint depressive line. Slowly her life-map was being drawn.

But instead of familiar irritation, Cheryl felt something more like pity. She knew they had come to the right place. It was only afterwards when she filled out her report that she realised why she had known so surely. It was the tattoo on the girl's knuckles. Not the words ... 'Love' and 'Hate' were common enough. It was the letters – the 'A' done in the same pointed style with a curl at the bottom and the 'L' with a loop at the bottom corner. Calligraphy instead of the usual crude square letters. And they were drawn in grey rather than the usual navy ink.

So they followed the girl along the corridor towards a smell of onions. 'He's making tea,' the girl said over her shoulder. 'Hotpot.'

The warden was younger than they had expected,

with a plump face and heavy glasses. He was bending over the kitchen table, wearing a navy-and-white-striped butcher's apron over jeans, holding a very sharp-looking carving knife. With a quick and expert touch he was busily slicing onions, and as they walked in he scraped them into the pot over the pink, raw beef.

'Tea,' he explained, with a wary glance at the overwhelming presence of the two police officers. 'Don't tell me one of them's been up to something again ... I really thought they'd settled down – apart from Dean.' His eyes narrowed. 'Have you brought him back?'

'No ... There's no trouble ... Please don't worry.' DC Alan King put his hat on the table.

The warden held out his hand. 'Mark,' he said. 'Mark Riversdale. I'm warden of this madhouse.' He had brown eyes behind the glasses, fringed with long, thick lashes and a frank, friendly smile. 'So what can I do for you?' His eyes were still faintly wary.

Cheryl Smith found herself wondering just how many times the police had visited The Nest.

'Trouble?' he asked.

'We hope not.'

Mark looked questioningly at Cheryl and smiled at her. 'Well, then?'

'How many young people live here?' she began.

Mark Riversdale blinked. 'Look,' he said, 'I know two police officers don't simply turn up at children's homes and make polite conversation. I don't want to appear unfriendly or over-suspicious, but what's going on?'

'How many?' Cheryl asked gently.

Mark gave a loud sigh. 'Three boys,' he said, 'and three girls. At the moment Sonya is the youngest – she's four. And Jason is the oldest. A couple of boys left about four months ago,' he explained. 'They have to leave care at 16.'

'Have you seen the papers?'

Mark Riversdale gave a quick glance from one to the other. 'Hardly have time to look at them,' he said. 'Why?'

'Do you have a boy aged about ten to 11,' Cheryl asked, 'with blond hair and an earring?'

Mark laughed. 'They all have earrings,' he said, 'and tattoos. Jason fancies himself as a bit of an artist. I have asked him not to, but the kids, they beg him.' His eyes looked suddenly weary. 'I have more important things to worry about than a bit of skin-art.' He gave a faint smile. 'That's what they call it. It seems a fanciful name for those crude love/hate things but – as I say – they like them. For the record,' he looked serious now, 'we do have a boy who answers that description, but he isn't here at the moment. He's absconded,' he said apologetically. 'I usually leave it a day or two. He often goes. Always gets back safe and sound. Keeps him out of trouble, you see, if I don't make too big an issue of it.'

'So you haven't informed the police?' Alan King failed to keep the accusation out of his voice and the warden picked it up.

'We'd never get any other work done if we reported every single absconder from a home to you and expected you to find him or her. As I've said, I usually wait – up to a week. If they come back, no harm's done. If not, then I inform you lot. Dean can look after himself.' He stared at the table. 'He absconds on average twice to three times a month, usually for two to three days – much less frequently in the last year. February it was a fortnight. He always comes back, you know, clean and well fed. Sometimes even with money in his pocket. He is a survivor, that one.' Sudden alarm crossed his face. 'What is all this about?'

Cheryl pulled out the photograph of the dead boy, placed it on the table and studied Mark Riversdale's face, knowing Alan King was doing exactly the same.

'Is this Dean?' she asked.

Mark stared at it disbelievingly. One hand reached out slowly, picked it up and held it nearer his face. 'It can't be,' he said. 'Surely this boy ...?' Then he looked up at the two police officers.

'Yes,' Alan said quietly, 'the boy is dead.'

Cheryl leaned across the table. 'Take your time, Mr Riversdale. Be sure. Is this boy Dean?'

Mark Riversdale studied the photograph again, then he nodded. 'Yes,' he said, 'at least I think so.' He looked again at the photograph then nodded slowly, deeper and more definite. 'Yes, it is him.' He bit his lip, gnawed at a nail, drummed one index finger on the table. 'How did he die?' he asked eventually.

'We're not absolutely sure,' Alan said, 'but it looks as though he was murdered. You will have to formally identify him, of course.'

Mark Riversdale looked again at the picture, brushed away a tear and muttered something about the onions. 'He could almost be asleep,' he said. 'He looks so peaceful.'

'He isn't asleep,' Cheryl said brutally. 'He's dead.'

'Who – where?'

'He was found dead on the moors early yesterday morning,' Alan King said.

Mark, looked up. 'So he was the lad. I heard something about a body being found on the moors. Wasn't it burning?'

'And you still didn't report him missing?'

Mark Riversdale sank down into one of the kitchen chairs. 'I just didn't connect it,' he said, pulling off his glasses and setting them down on the table. 'I never thought for a minute it was Dean ...' He passed his hand over his brow in a gesture of hopelessness. 'But he was a survivor. He was always going. But he came back – every time. Not only came back but was clean and well fed.'

'Not this time,' Cheryl said quietly.

'It wasn't exposure?'

'No.'

Cheryl felt suddenly sick and angry. All she could think of was the fact that the dead boy now had a name. Dean.

'Dean what?' she asked.

'Dean Tunstall. He was ten years old.'

And her mind toyed with another idea. He had been a victim of long-term sexual abuse. She looked carefully at Mark Riversdale and wondered.

'When did you say he was found?' Mark asked.

'Yesterday, very early in the morning.'

He passed his hand across his brow. 'All the time, I thought he'd be back.' He stared again at the photograph.

'Mr Riversdale,' DC King's voice was toneless, 'I'm afraid we'll have to ask you to come down to the mortuary for a formal identification. Also we shall want to speak to the other occupants of the home.' He hesitated. 'We'll have to report back to the station. I think it's best if you tell the other children.'

Mark nodded.

'Do you know what's puzzling me?' Cheryl said as they

were driving back to the station.

Alan King shook his head. 'Come on, brain-box,' he said, 'what is it?'

'Clean and well fed.' She looked at her colleague. 'Does that sound like a boy who's been sleeping rough?'

Joanna held the briefing early that afternoon. She faced the team allocated to her. 'Thanks to some legwork by DC Alan King and PC Cheryl Smith we have a name for our burning boy. I just want to say that they may have been to the right place but all of you have helped to identify this child. You are all equally important. It's just luck who happens to visit the right place. My thanks extend to every one of you. I don't need to tell you that finding out who he is was the first step to finding out who killed him.' She smiled. 'The boy's name is Dean, Dean Tunstall. He was resident at the children's home just off the Ashbourne road, known as The Nest.' She ignored the titters at the name that rippled around the room. Sometimes in a murder case – especially the murder of a child – it was only the light relief that kept morale from dipping into depression. 'He was ten years old and a frequent absconder from the home – we'd returned him there ourselves once or twice. He had apparently lived there for most his life.' She glanced at Cheryl Smith, who was seated in the front row, her dark eyes fixed on Joanna's face with rapt attention. 'PC Smith' she said, 'as you have already been to The Nest, I would like you to go back there. Find out as much as possible about Dean's life ... his origins ... parents, friends, relatives, etc. I'd like you to begin as soon as formal identification has taken place later on this afternoon.'

She looked back at the workforce. 'It's early days yet,' she said, 'but already we know a few details. The warden at the home is 27-year-old Mark Riversdale. As far as we know, he's clean with no previous convictions. However, please remember, Dean had been abused over a number of years. Obviously any male who came into contact with the boy is under suspicion. Broach the subject carefully. At the moment he has to be on our suspect list. PC Smith ...' she glanced at Cheryl, 'go gently, but we will need statements from the children at the home, in the presence of social workers. Also we'll interview Mark Riversdale. Get an alibi if possible.' She paused. 'There is another avenue that we would be negligent not to explore. Dean was as we know a frequent absconder. I want a couple of you to speak to the homeless in Leek and find out if they knew him. Although we know that when he returned ...' she glanced at the notes she had made, 'in mid-February last year following a disappearance of a fortnight, he returned clean and well fed.' She looked up. 'I don't know if any of you remember that particular fortnight, but according to the Met Office it snowed and the temperatures remained well below zero for most of that period. So where was Dean? Who looked after him? Who kept him?' She nodded.

'I want to make another point. The press will be on our heels wanting an early arrest, but our forensic evidence is, quite frankly, so far disappointing. It is important we arrest the right man for the right reasons. I am not in a hurry but I am determined. No mistakes and play it all by the board. We can video the children's evidence and it will be admissible in the courts. According to our latest guidelines children do not lie.' The ripple that swept through the room was louder this time and one or two laughed. She held up her hand. 'I know, I know,' she said, 'but they are our guidelines. We can sift through their statements carefully and see where they lead us. Also, I have spoken to the coroner. The inquest can go ahead and Dean be buried just as soon as we've contacted his next of kin.' She stopped briefly before saying quietly, 'I believe there is a mother – somewhere.' Then she added, 'The verdict will almost certainly be murder.'

She paused to glance through her notes again. 'We're following up the lead on the ring but still haven't managed to get hold of either Mr Robin Leech or his mother, Mrs Gill Leech. It seems they are away from home for a long weekend. When they do return I want you to remember – we will have to go cautiously. Mr Ashford Leech was a man who was very vocal at the House. His wife and son are both members of some pressure groups – also very vocal. The Leech family will know their rights and you can be sure they will be the first to complain of any departure from recommended police protocols.' She paused. 'Any questions?'

One of the detective constables at the back raised his hand. 'The two soldiers who found the body, ma'am, are they under suspicion?'

Joanna nodded. 'The boy soldiers,' she mused. 'Yes.' She turned back to the board and the enlarged photograph of the tattoos on Dean's knuckles. 'I expect some of you noticed these tattoos. Private Gary Swinton appears to have at least the same tattoo artist as Dean. We're looking into Swinton's past at the moment and will let you know of any further developments in that direction. We do need to know a little more about these boy soldiers – their whereabouts for the night in question, alibis and, most important of all, I want to know this: did Swinton have any previous contact with the dead boy?' She grinned at the DC. 'Well done.'

She scanned the room. 'Does anyone have anything further to add?'

This time it was Roger Farthing who spoke. 'I visited the shoe shop,' he said, and reported the uncertain record of stock. 'When I got back from the shop,' he said slowly, 'I looked up Keithy Latos – the guy who owns the shop. He has a record for soliciting young boys. He's been caught once in some public toilets in Hanley with an under-age.' He sat down with a flushed face. 'I thought you ought to know.'

Joanna nodded. 'So,' she said, 'he has to go on the list. We'll watch him for a day or two.' She glanced at Roger. 'Did you say he's going to stock-take?'

'Yes.'

'We'll call back there later on today. Mike?' He nodded. 'We'll go together. If we can see anything out of the ordinary we'll get a warrant and search his flat.'

Mike touched her on the shoulder as the officers filed out of the room. 'Have you heard from Dr Levin?'

She shook her head.

His face was almost mocking. 'Not even a picture postcard, Joanna?'

'I told you,' she said sharply. 'He's on a family holiday.'

'Oh yes, I was forgetting.' His eyes were very dark and unreadable. 'A family holiday.'

They called at the shop just as Keithy Latos was switching off the lights. He started when he saw them, and opened the door very slowly, giving a strained grin.

'I thought you'd be back,' he said.

Mike spoke. 'We wondered if you'd had time to go through your books yet, Mr Latos.'

Keithy Latos took a step backwards. 'I did actually,' he said. 'It was quiet in the shop. I am missing a pair. Did you say size sevens?'

'When did they go?' Joanna glanced around the shop, wondering if it had been here that Dean had died – or upstairs?

'I ... I'm not that sure.' He licked his lips.

'Were you just closing?' Joanna asked innocently. 'We could come up, help you look through the books.'

He opened and closed his mouth like a fish.

Mike smiled. 'A cup of tea would be lovely,' he said.

It was a tiny flat upstairs, beyond a square foot that served as a landing. Through a half-opened door Joanna glimpsed an unmade bed with dark sheets and quilt thrown back. To the side was a white toilet with curling lino on the floor. Ahead was a square sitting room and a tiny kitchenette. It was a far cry from the smart shop below.

'No palace,' Keithy called, 'but it does – know what I mean? Go in, sit down. I'll put the kettle on.'

While he disappeared into the kitchen, Joanna and Mike walked into the tiny sitting room, decorated in cream and brown, dominated by a huge television set and video. They scanned the room but saw nothing more suggestive than a pile of gay magazines. Keithy walked in carrying three steaming mugs.

'I'll just get my books.'

The books were poorly kept, with Tipp-Ex and crossings out, but as far as they could see the list of stock was short by one pair of trainers. But as the previous accounts had been done almost three months earlier, the shoes could have gone at any time in the last 12 weeks.

Joanna closed the book and looked at Latos. 'Can you give me a better idea of when the trainers might have been stolen?' she asked. 'When did you put them outside in the basket?'

Here he could not be much more help. 'About a month ago,' he said, 'I think.' He studied his fingernails. 'I'm not really a very precise sort of person.'

'Mr Latos.'

'Please, call me Keithy ...'

'Keithy,' Joanna said firmly. 'The boy who was killed. Did you know him? His name was Dean – Dean Tunstall.'

Mike slid the photograph in front of the man's face.

'You see,' Joanna said softly, 'we know that you have been in trouble before – with boys.'

A look of panic crossed Latos's face. 'I swear, I don't know anything about him. 'You see ...' his eyes pleaded to be believed, 'I got a steady friend now. The guy I went to Buxton with. We're very faithful. I wouldn't ... I really wouldn't. I couldn't do anything to risk things between us two.'

They finished their tea and left.

In the car outside, Joanna looked at Mike. 'Well?' she said. 'What do you think?'

'Very eager to please.'

'Come on, Mike,' she said. 'You know these past sexual offenders. They feel they get hauled in for about everything that goes on – all the slightly deviant crimes. In his place you'd be eager to please.'

He turned towards her. 'I wouldn't be in his place,' he said. 'But just remember, Jo, there is a coincidence. The shoes came from here. Dean was abused. This man has been convicted of soliciting boys ...'

'We don't have enough to get a warrant,' she said. 'Circumstantial. That's all.' She paused, then bit her lip. 'Do you think his name's really Keithy?' she asked.

He drove her back to the station to pick up her bike.

'Fancy a drink?' he asked.

She frowned. 'I want to get back. I have a sudden strong desire to be alone. Besides ...' she grinned, 'it's a steep ride home.'

7

There seemed no time at all between the ride home and the return journey into work. Mike was moving into his parking slot as Joanna locked her bike against the railings. He gave a swift, appraising glance at the slim figure in black cycling shorts and a pink T-shirt.

'Good morning, Jo,' he called. 'What's on the agenda?'

'Nothing until I've got changed.'

She emerged from her office ten minutes later in a straight black suit with a scarlet blouse and some low-heeled, black leather pumps.

'I want to speak to Mark Riversdale,' she said.

The Nest looked grey, old and forbidding as the car rolled up the drive. A young face was peering through the window but jerked back when the child saw it was observed.

Joanna stood, staring for a moment, then she and Mike walked briskly up the four steps to a huge front door. It was opened almost immediately by a young man with brown hair and a plump face with heavy glasses. He was dressed in a navy sweatshirt and blue jeans.

'Hello?'

Joanna held out her hand. 'Mark Riversdale?'

He gave a rather weak smile. 'That's right,' he said. He gave a deep sigh. 'I suppose you're the police.'

'That's right. I'm Detective Inspector Piercy. This is Detective Sergeant Mike Korpanski. May we come in?'

They were shown into one of the large, shabby front rooms. A dusty grand piano stood in the corner, a box of toys underneath it. The carpet was plain blue; the curtains a different shade of blue. They sat in soft low armchairs of brown Draylon.

'There's going to be a devil of a fuss,' Mark Riversdale said with a worried look. 'Typical of Dean. He was always the odd one out – the unexpected one.' The two police officers noted that the warden – or 'carer' as they had been informed – was not unduly upset at the tragic end of one of his young charges. 'I suppose he was lying there dead when I was believing a pillow was him.' He seemed cross at the deceit.

Joanna looked at her notes. 'Was that why his disappearance wasn't reported?'

'I went into the bedroom Monday morning to get the lads up for school. Jason and Dean shared a bedroom.' He looked suddenly defensive. 'It isn't bad – two of them sharing a room. It's a bloody sight better than it used to be.'

'So what happened?'

Mark Riversdale flushed. 'I saw the hump in the bed,' he said, pulling his glasses off in an embarrassed way. 'I thought it was Dean.'

'You didn't check?' Mike could never quite keep

the critical note out of his voice.

Mark Riversdale put his glasses back on. 'One of the boys distracted me.'

Joanna looked again at her notes. 'Jason?' she asked.

Riversdale nodded. 'Yes.'

'What about Sunday morning?' Mike was watching him intently.

'I never disturb them Sunday morning,' Mark said. 'They have to have a bit of freedom.'

'We'll have to talk to Jason.'

Mark's eyebrows lifted. 'I'll have to be present,' he said apologetically, 'and a social worker. And if there's any possibility of his being charged ...'

'Definitely not at this stage.' Joanna paused. 'Mr Riversdale,' she said with some difficulty, 'tell me – what was Dean like?'

Mark sat right back in the chair, his eyes half-closed. 'Like a lot of them,' he said, 'he was naive, gullible ... longed for something better without a clue how to go about it. He was so typical of these lads ... streetwise and crafty. Clever. He could con the trousers off anyone.' He frowned. 'Such a pretty kid. Blond, you know – blue eyes innocent as a baby's. But he had this tough exterior – like they all have.' He looked suddenly upset. 'The tattoos and the earrings ... They're all a badge. "I'm tough. Leave me alone."' He smiled. 'He was fond of doing that ... Shrugging his shoulders, pushing your hand away. "Leave us alone," he'd say. But he could be so damned secretive ... And this last few months he's gone from bad to worse.'

Joanna watched Mark Riversdale's face very carefully.

'Where was he going,' she said, 'when he

absconded?'

'I don't know.' Mark seemed angry and insulted at the question. 'If I knew I would have gone and got him back.' He thought for a minute. 'Where do they all go?' he asked.

'But he wasn't sleeping rough, was he?'

Riversdale shook his head. 'I don't think so,' he said. 'But I've often wondered. I mean, where else? He had no family. Mother walked out years ago,' he explained. 'I don't think she's seen him for many years – possibly not since Dean was about two. The last I heard she was in Portsmouth ... but that was seven years ago.'

'Perhaps you'd let us have the address.'

'Yes, of course.' Mark Riversdale wriggled uncomfortably in his chair. 'Look, the person you really ought to be talking to is Maree, Dean's social worker. Maree O'Rourke.' He gave them the number.

'And Dean's father?' Mike asked.

'No sign of a father at all – not even on his birth certificate.'

'Was he resentful at all – envious?'

Mark Riversdale thought for a moment. 'No, I don't think so.'

'He wasn't envious of others with families?'

'He said to me once ... he said he had a family.'

'Do you think he meant here?'

Mark Riversdale thought for a moment. 'I thought so at the time. I must admit now I'm not so sure. Maybe he meant here. But perhaps ...' He hesitated. 'Some of the kids here – they make up things. They're not a particularly truthful lot, and deep down under all that bravado and swagger they really do wish they were like other kids ... You know – mum, dad, brothers and sisters. It isn't unusual for them to invent them.'

'But in Dean's case,' Joanna pursued, 'he returned clean and well fed. Didn't you wonder?'

Riversdale pushed his glasses up his nose. 'He was canny,' he said. It was not an answer.

'The tattoos,' Joanna said next. 'Who did them?'

'Jason,' Riversdale said reluctantly. 'Considers himself quite an artist.' He looked at Joanna. 'I know ... I know they're awful. But all the kids were clamouring to have them.' He sighed. 'What could I do?'

Joanna opened the next line of enquiry very gingerly. 'The post-mortem shows evidence of both physical and sexual abuse,' she said.

Riversdale's eyes flickered.

'Someone had burned him repeatedly with a cigarette. Do you have any ideas?'

Riversdale flopped back into the chair. 'Is this official?'

'Off the record – at the moment,' Joanna said evenly, fighting away the wave of disgust.

'He never complained,' Riversdale said. 'He never said anything ...'

Mike moved forward. 'But you had your suspicions?'

Riversdale nodded, cowed by the burly form of the detective sergeant.

Joanna took a deep breath in. 'Can I get this quite straight?' she said carefully. 'You were aware that Dean was being abused here – in the home. But you did nothing?'

Mark Riversdale dropped his eyes and looked suddenly shifty. 'He never complained,' he said again. 'The cigarette burns,' he began. 'It was a sort of game with the kids. They'd see how much they could stand.'

'And who was the ringleader of this sadistic game?'

'He left,' Riversdale said, and suddenly it was clear to Joanna. The tattoos ... the grief when he had found the boy's body. Why? Because he had known him. She glanced at Mike and knew he had reached the same conclusion.

'Swinton,' Joanna said quietly, and Riversdale nodded.

'I was glad to see him go. There was nothing like that after he'd left.'

'To join the army ... Glory be,' she muttered. 'What an incestuous little murder investigation this is proving to be.' She stared at Riversdale. 'Did you know he was the one who found Dean's body – still burning?'

Riversdale's face was ashen. 'No,' he said hoarsely.

'And the sexual abuse – was that down to him as well?'

Riversdale gulped. 'I don't know,' he said hoarsely. 'I don't know. I was never sure about the sexual abuse.' He looked defensive. 'Without actual medical proof you can't be sure.'

'But you suspected it?'

'I wondered,' he said, and Joanna found herself staring at him. Had Mark Riversdale had a penchant for little boys? Was it this dirty little secret that had lured him to the post of warden at the children's home?

Under Joanna's stare he looked uncomfortable.

'Rotten apples,' he said unexpectedly.

'Pardon?'

'I come from the West Country,' Riversdale said. 'One rotten apple's enough to turn the whole barrel. It's the same with these kids in homes. You get one or two bad ones.' He sighed. 'We do what we can. The trouble is, the kids flatly refuse to testify. They won't say who it is. Result, you can never charge them with anything. But we knew it was him that did the burns.'

Before she left, Joanna asked her final question. 'A ring was found on Dean's finger.' She produced the ring, still in its SOC plastic bag. 'We've traced it to the Leech family, Ashford Leech, the MP who died last year. Can you think of any connection between the Leech family and Dean?'

'That's easy,' Mark Riversdale said. 'He was a sort of benefactor of The Nest. He was very kind to Dean and Dean seemed genuinely fond of him. He was quite upset when Mr Leech died.'

'How do you think Dean came to be wearing the ring, Mr Riversdale?'

Mark Riversdale looked puzzled. 'I don't know,' he said. 'I really don't know.'

'There was a burglary last year at Mr Leech's home,' Joanna said. 'It is believed that this ring was stolen then.'

Riversdale looked dubious. 'I don't think Dean would have stolen from Mr Leech. He really liked him.' He gave a shy, tentative smile. 'You see, the kids, they don't think it's wicked to thieve from shops and companies and things – but I don't really think Dean would have stolen something from someone he was so obviously fond of.'

'And these shoes?'

Joanna put the Reeboks on the floor, still faintly bearing scorch marks.

Riversdale looked at them carefully. 'I don't think they're Dean's,' he said. 'He was due for a new pair of shoes. His were really old.'

'Did he ever shoplift?'

Mark Riversdale seemed reluctant to answer.

'The boy is dead,' Joanna said gently. 'It's not like we're going to prosecute him ...'

Mark Riversdale nodded slowly. 'I think he probably did. I've got no proof but I think he did.'

'And where were you Sunday night/Monday morning?'

'In,' he said quickly. 'I stayed in all night.'

'Witnesses?' Mike asked.

'The kids.' Mark gave him a grin. 'They'll soon tell you I was in all night. You can't hide much from them.'

Later that morning Joanna met a few of the investigating officers in the incident room and began filling them in about the interview with the warden of the home.

'So – we know a little about Dean's life and will soon find out more from the social worker. He was ten years old – his eleventh birthday would have been in three months' time – on Christmas Eve.'

Those few words seemed to penetrate the entire room deeper than all the forensic evidence that had been spread in front of them – all the photographs ... The officers sat motionless, stopped writing, stopped whispering, stopped looking at one another. They stared at the floor. This brought Dean to the level of their own children – birthdays, Christmas Eve ... Santa Claus ... presents. Someone cleared his throat noisily. A pall hung over the room.

'The burns were done by a boy in the home. Surprise, surprise, when he left the home he joined the army as a boy soldier. Three guesses as to his name.'

She turned to the board, pointed out Gary Swinton. 'Coincidence?' she said. 'One hell of a coincidence. And we still don't know who put the little bunch of flowers beside the body. *Someone* put them there. Murderers don't usually make little bouquets of flowers to put by their victims, do they? So who was it?'

There was a short silence. Then someone spoke. 'What about the shoes, ma'am?'

Joanna nodded. 'Thanks to PC Farthing we think we have a lead on the shoes. The owner of the sports shop has denied knowing Dean, but from his books it seems probable that a pair of Reeboks answering the description and sizing are missing from his stock. Two things here. Dean might have stolen them. Mark Riversdale, warden at the – home, has admitted Dean was not above some shoplifting. He could have stolen them. They were in a wire basket outside the shop. Alternatively, Dean could have been given them by someone else. Certainly someone was in the habit of looking after this young lad on frequent occasions. Please remember the sports shop sells its shoes laced parallel. Dean's were laced criss-crossed. They were newish shoes. Someone – possibly Dean – threaded the laces again. Also – and I don't want you to start reading too much into this – Keith Latos, the man who owns the sports shop, has a record for soliciting young boys. He is a known paedophile.'

'Why don't you bloody arrest the pervert now?' The voice came from the back, from a young DC – Greg Stanway.

'Prove it, can you?'

'No,' he said, 'but you might search his premises before he gets rid of anything.'

'We haven't got the evidence to get a warrant,' Joanna said, appalled. 'God,' she appealed to the room, 'is this how far the force has gone – genetic coding, 1995 ... For God's sake, this isn't good enough. We don't nab the nearest gay and bung him in the cells for murder ... The CPS expect a case.'

'And if we can't get one?' The voice from the back was persistent. 'He gets off scot and does another kid in?'

'He gets off "scot" if we don't have enough to convict him,' Joanna said.

'So he's your top suspect?'

'Not yet, no.' She gave a quick, helpless glance at Mike.

'Forensic evidence,' he prompted.

'Forensic evidence shows that Dean was murdered elsewhere. His body was moved after death. The pattern of lividity proves that his body lay on its side for a number of hours, then he was laid on his back on the moor before being set alight. By the way, the propellant used was petrol. Unfortunately, not much of a clue but remember it. Gallon containers, I know, are common, but one was certainly used to pour petrol over Dean's clothes ...' She glanced at the picture of the small white body lying motionless on the mortuary slab. 'The shoes were clean. Luckily no petrol splashed on the shoes – otherwise they would certainly have been destroyed, and with them a valuable piece of evidence. It was quite windy early on that morning. We think the murderer stood to the side of the body, to the west, the wind behind him – which is why most of the petrol was blown onto the surrounding grass. Forensics did uncover a few fibres of a dark red wool from his sweatshirt. They could be carpet fibres. Possibly from a car boot. He had to be transported to the moors somehow. But the fibres could be from clothing or even upholstery or a rug.'

She blinked. 'Incidentally, the shoes were the wrong size. Dean's feet were fives. The Reeboks size sevens. If he did steal them he stole the wrong size. We think the jeans weren't his either. They were Jason's.'

'Please bear in mind,' she said quietly, 'this boy was the victim of repeated abuse. In all our enquiries I want you to remember this. Someone – probably someone close to the boy – was molesting him. I want you to be aware of this fact. Unfortunately, it might not even have always been the same person. Different people might have been the perpetrators at different periods in the boy's life. Also it would be an erroneous assumption to make the killer and the molester one and the same person. According to forensics, Dean had not been touched for a long period – a number of months, possibly up to a year. For some reason the abuse had stopped. Now whether Dean was getting older, objected, and this led to his killing, or whether we are talking about two different people remains to be seen. In other words don't rule out anyone because they aren't a known paedophile. It could lose us the killer.' She glanced at Greg Stanway. 'And don't just home in on all the people who have a record for sexual crime. Keep your minds as well as your eyes open.'

A few of the uniformed boys at the rear of the room moved uncomfortably. Joanna stopped talking for a moment. Something was pricking the back of her mind. Keith Latos ... It was a phrase he had used. He had a regular friend now. Perhaps he hadn't needed a small boy anymore. Perhaps the boy had become an embarrassment. She glanced at Mike and decided she would talk to him later. For now she should continue with the briefing.

'Have we got a lead on a car yet?' one officer asked.

'Nothing,' she said. 'There were no tyre tracks at the nearest point to where Dean's body was found. The road behind the Winking Man, however, is much quieter. The car would not necessarily have had to pull off the road for the killer to dump the body. I rather think this was the route he took. But as yet the inch-by-inch boys have not found anything to support this theory.' She made a face. 'It's a very wide moor. We're also a bit disappointed that there were no recent footprints by the body. The ground is soft but rather springy and we haven't got much there.

'Now tell us about the ring, Phil.'

Phil Scott stood up, faced the front. 'It's been difficult,' he said. 'The ring was reported stolen last December by the then MP Ashford Leech. He claimed, at the time, that the ring had been stolen after a house break-in. Between ourselves ...' He looked round at the ring of faces. 'Between ourselves,' he repeated, 'there wasn't any sign of a break-in. It was all very fishy. There were a couple of things wrong. He claimed they'd got in through the bedroom window. But the window had been smashed while it was open. Fragments of glass were both inside the house and outside on the glass roof that they would have had to have climbed to get in that way – while the back door was open.' The atmosphere in the room was still.

Scott carried on. 'The things that were taken in this rather strange burglary were very odd. A photograph album and this ring.' He hesitated. 'When there was a telly, a video – even money. Also there was a car parked right outside. You know how they hate company. So why go when there's obviously someone in?' Again he paused – for effect. 'And lastly the alarm never went off. Funny, says my sarge to me. We did wonder if it was an insurance job – or something. But old Leech – he wasn't that stupid. We all know burglars just grab the first thing that their greasy little fists close on. They don't climb glass roofs, pass silver photo frames, leave the telly, the video, tiny antique miniatures that any crook knows are worth a fortune and damned easy to turn into cash.

'Lastly – and to my mind most suspicious – he rang up a couple of days later and said he didn't want us to continue with the investigation.'

Someone at the back cleared their throat. 'And now his ring has been found on a dead boy. Perhaps we'd better speak to the Right Honourable Ashford Leech.'

Phil Scott shook his head. 'No can do,' he said. 'He's dead.'

The words had their effect. Each one of the ring of faces looked puzzled now. But Phil Scott had one more card up his sleeve. 'He died six months ago,' he said. 'Bronchopneumonia was on the death certificate. I've spoken to the coroner. He seemed young to die of pneumonia. The coroner told me confidentially that whatever appeared on the death certificate, Ashford Leech died of Aids, or, to quote him, he died of an Aids-related disease.'

The ripple that went round the room now was tangible as well as audible. In the force they had a hetero horror of HIV. Phil Scott sat down, his dramatic effect complete. Joanna sighed and knew this promised to be another murky case.

When the briefing had broken up she spoke to Mike. 'Did I handle that prejudice thing a bit roughly, Mike?'

'Jo,' he said, 'give the lads a break. You know as well as I do it's the way their minds are bound to work.'

'It doesn't solve crime though,' she said.

He looked at her quizzically. 'Doesn't it?'

Maree O'Rourke, Dean's social worker, was tiny with spiky hair, dressed in a very short skirt that revealed an expanse of plump, pale thigh as she sat down in Joanna's office and crossed her legs. Her face was caked in thick, pale make-up, eyes black-lined in a Cleopatra look and hair unnaturally black. Her lips were carefully outlined in dark pencil and filled in with a deep coral lipstick.

She linked her hands around her knee and looked mournfully at Joanna. 'I'm heartbroken about Dean,' she said, sniffing. 'What do you want to know? I don't think I can tell you much but it'll be more than you'll get from anyone else. The other kids won't say nothin' in case they get someone into trouble. And I don't think any other adults really spent much time with him.' She stroked her chin. 'But I certainly haven't a clue who "got him". He could be very secretive, you know. Vulnerable – like they all are. They're dying to be like other kids – really privileged – but at the same time they're all terrified of rejection. That's why they build such high walls around themselves. Dean was not a bad boy. Used, manipulated – sometimes very gullible, at other times he could really be quite clever, like his disappearances.' Her heavily made-up eyes stared straight at Joanna. 'I never got to the bottom of those. I don't think anyone ever did – unless Jason or Kirsty knew. He was very thick with both of those two.'

Maree scratched her head. 'How official is this?' she asked.

'Totally off the record,' Joanna said. 'It won't be used in court. I have to find his killer. These sorts of crimes tend to become more frequent if the killer gets away with it.'

'I'll do all I can,' Maree was swift to reassure her.

'How well did you know Dean?'

'I've known him practically from birth,' she said, biting her lip. 'Do you know, he was such a pretty child – like an angel. On the at-risk register right from birth – not violence but extreme neglect, left alone while Ma went out on the town.'

'Very young, was she?'

Maree shook her head. 'No,' she said, 'she wasn't. She was in her twenties, but she wanted a good time. He was two months old when I first saw him – very skinny.' For a second she looked too upset to continue. She dabbed her eyes, sniffed and regained her self-control. 'We kept taking him into care and then trying him back with her. In the end she just dumped him outside the social services in his little push-chair with a note pinned to his anorak.' She gave a wry smile. 'We'd even bought him the bloody anorak,' she said. 'He was a lovely baby. He had lovely pale hair – almost silver – and enormous blue eyes.' She looked at Joanna. 'Detective Inspector Piercy, he was the most neglected child I'd ever seen. His bottom was sore from never having his nappy changed. He had scabies. He was dirty and terribly undernourished. Like I say, she'd never been physically violent toward him – never beat him or anything. He was just totally ignored for the first two years of his life — apart from when he was in local authority care.'

Joanna shook her head.

'At first she wouldn't let Dean be put up for adoption. She kept saying as soon as she had a proper home she'd have him back.' Maree looked at her earnestly. 'The law was different then. She had absolute right. So little Dean was fostered by a succession of unsuitable people. Every time they rejected him for whatever reason – usually that he didn't measure up to their image of a perfect child – he was sent straight back to us for a few months while we searched for another "suitable" family. By the time he'd reached ten years old the law changed. Dean wanted to stay in The Nest. And for the first time in his short life we listened to him. He was happy there.'

'But he absconded.'

'I believe,' Maree said slowly, 'that he was encouraged.'

'By whom?'

'I don't know. Someone was stringing him along. Each time he returned he'd have that horrible, secretive look. I learned to recognise it.'

Maree looked past Joanna at the window, which faced a brick wall. Joanna often thought it highly symbolic when on a particularly frustrating case.

'I don't know what Dean looked like when you saw him,' Maree said, 'but he was a very beautiful child.'

Joanna nodded. 'We could see that.'

'I had suspicions,' Maree continued. 'I was afraid ...'

'That he was being molested?'

Two large tears appeared in Maree's dark eyes, and the black lines that drew them seemed to blur. 'He denied it. We moved him,' she said. 'But I think it happened again.'

Joanna stared at her. 'Did you ask him?'

Maree shook her head. 'It's hopeless,' she said. 'He always denied it. Sometimes it's other boys at the home – sometimes the wardens. Sometimes they frequent public toilets ... Somehow these children ...' Her voice trailed away. 'They're the lost boys. We couldn't force an examination on him.' She swallowed. 'I know some of the older boys were quite cruel to him. One of them burned him – another tattooed his knuckles.' She stopped. 'I asked him but he wouldn't say a thing. So I could never prove anything. But I just had the feeling he was being abused. It was the ... how can I put it... the knowing way he would look at me. But it made him very confident.'

Joanna frowned. 'Confident?'

Maree looked confused. 'I can't put it any other way,' she said. 'At eight years old he knew things he shouldn't have done.' She stopped. 'They're all like that, these lost children.' She sighed. 'All I can do is to be around – be available. After that my hands are tied.'

It had been a long, hard day, so when Mike offered to buy her a drink at the pub, Joanna accepted, knowing she would value his thoughts on the case.

'I had an idea,' she said when they had found seats. 'It's about the abuse stopping. What if it was Latos who was touching him up?'

He looked at her. 'Why stop?' he asked.

'He's got a friend now,' she said. 'The one he went to the opera with. He didn't need Dean anymore.'

Mike took a long, slow drink from his beer glass. 'I've thought of something else,' he said. 'What if Leech was the one abusing little Dean? Then Dean might be

HIV positive. The killer had been at him too ...'

'And stopped because he was worried he might get it as well?'

Mike nodded. 'And you see what that means, Jo?'

'Killer and abuser were the same person. Bloody hell.' She made a quick decision. 'We should get Dean Aids-tested,' she said, then looked at Mike. 'And what about Riversdale?'

He shook his head, offered to buy another drink, but she stood up.

'My turn,' she said.

8

Tom Fairway called round unexpectedly on the Thursday morning, just as she was swallowing the last of her breakfast.

'I felt I ought to warn you,' he said. 'Caro's on your tail. She's sniffing around for what she calls an "angle" on the case. She was just on the telephone.'

Joanna offered him a coffee and they sat down together.

'What did she say?'

'Just that in London the image of a young boy's body alight on the moors is ... to quote her, "wonderfully atmospheric". She particularly likes the image of the rock man, winking at passers-by and guarding the corpse.'

'She would,' Joanna said gloomily.

'So expect her any day.' He looked at her with sympathy. 'How is the investigation progressing?'

'Slowly,' she said. 'I have to interview a horde of kids tomorrow. And I still haven't got hold of the chief people I want to interview – Mrs Leech and her son. They're away, so the answerphone keeps telling me.'

'Be careful, Jo,' he said. 'Caro will soon be here.

And you know how predatory she can be.'

'I do,' Joanna said with feeling. 'And that's all I need. The press's chief bulldog.'

'Well, the burning boy would be enough,' he said grimly, 'even without the MP connection.' He paused. 'I'm not trying to pry, but it seems a nasty, sordid little business. And the more I read in the papers the less I like the sound of the story – and the implications on our society.'

'I know, I know. The whole case does seem an indictment on the way we treat children if the parenting system fails them.'

Tom nodded, and finished his coffee. 'Well,' he said, standing up, 'I mustn't delay you.'

'Thanks for warning me,' she said, and he faced her.

'I don't know what I'm doing – warning you. I'm sure you can look after yourself.'

She grinned. He bent and kissed her cheek, then left.

Mike was seated at her desk when she walked in the next morning.

'Trying it for size, Mike?' she asked coolly.

He flushed and stood up too quickly, knocking over the waste-paper basket. 'Just waiting for your instructions for the day.'

'Well, if you'll excuse me,' she said, 'I have to get changed.'

He beat a hasty retreat.

At nine o'clock exactly the telephone rang. Gilly Leech had come home. And in a crisp, sharp voice she informed: 'Inspector Piercy, if you would like to call this morning it would be convenient. About 11?' Her tone sounded as though she was summoning the dustmen to empty her bins.

In the car Mike glanced at her. 'You know – you could do with a holiday too, Jo.'

She kept her eyes on the road. 'When this is over,' she said. 'When we've got the person who killed that poor boy, I'll have myself a holiday.'

'On your own?'

She was silent.

Rock House was an enormous Victorian mansion with its back to craggy rocks and fine, huge bowed windows that opened out to long green lawns sweeping straight down to the canal.

Joanna glanced at Mike. 'Money,' she said. 'Lots of it. He could afford to be a benefactor.'

'And die of Aids?' There was a scornful note in his voice.

She steered the car around a sharp bend.

She had not slept at all the night before but had spread out on the sitting-room floor Matthew's letters and cards – birthday, Christmas – and the photographs of snatched minutes and the few whole nights they had managed to spend together, when she had not slept either – for fear of wasting precious moments. She had recalled all the sayings she connected with him, the books and pieces of music they had shared. There could never be anyone to touch her heart as he had done – or her body either. So she had sighed, opened the curtains and watched the dawn climb over the hills and spill into the small valley with its black snake of a canal flowing along its bottom until it reached the motionless lock gate.

But the deepest, most lasting picture that had stuck in her mind was the haunting image of Jane, Matthew,

Eloise ... one happy family. Under blue skies, in sparkling water, on golden beaches – together.

They reached a sharp bend in the road bordered by a high stone wall. 'I think we're here,' Mike said, and swung the car through tall wrought-iron gates, standing open.

'We don't know yet how he got it,' she said.

'Don't we?'

'Don't jump to conclusions, Mike. Assume nothing. Wait for the truth.'

'You're a real Mrs Plod sometimes.' He grinned. 'I'm crossing a bridge over a very narrow stream – not leaping to conclusions. And you know as well as I do we're going to find it very difficult to get to the bottom of how Ashford Leech contracted HIV.'

'Well, let's start here, shall we?'

She knocked on the door. It was opened immediately by a hatchet-faced woman with fading golden hair scraped into a wispy pony-tail and secured by an elastic band. She was, Joanna noticed, extremely thin and the stretch trousers and baggy sweater she wore only emphasised her boniness.

She held her ID card up in front of the woman's eyes. 'Mrs Leech?' she asked. 'I'm Detective Inspector Piercy. I rang to say we were coming.'

Gilly Leech tightened her thin lips until she looked even more severe. 'I really don't see how I can help you,' she said. 'The child's death has absolutely nothing whatsoever to do with me.'

Joanna nodded. 'I'm sure you're right,' she said soothingly before she produced the ring. 'But this is your husband's?'

'*Was*, Inspector.' Gilly Leech's eyes were so pale that a light seemed to come from them. Her face was crumpled and unhappy. Embarrassingly her eyes began to water.

'Look, wouldn't it be better if we came in,' Joanna said, 'instead of standing on the doorstep?'

Gilly Leech's eyes hardened. She gave a quick expression of extreme distaste. 'If you must,' she said ungraciously. Joanna and Mike followed her across a large, square hall, polished dark parquet with a central red circular Chinese rug and a tall grandfather clock in the corner. To the left a large staircase swept upwards to the first floor.

'You live here alone, Mrs Leech?'

'No, I do not,' she snapped. 'At least – not exactly. Look, Inspector.' She turned and faced Joanna. 'Is this all part of your investigation? It looks like my late husband's ring. It probably is ... was,' she corrected quickly, 'his. But obviously it can't possibly have anything whatsoever to do with myself or my son. You're wasting your time. You ought to be out there – hunting for the real murderer of the poor child.'

Joanna felt a sudden flame of anger at this grim-faced woman. 'Plenty of people are,' she said. 'We will follow up every single connection – however tenuous. One never knows in this work quite where clues may take you, but we can't afford to ignore anything. A young boy was found murdered, his body ablaze on the moors. He was ten years old, a young, blond child. On his finger, Mrs Leech, was found your husband's ring, supposedly burgled from this house.'

Her lips tightened. ' "Supposedly," Inspector,' she said sharply. 'Exactly what do you mean by that?' Her pale eyes shone with disdain and dislike.

'We never caught the burglar,' Joanna said smoothly. And behind her she felt Mike relax.

Gilly Leech gave a staccato mutter of impatience, her hands stuck rigidly against her side, like a doll's. Then she moved to a door to the left, at the foot of the stairs, and they followed her into the sitting room.

She sank down onto a chintz-covered armchair, facing wide, bowed windows with thick brocade curtains draped across. For a moment she stared out over the sweeping green lawns. Joanna sat too. Mike stood near the door as though on guard, grimly watching.

'My husband is dead, Inspector ...' Gilly Leech was struggling to keep control. 'He died six months ago ...' she chewed at her lip, 'very painfully. Inspector, he was not an old man. He owns nothing now – not this great bloody barn of a place. Not even that small ring.' She held out her hand. 'May I hold it – please?' She took the ring from Joanna and held it in the flat of her hand where it looked like a chunk of pig gold. She stared at it for a few minutes without speaking.

Mike shuffled uncomfortably at the door. The silence was painful.

Then Gilly Leech looked up. 'What was the name of the poor child?'

'Dean Tunstall.' Mike spoke from behind in a hard, hostile voice. 'He was a ten-year-old from the children's home along the Ashbourne road, The Nest.'

Gilly Leech hardly moved a muscle. 'I thought it would be,' she murmured. 'I did warn Ashford – more than once – that he was taking a chance.' She hesitated. 'Which one was he?' She lifted her eyes very slowly, as though afraid to meet their faces.

'He was blond,' Joanna said, 'quite small.'

'A pretty little boy,' Mike said. In his voice there was accusation.

Her eyes flickered and Joanna cursed Mike for his gaucheness. She cleared her throat. 'Is this your husband's ring?' She met Gilly Leech's pale eyes. 'We do need a formal identification.' She paused. 'I thought you would prefer it if we came here rather than ask you to attend the station.' It was politely said but the implication was quite obvious. It was a murder inquiry and whoever the person was and whatever their status, if they were needed to answer questions the police had definite powers. Exposing them seemed to soften Mrs Leech's attitude.

'Yes, of course,' she said humbly.

She stared at it in the palm of her hand. 'Yes,' she said at last. 'It is my husband's ring.'

Behind her Joanna could feel Mike shifting his feet.

'Can you tell us positively that this is the same ring that was stolen during the reported burglary, Mrs Leech?' She used the word 'reported' deliberately, but if Mrs Leech noticed she gave no sign, simply held the ring loosely in the palm of her hand, rolling it one way and then the other. Then she swivelled round and looked up at Mike, her head on one side as though she sensed his hostility but was trying to convince him that she was telling the truth. She hesitated, began to speak, but her throat was dry and she coughed instead, a harsh, dry cough. 'It must be his ring,' she said. 'I had it made for him myself when we were married.'

'And you last saw it?'

'I don't know,' she said impatiently. 'Around the time of the burglary.'

'Who did you think was responsible?'

Gilly Leech said nothing.

'Then tell me about the children,' Joanna said, 'the ones from The Nest.'

Gilly Leech blinked. 'My husband,' she began, then covered her face with her hands. 'My husband was a kind man,' she said defiantly, 'with a social conscience. He was very fond of children.' She stopped speaking for a minute. 'He knew the children from The Nest. He met them one Christmas soon after he was elected to the House.' She gave a weak smile.

'You said you don't live alone, Mrs Leech. Who else lives here?'

Her pale eyes fixed on Joanna. 'Properties like this are difficult to sell at the moment,' she said. 'My son, Robin, has recently left his wife. He lives in the stable block. We had it converted into a flat a few years ago – for friends. I also have a daughter,' Gilly Leech said tightly. 'She lives in the States and has not been in England for ten years.' She dropped her face suddenly into her hands. 'Oh, God, will all this never end?'

Mike gave Joanna a questioning glance ... What the hell is all this about?

'Mrs Leech,' Joanna said softly, 'who did you think, at the time, had broken into the house?'

'Some kids,' she said.

Joanna shook her head. 'I don't think so, Mrs Leech. I've read the report. You see, young burglars tend to take videos and televisions, money, credit cards. They don't take a ring, a photograph album. They don't climb over glass roofs, break windows that are open. And last of all they don't enter houses where someone is home.'

Gilly Leech narrowed her eyes. 'What exactly are you suggesting, Inspector?' she asked in a dangerously quiet voice.

'Who took the ring?' Joanna asked.

Gilly Leech closed her eyes for a moment then wearily opened them again. 'All right,' she said. 'We thought it was probably one of the kids who came here from The Nest. Ashford ...' Her face softened for a moment. The deep lines flattened out. 'Ashford broke the window himself,' she continued. 'We simply forgot about the glass roof. It was rather silly, I know – but it was a valuable ring. We were very upset to lose it. The photographs didn't matter much but we wanted to claim for the ring under our household insurance cover.'

Joanna felt suddenly curious. 'What were the photographs of?' she asked.

The question seemed to cause Gilly Leech some discomfort. 'Nothing in particular,' she said, flushing. 'Family snaps – that's all.'

'Family snaps?'

'My daughter,' she said haughtily. 'She can have no bearing on this.'

'Is this the one who lives in America?' Mike asked casually.

Gilly Leech turned and glared at him. 'Yes,' she said.

'Did she get back for her dad's funeral?'

'Fleur is a busy woman,' Gilly Leech said savagely. 'A businesswoman. She is in banking. She can't just have time off for funerals.'

'Really,' Mike said.

Joanna sneaked a look at him. His face was impassive, features quite wooden. She knew Mike. This was when he was at his most thoughtful. She resolved to speak to him later. What was he thinking?

Gilly Leech paused for a moment then spoke softly. 'Ashford was so disappointed when we realised one of the children had stolen it. It was horrible. You see, Inspector, we'd opened our house up to these children. For them then to steal things ...' She stopped speaking.

'Quite unpleasant ... So ... we decided to pretend there'd been a burglary.'

Joanna felt furious. 'You understand,' she said, 'that you could be charged with wasting police time?'

Gilly Leech nodded. 'We didn't think at the time. And you can't charge Ashford now, Inspector. We simply wanted to protect the children,' she said again, picking a tiny piece of fluff up between her forefinger and thumb.

Joanna stood up. 'I shall want to speak to you again,' she said. 'In the meantime, perhaps you'll tell your son we shall want to see him too.' It was a shot in the dark but Gilly Leech looked anxious.

'Why?' she asked. 'Why do you want to speak to Robin? He has nothing to do with this. He didn't even live here when the ring was stolen. He only moved back less than a year ago. He never even knew the boy. They never met.' She rubbed her temple in a sudden, anxious gesture. 'They never met, I tell you.'

'Just routine, ma'am.' Again Mike was at his most impassive. Joanna raised her eyebrows and met his glance.

They were glad to leave the house. It's cold, expensive air only emphasised the deep unhappiness of its owner, though due whether to her husband's death or to other factors neither of the two police officers had decided yet. Joanna glanced up at its grey facade as they drove past the front door. 'If ever I wanted certain proof that money can't buy happiness,' she said, 'I couldn't find a more suitable place.'

'Grim, isn't it?' Mike said. 'So what do you think, Jo?'

'I am very curious about the late Mr Leech,' she said slowly. 'Very sorry for the current Mrs Leech who seems to have inherited a legacy of sheer misery.'

'And Mr Robin Leech?' he asked.

'I've got a feeling he will be a very hard man to like,' she said. 'But then I can't just mix with nice people.'

'Joanna,' he said slowly, 'why didn't she come to the funeral?'

'Who?' she asked, puzzled.

'The daughter,' he said, his voice sounding alert.

Joanna looked at him. 'Do you think it has any bearing on the case, Mike? Surely pressure of work.'

'Did you miss your dad's funeral, Jo?'

She shook her head.

'I rest my case,' he said.

Joanna frowned. 'But Fleur Leech hasn't been in England for ten years.'

'All I'm saying is it could have something to do with Dean's death.'

'Apart from the fact that he was ten years old, I doubt it.' Joanna remained unconvinced. 'Just consider this, Mike. If – and it's a big if – Ashford Leech was sheltering Dean and at the same time abusing him, where the hell was his wife? She doesn't exactly strike me as the type of woman who would turn a blind eye to that sort of thing.'

'But the daughter,' Mike persisted.

'It could be coincidence,' Joanna said. 'Even a policeman has to acknowledge there is such a thing as coincidence.'

Mike grunted.

By now it was seven o'clock, and the evening was pink and beautiful and very warm with a hint of the gold that illuminates late September. Joanna turned to Mike. 'Is it your body-building night?'

He shook his head. 'Not tonight. Why?'

'I'd like to go up there for myself, get the feel of the moors, check on the SOC team. I've a feeling if they try a slightly less obvious route they might pick something up. Come on,' she said. 'I'll buy you a drink in the Winking Man afterwards.'

Up in the sheer huge emptiness of the moors the world seemed a different place. A world of extremes – black and white, containing not all the variations of life in the towns but either pure good or pure evil. With the dark shapes of the hills behind them they drove towards the Winking Man, passing the yellow lights of the police vans. They would soon be going home. It was too dark now to continue searching the moors.

Joanna suddenly spotted a narrow track leading off to the left. 'That isn't on the map,' she said.

'It's the road to Flash,' Mike said, looking at her. 'Then it goes on to just one farm.'

'Take it, Mike. It must lead to the area behind the crag.'

Obediently he turned the car and they drove along the narrow one-lane road behind the Winking Man. 'But why go up there? He would have had to carry the boy's body over the ridge.'

'Perhaps he knew the army trucks would be arriving at dawn,' she said thoughtfully. 'Maybe he didn't want the car to be noticed by any passing travellers.'

'Maybe ...' Mike echoed.

When they reached the spot, Joanna got out of the car, wrapped her coat around her, changed out of her court shoes into a pair of Wellington boots and looked around at the clear air. 'I never knew anywhere so empty,' she said as they climbed towards the top of the crag, found a flat stone and sat, staring far down below at the wide valley, the toy-town of Leek where lights were being switched on and car headlights swept along the roads like a Scalextric set.

For a long time Joanna sat and stared until Mike spoke. 'Do you need inspiration?'

She nodded. 'Silly, isn't it?' She gazed around her at the huge expanse of nothing. 'I thought I might see things clearer up here.' She turned to look at him. 'But I don't know that I do.' She frowned. 'Who did he have, Mike? Where were his parents, grandparents, godparents, aunts and uncles? Where were they all? How is it possible for a child to be so neglected?' She drew another deep breath in. 'Even the children's home. Mark Riversdale and Maree. They weren't with him, all the time, as a parent would be. He was gone for a long time before anyone even knew.' She pondered the point for a while. 'You know – I don't think Eloise Levin could be missing for more than 15 minutes without there being a hue and cry. Do you know what I'm saying?'

He nodded.

'It's the difference between the pampered middle classes and these young tigers of survival. And for most of the time, who are the real survivors? The tough, young tigers,' she said.

'Not Dean Tunstall,' Mike said grimly. 'If there's one thing he wasn't – it's a survivor.'

'True.' She was forced to agree. 'And yet,' she said, 'I have the strangest of feelings that the neglect was the key. It gave him the opportunity and maybe a naivety about people's motives. I don't know ...' She tailed off. 'I'm not being very clear.' Then she frowned. 'That's because I'm not very clear myself. I just know his murder is bound up with his life. I keep thinking these same thoughts over and over again. Who was really responsible for him?'

Mike said nothing and she looked at him.

'I'll tell you who, Mike. No-one. No-one was really responsible. No-one really cared. No-one will mourn his passing. And that is why he died ... Oh, God,' she said, 'sometimes this job gets me down.'

She stood up. The gloom of the night was pressing in around them.

'Right, let's get on with it. My theory is that he or she brought the boy's body up this way. Not straight from the main road at all but parking on this little side road, out of sight of the army trucks. They all parked in the lay-by and there was no other vehicle.'

'It's a steep climb,' Mike objected.

'But safer,' she said. 'And it would give him more time, the vehicle being hidden. Besides, it isn't that steep. We've just done it in about 15 minutes.'

'Not carrying a body,' he said.

'Our murderer might even have still been on the moors when the army trucks arrived,' she said. 'We didn't ask the soldiers if they heard vehicles on the move after they began their exercise, did we? Only whether they met anything on the road.'

'True,' he agreed. 'True.' He gazed at her. 'You know, Jo,' he said, 'I've been thinking. The boy's death – what if it was an accident? A game that suddenly went wrong?'

She nodded. 'It could have been – according to Cathy Parker. It could have been just a shock ... Vasovagal inhibition she called it.' She grinned. 'If I remember rightly, she said it would have been rapid, not accompanied by congestion and haemorrhaging, which is why he looked so beautiful and peaceful. A quick and sudden death.'

'Very good,' he said with a touch of sarcasm. 'Dr Levin would be proud of you.'

'You can't resist an opportunity to have a dig at him, can you?'

Mike grunted.

She shot him a meaningful look. 'Perhaps the real crime we're investigating ought to be the abuse – year after year ... Maybe the abuser was the only villain.'

'But the fact remains,' he said, 'someone did kill him – put their hands around his neck and drag his body up here, douse it in petrol and set it alight. Until we know who, we can't know why or how serious the crime is. We have to catch this person to understand the motive.'

The evening turned to deep dusk. The light was fading and in the blackest part of the crag Joanna saw a movement. She clutched Mike's arm. 'What the bloody hell is that? Surely the SOC boys have clocked off by now. It's too dark to see anything.'

He laughed. 'Spooked?'

She peered into the gloom. 'Yes,' she said, 'I bloody well am.'

'Shall I tell you a story?' he said. 'It's why I find this place so threatening. It was about eight or nine years ago – before you got here. Four people were travelling from Leek to Buxton. The snow blew up and they were trapped in their car. Their bodies were found four days later, frozen. Their car had been so smothered in snow, nothing – not even the aerial – was showing. Friends in Leek assumed they'd got through. The Buxton friends assumed they'd never set out. Telephone lines were down. It was only when the snow plough touched metal that they realised. They told me the four bodies were so frozen together the undertakers had to break their bones to get them apart.'

Joanna shivered. 'What a horrible story,' she said, looking around at the deepening gloom closing in on them. It would be difficult to find their way down. 'Let's go, Mike. Come on, I'll buy you that drink.'

Alice watched them stumble down the side of the ridge, heard them roll loose stones. Then she crawled back into the cave.

9

After the hostility of the moors, the bright warmth of the pub was welcome. The Winking Man was an old-fashioned pub, untouched since the late 1950s. It consisted of a large, square lounge bar lit by one electric light bulb that swung in the centre of the room from a long, brown plaited flex. Bench seats, covered with wine-red plush reminiscent of 'tween-wars railway carriages, sat uneasily on bumpy stone flags. The tables were round with wooden tops stained with beer rims and stood on wrought-iron legs. Apart from two men huddled in the corner and the barmaid it was empty. All three looked up briefly as the two police officers walked in, and Joanna and Mike both knew they had been recognised. It was not a pub for strangers.

Joanna approached the bar. 'A pint of Theakston's,' she said, 'and a glass of wine, please.'

In the corner the two men sniggered.

The barmaid was a pleasantly plump lady with strong-looking arms and plenty of wrinkles around her eyes. 'I'm sorry,' she said, 'we don't serve wine by the glass. Would cider do?'

Joanna nodded, and when the barmaid slid the

glasses over the Formica counter she broached the subject. 'I suppose you've already been questioned by the police,' she said. The woman's eyes grew round. 'About the dead boy,' she said.

'We have.' Her face seemed to sink in sadness. 'Poor little thing.' Her eyes narrowed. 'You police, are you?'

'I'm the detective in charge of the case,' Joanna said. 'Do you live on the premises?'

The barmaid nodded vigorously. 'With my husband,' she said. 'We have a few sheep and run the pub.' She chuckled. 'It don't make us rich but it does us a livin'.'

'What time do you usually rise in the mornings?'

'Late.' She grinned. 'Sometimes not long before 11. We keep late hours, you see – pub hours. I always clears up before going to bed.'

'I suppose you've already been asked if you heard a car on the morning the boy's body was found.'

'I didn't.' She spoke forcibly. 'But I heard those ruddy army trucks. Noisy bloody things they are.'

Mike lifted his beer glass to his lips, took a long swig and set it down again, then glanced at Joanna. 'What about the Flash road, miss?'

She looked with undisguised pleasure at the tall, muscular policeman with his black hair and dark eyes, then she gave him a coquettish smile. 'Nobody's asked me about the Flash road,' she said. 'The main Buxton road was what I was asked about and nothing – only the army lorries – went along there.'

'I'm asking you about the Flash road, miss,' he said.

'I'm Mrs.' She giggled. 'I did hear something along the Flash road, I remember. It was Monday morning.

And I thought, Herbert's taking his cows to Newcastle market a bit early. It was four o'clock. I said to my husband, "What's he going so early for?"'

'And what did he say?' Joanna asked quietly.

The barmaid gave a look of disgust. 'He said it weren't Herbert's Land Rover at all. He said it were a car what had gone up a half-hour or so before. My husband – he don't sleep too well, you see. He gets arthritis – and terrible wind. The doctor's given him some medicine.' She shook her head. 'It 'aven't done him no good – no good at all.'

She paused and Mike prompted her. 'The car?' he said.

'Well ... it's that quiet up 'ere we notices any noises.'

'I'm sure.' Joanna found it hard to contain her excitement. She glanced triumphantly at Mike and his lips moved. She knew what he was saying. She had been right. The vehicle for some reason had approached from behind the crag not in front. The driver had left the car blocking the Flash road.

'Did your husband note anything about the car?' she asked. 'What sort of sound it made? Rattles, silencer, noisy?'

The barmaid leaned right across the stained lemon Formica. 'I still thinks it was Herbert's,' she said, still looking Mike Korpanski full in the eye. 'It sounded exactly like his old thing.' Then she fluttered her eyelids in a gesture meant to convey all that sex might offer but instead managed to look comic. 'Heavy and slow, if you know what I mean, just like my husband.' She chuckled chestily. 'And noisy. It was definitely noisy.'

'Would you both be prepared to come down to the police station and make a statement?'

The barmaid reluctantly peeled her eyes away from Detective Sergeant Korpanski and looked instead at Joanna. 'Course we would,' she said. 'Anything what'll get the bastard what did that to the little kid.' Her doughy face dropped. 'Fancy settin' him on fire. Poor little thing. Do you know who the little beggar was yet?'

'His name was Dean Tunstall,' Joanna said. 'He was from the children's home along the Ashbourne road. He was just ten years old.'

'Poor little mite,' the woman said. 'Poor little mite.' She looked again at Joanna. 'What I want to know is – where was his mother?'

It was an important question but one that no-one so far had any answer to.

They drank in silence for a while as outside the moors darkened for the night, then one of the men who had been seated silently in the corner cleared his throat. 'I'm surprised,' he said gruffly, 'that you haven't come across the King and Queen yet. They could 'elp you,' he insisted, looking around the room. 'They could.'

His companion nodded solemnly into his beer glass. Both were dressed in moorlands best – ancient, ill-fitting matted suits covered in suspicious farming stains, exposed braces, collarless shirts and strong, practical boots as durable as clogs. It was hard to be sure from their complexions what was owed to dirt and what was pure weather, but their skin had a dark, prickly look.

Mike shot Joanna a sideways look. 'Nutters,' he muttered out of the side of his mouth.

But Joanna crossed the room. 'Sorry?' she said politely.

The man gave a toothy chuckle. 'Didn't know, did you?' His voice held a note of triumph. He had scored – knew something the police didn't.

Joanna sat down opposite him on the plush seat. 'No,' she said gently, 'I didn't know.'

She could almost hear Mike snort his scorn from his place at the bar. She knew what he was thinking – that she was a sucker, listening to nutters.

'Alice and Jonathan.' The man was going to take his time over his story. Without hurrying he took a small drink out of his pint glass, swilled it deliberately around his mouth then swallowed it. He pointed in the direction of the dark crag barely visible through the tiny window at the back of the pub. 'They lives there,' he said. 'If anyone saw something it will be Alice. She don't miss nothin' what happens on these moors.'

'Hang on a minute,' Joanna said, frowning, turning away from the man and staring out of the window. 'Lives where?'

'Right by the ridge,' the man said impatiently. 'In the cave.' He took another deep swig out of his pint pot. 'Don't tell me you didn't know.'

'Somebody lives up there?'

The other man cleared his throat now. 'Calls themselves the King and Queen of the Roaches they do.'

Joanna sat back and gave a deep sigh. 'Mike,' she said, 'do we really know *anything* about this case?'

Joanna cycled into the station car park the following morning and glanced at her watch. Not bad – 17 minutes and 35 seconds. She took a deep breath of undisguised pleasure. The day was warm and balmy, the sunshine bright. There had been road works on a bad bend between Leek and Cheddleton with long queues either side. She had cycled straight along the pavement and known again she had been quicker than a car. She stretched her arms, ran her fingers through tousled hair then headed towards the station door. A wash, a change, a cup of decaffeinated coffee.

Then her good humour evaporated. A gleaming red Honda was parked in the visitor's space near the entrance. Caroline had arrived.

She was waiting for her as Joanna walked in through the double doors. She moved forwards with the controlled elegance of a cat, in black ski pants and a beautiful white sweater.

'Jo, darling. It is so good to see you.' She gave a swift glance at the cycling shorts, baggy T-shirt and bare legs. 'God,' she said explosively, 'I wish I had my cameraman with me.'

Joanna gave her a wary look. She had not forgotten a particular case where Caroline had used friendship and an intimate dinner party to find things out and leak details in the press. She would never again trust her as a friend.

'The press conference is tomorrow,' she said formally. 'Saturday at 11.'

'Oh come on.' Caroline raised her shaped eyebrows a little, threw back a handful of sleek pale hair. 'We're friends, Joanna. We know each other's little secrets.' She smiled. 'And a few big ones too.'

It was a distinctly unsavoury warning and although Joanna had been half-expecting something like this she felt as though she had been punched hard in the chest.

'I can't say much,' she said. 'We're still in the early stages of the inquiry.'

Caro looked sulky. 'But I don't want to battle in one of those dreadfully overcrowded press conferences. Uncivilised – that's what they are – un-civ-i-lised.' She pouted again. 'Of course,' she said airily, 'if I can't get enough of a story from this case I might just decide to take a holiday in Greece, follow up a few leads there. You have to admit,' she said with one eye firmly on Joanna, 'it sounds an interesting story. A married, adulterous pathologist. Scandal involving a female police inspector.' She gave Joanna a sideways glance. 'I could have a damned good holiday running an exclusive on that one. I think it has a lot of mileage. Don't you?'

Joanna thought how very easy it was to hate Caro. Human interest, child abuse, rape and suffering were nothing but valuable, tradable commodities to her.

'You utter bitch,' Joanna said under her breath. She stared at Caro for a minute. How light and flippant her tone was over something so vital. She sighed. 'You'd better come into my office. Just wait for me to get changed.'

'Good.' Caroline looked pleased. 'My editor knew I'd get far more out of you alone than with that pack of piranhas.'

'If they are piranhas,' Joanna said as they passed along the corridor, 'you are the original great white shark. You are so perfect for your job, you know, Caro.'

Caro smirked. 'I know. Marvellous, isn't it?'

They reached Joanna's office and she opened the door. 'Just give me five minutes,' she said.

They sat facing one another. 'God, Jo, you look as though you haven't slept for a week.'

Joanna said nothing.

Caro switched on her tape recorder and settled back in the chair. 'Now what can you tell me about the dead boy?' she asked.

'He was a ten-year-old.' Joanna paused. 'A rather pretty, blond ten-year-old. His name was Dean Tunstall. He came from a local children's home, had been there for practically all of his life.' She passed one of the photographs of Dean across the desk.

Caro looked at it then put it down. 'Yes, he was rather sweet, wasn't he?' She paused. 'But I could have read all that yesterday in any one of the tabloids.' Her eyes were sharp and intelligent. 'What about his mother?'

'We haven't traced her yet. She had had no contact with Dean since he was two years old. The last address we have is from six years ago. She moved around a lot.' Joanna felt this was a great failure on the part of the police. The mother still did not know her child was dead. She may have failed to care for Dean, not given him love or money or even a father, but surely she had a right to know the child was dead. She had given him a name – and life. Someone else had taken that life away. She had a right to know.

Caro leaned forwards. 'Joanna,' she said, 'use the press as they use you. We can find her. Let me offer a reward.'

'And then you'll get an exclusive?' Joanna could not keep the note of cynicism out of her voice.

'Yes, all right. But we can find her for you.' Their eyes met. 'Do you want me to try and find her?' she asked. 'You know the sort of thing. *Is This Your Son?* etc, etc.' She narrowed her eyes, flicked some hair off her face. 'I'm afraid much as people loathe cheque-book journalism it does bear fruit. She'll come forward for money.' She tightened her lips. 'Given love or money, they choose money every time. Sod love. We'll find her. I bet you £20 she'll come to us for the money where she wouldn't have bothered attending the child's funeral just in case someone asked her to pay.' She glanced again at the picture. 'Poor little bastard,' she said.

'Probably.'

'So you don't know the father? No family.'

Joanna shook her head. 'No.'

'Cause of death?' Caro asked briskly. And when Joanna didn't answer straight away she looked up. 'The body was found burning,' she said, 'by soldiers on exercise. You're not going to tell me he burned to death, are you?'

Joanna almost exploded then. 'You know what,' she said, 'you are as hard a woman as they come.'

'I have a job to do.' Caro's voice was faintly defensive.

'So have I,' Joanna said sharply, 'but even I have some bloody feelings.'

'Cause of death?' Caroline repeated.

Joanna frowned. 'He was manually strangled ... We think the body was probably burned to try and destroy forensic evidence, possibly to delay identification.'

She paused. 'We also believe it was pure chance that the burning body was found so early. The moors,' she added drily, 'are not exactly crowded at that time of day. It so happened some boy soldiers were on exercises at 5 am.'

'The boy soldiers are the under-eighteens.' Cam looked up. 'Is that right – sort of cadets?'

'That's right.'

'And there's no connection?'

'We're working on it,' Joanna said cautiously. But she knew this was the one area they would have to return to. They had had one brief interview with the soldiers – that was all. And Swinton had been the one who had burned Dean with the cigarettes.

Dean's body had been found alight – by Swinton. The long arm of coincidence?

Caro was watching her very carefully. 'Rumour has it,' she said, 'the boy had been molested – from an early age.'

Joanna looked hard at her friend. 'I don't think anything can be achieved by printing that, do you?'

'Joanna, you may as well come clean,' Caro said. 'Is this promising to be another children's home scandal? Perhaps on the scale of Pindown?'

'I hope not.' Joanna gave a heartfelt sigh. 'I hope not. We've had enough of that particular Pandora's box in Staffordshire over the last few years. I believe this was an isolated case – not a full-blown scandal.'

Caroline glanced at her pad. 'Is it true the shoes he was wearing were too big for him?'

Joanna nodded. 'Two sizes too big,' she said. 'Dean was a size five. The shoes were sevens.'

Caroline looked up. 'New?'

'Almost.'

'Where did they come from?' Her eyes were blue and intelligent. 'Had somebody bought them for him? Given them to him?'

'We think,' Joanna said cautiously, 'that it's possible he might have shoplifted them. We don't know.'

Caro's face grew rat-like, almost twitching in her anxiety to sniff out the truth. 'Where from?'

Joanna knew she dared not say. With Keith Latos's previous record the press would have hanged him before proving anything. Trial by headline. Even if – and she had to admit it was a big if – he was guilty, they still had to prove it beyond reasonable doubt, in a court of law. She had already applied for a search warrant to comb through Keith Latos's flat. And she would have laid a moderate-sized bet that they would stumble across something there with which to connect Latos with Dean. So to Caro she said, 'We don't know that he did steal them – let alone where from. Enquiries are progressing.'

Caro shot her another very sharp, perceptive look. 'I see,' she said.

Joanna glanced enquiringly at Caro. 'Is that all? I have a briefing at nine.' She looked at her watch. It was five past.

'Just one more thing ...' Caro's voice was deceptively casual. 'Whose was the ring?'

Inwardly Joanna groaned, and then she thought very quickly. Use the press, Caro had said. She could use them ... perhaps to flush a sly fox out of his hole. 'The ring,' she said slowly, 'has been positively identified by Mrs Gilly Leech as belonging to her late husband.'

Caro sat up. 'So how did it get on the finger of the dead boy?' she asked.

'All we know,' Joanna said carefully, 'is that the ring was missing after a reported break-in at the Leech home, Rock House.'

Caro was quick to spot the flaw. '*Reported* break-in,' she said, her eyes very clear, the pupils like pin-points.

'That's right,' Joanna said deliberately. 'Reported break-in.'

Caro's eyes flickered. 'I see,' she said slowly. 'I see.' She wrote something down in her notebook. 'When was this?'

'About a year ago.'

'Mr Leech died ...?'

'A little while after.'

Caro looked up. 'He died of ...?'

'Pneumonia.'

'Rumour has it,' Caro said carefully, 'that Robin Leech is consulting solicitors about a visit you recently made to his mother.' She looked up. 'Would you care to comment?'

'He's perfectly within his rights,' Joanna said calmly.

Caroline regarded her curiously. 'So will you be interviewing Robin Leech?'

Suddenly Joanna grinned. 'If you run half the story I think you will,' she said. 'I expect Robin Leech will want to talk to me, probably with his own solicitor.'

Caro frowned. 'I gather a murky separation followed by an even murkier divorce is about to hit your local rags,' she said.

Joanna looked at her. 'Not the London papers?'

Caro shook her head. 'He isn't big enough, and neither is the scandal. Nothing more than a teenage waitress.' She shook her head again. 'The waitress, so rumour has it, isn't even very photogenic. Naive, a bit silly and stupid. In fact, I think you could say it was a sordid little kitchen-sink drama.'

Joanna smiled. 'Well, thank you,' she said. 'I'm glad to be armed with that little fact before I meet Robin Leech for myself.'

'For what it's worth,' Caro said, 'he is one of the most pompous, snobbish and incredibly boring men I have ever met in my entire life. He is one of the by-products of the English caste system. And don't tell me all men are equal. No-one meeting Robin Leech would ever believe that line. Not in a thousand years. Now,' she said briskly, 'in exchange for that little opinion, perhaps you can fill me in with a detail or two. Off the record, of course. Rumour has it that Ashford Leech was a paedophile with a penchant for young boys. I would imagine they were pretty young boys. Rumour also has it that Ashford Leech's terminal illness was due to the fact that he had Aids.' She was watching Joanna carefully, like a tiger stalking its prey.

'No comment,' Joanna said, and Caroline closed her eyes wearily.

'So he did,' she said.

'Really?'

'I do understand police speak,' Caroline said. 'So please don't insult me.'

'The trouble with you, Caro,' Joanna said suddenly, 'is that I can never say something off the record. As far as you're concerned it's all on the record. So I have to guard my comments. You've tested our friendship too far'

'It's got me some good stories,' Caro said smoothly.

Joanna stood up. 'I do have to go. I have a briefing.'

As she reached the door Caro spoke again. 'Good luck. I hope you get him.'

Joanna turned and gave her a watery smile. 'Thanks,' she said. 'So do I.' And she was left to wonder whom Caro had meant.

The briefing was held in the large office at the front of the building. Joanna stood near the blackboard and faced the assembled officers. Mike sat on the corner of the table.

'The Gypsy's looking fierce today,' DC Alan King whispered to PC Cheryl Smith.

'Did you see the blonde?' she whispered back. 'Press.'

They looked at each other knowingly.

Joanna cleared her throat. 'There are quite a few leads that need following up,' she said. 'The first is we need to speak to the soldier again, Gary Swinton. I'd like us to get him in. He is the person who found the body. He also has tattoos identical to the ones on Dean's knuckles. Private Gary Swinton. We'd better get him in sometime today, please.' She glanced around the room. 'For those of you who are not aware, Gary Swinton was, until last year, living at The Nest.'

There was a mutter around the room and she held up her hand.

'He is not the only suspect. But obviously he moves to the top of the list. DC King. Perhaps you'd visit the army camp. Speak to the other one ... what's his name?' She read from her notes. 'Tom Mayland, the Welsh boy, and any others who might have seen Swinton at the disco on Sunday night. Let's find out if he did have the opportunity to commit this crime. We have narrowed the dumping and setting fire to the body to around 4 am. Find out if he could have got out of the camp. Also ...' she frowned at King, 'see what you can dig up about him. What sort of person is he? Violent? Paedophile tendencies? You know the sort of thing. Look particularly for anything that connects him with Dean Tunstall.'

DC King nodded, scribbled something down on his notepad and folded his arms ... 'Excuse me, ma'am.'

She waited too.

'We've uncovered something about the warden at The Nest.' He surveyed the room, enjoying the expectation on the watching faces. 'Mark Riversdale ...'

He glanced at his pad. 'Apparently he spent six months in a psychiatric ward – drying out. He was an alcoholic. I spoke to the psychiatrist in charge of his case. As usual ...' he made a face, 'he was not keen on divulging information, but he said Riversdale was an unstable character and that after one of his drinking bouts he suffered from amnesia ... didn't remember a bloody thing of what had gone on.'

DC King paused. 'Riversdale referred himself to the psychiatric unit after he exposed himself to a young lad. No charges were pressed. I've checked. He doesn't have a record but the mother of the boy – a ten-year-old, by the way – threatened him with the law if he didn't do something about his problem. According to Riversdale he never remembered a thing about it.'

King sat down, pleased with the effect of his words. Everyone in the room was watching him.

Joanna nodded. 'And he is the one in charge of the home.' She looked around. 'I don't think I need to say anything more about Riversdale – except to say watch him. Is he still drinking? Have we any evidence of deviance since he became warden of The Nest?'

To Mike she said quietly. 'Did they check him out before they put him there?' He shrugged his shoulders and she met his eyes. 'It makes me so bloody cross,' she said. 'Imagine – putting a man with that sort of record in charge of a children's home.'

'Joanna ...' he touched her arm, 'Riversdale didn't have a criminal record. When the council checked him out – if they bothered – he would have come out spotless. He had a medical record – not a criminal record.'

She stared at him for a minute before turning her attention back to the briefing. 'So far the SOCs have covered the west side of the Roaches – that is the area between the Buxton road and the spot where Dean's body was found. However, due to information received from the landlady of the Winking Man – she and her husband heard a car travelling along the Flash road – I believe that the murder vehicle could have approached the Roaches from the Flash side.'

'Excuse me ...' One of the DCs put her hand up. 'We thought of that, but it's a narrow track. A car pulled up there would have completely blocked the road. Besides, there's nowhere to turn.'

'Nevertheless,' Joanna said, 'I think this is what our killer did. I'd like some of you to speak to Herbert Machin. He's a farmer from Flash.'

'We already did.'

'Ask more specific questions,' Joanna said slowly. 'Ask him if a car or even a Land Rover turned round in his gateway. I feel it's worth a second go.'

The DC nodded and Joanna carried on. 'So I want the search area widened to include the other side – the east side of the Roaches. Take a good wide sweep of the area after a corridor has been cleared and marked. Please,' she appealed to the clump of uniformed officers in front of her, 'be thorough. I believe we will find forensic evidence that this is the route the murderer – or at least the person who dumped the body – took to X, the place where the body was set alight. I don't need to impress on you that the tiny fragment of evidence might just be the one item we need to connect a person with this place. It might make the difference between a conviction and none, the difference in a crime repeated or a person in prison.'

One of the probationers at the front put his hand up. 'Inspector,' he called, 'was it definitely a man?'

Joanna frowned. 'This is difficult, isn't it?' she said slowly. 'Abuse of a young boy would normally imply a man. But please all of you remember it does not have to be the abuser who killed Dean and set his body alight. Remember – he had not suffered abuse for some time before his death. No,' she said, 'it does not have to be a man, but I am strongly suspicious that it was.' She scanned the room full of police.

'The second thing is, I do need to talk to the other children from the home – I believe there are five of them. They will almost certainly want a social worker there as well as the warden.' She caught sight of Cheryl Smith. 'Perhaps you and DC King can set that up – probably this afternoon.

'Also … did any of you know that two people inhabit a cave on the Roaches?'

Phil Scott gave a sharp exclamation. 'I'd forgotten about them,' he said. 'I thought they were evicted a few years ago.'

Joanna sighed. 'You can imagine …' she said. 'We've been up there for a few days and didn't even realise they were probably watching us – let alone the fact that it is a distinct possibility that they saw part of the crime, at least the attempted destruction of Dean's body, if not the actual murder act itself.' She sighed again. 'You can imagine how incompetent it will make us look if this fact comes to light.'

Around the room they nodded with dropped shoulders. Police incompetence … It was the one phrase hurled at them from all quarters – general public, officers in charge, the press.

'Well, somehow we've missed them on the moors. I believe they are still there. DS Mike Korpanski and I intend driving out there later on this morning and speaking to them. I'd also like to talk to the landlord of the Winking Man and his wife, and I want you,' she looked at the two PCs in the corner, 'to keep trying to find Dean's mother. How far have you got?'

One of them stood up. 'We had an address in Plymouth,' he said, 'but she left there two years ago, owing rent. We've got a couple of friends but she seems to have been rootless. No-one's seen her for two years.'

'Keep trying,' she said.

One of the young policemen stood up. 'Why? She hasn't even seen him since he was tiny.'

Joanna held her finger up. 'I'll tell you why,' she said. 'We don't know yet who Dean's father was – if he had any family. And besides that, don't you feel a woman has the right to know whether her child is alive or dead?'

Not one of them had an answer to that, and when they had all filed out of the room Joanna asked Mike, 'Do you believe two people can survive up there in a cave?'

'I don't know ...' He looked confused. 'I suppose the only thing we can do is to climb the Roaches and see. By the way, Jo,' he said, 'message came this morning from the coroner's office. The inquest's been set for next Monday.'

'And there will be the police and the social worker, the warden. No family, Mike,' she said. 'No mother, father, brothers or sisters.'

10

For once it was light, fresh and golden on the moors – and as clear as ice. As they climbed towards the crag and the Winking Man, Joanna could see, far below, the wide spread of moorland, a distant town, dotted farms and the men combing the east face of the rock. She and Mike climbed towards the black hole that marked the mouth of the cave. It was a stiff climb and the wind whipped their faces as they gained height, howling around them like a banshee. They were both panting as they reached the ledge. Joanna turned near the top and looked back. It was an excellent vantage point. From here she could see both sides of the rock and yet not be seen. They climbed a few feet further and turned to face the tiny mouth that marked the entrance to the cave, hidden from below by a headstone of rock. It was only then that she realised they had been watched – probably all the time.

'Good mornin'.'

The woman looked monstrously huge. Only later did Joanna discover this was an illusion created by layers of thick, filthy clothes that blended perfectly with the stone. Her hair was granite grey, straggling below her shoulders, topped by a dirty red bobble hat. Her eyes were hostile.

'I seen you before,' the woman said.

'Last night?'

The woman nodded.

'Are you Alice Rutter?' she asked, having to shout the words to be heard above the wind whipping across the grey stones.

The woman agreed warily. 'Police, are you?'

Joanna nodded. 'That's right,' she said, and instinctively knew this sharp-eyed woman with iron strength to her body and iron will in her character held at least part of the answer.

She indicated the mouth of the cave. 'Is Jonathan at home?' she asked, but Alice was reluctant to invite her in. Instead she scowled.

'There's no reason for you to talk to him,' she said. 'He slept.'

It was unnecessary to ask Alice when he slept.

Joanna sat down on a small flat depression in the rock. Alice leaned against the crag.

'I want to know who killed the boy,' Joanna said baldly.

Alice nodded very slowly.

'He was very young, had had a short and unhappy life,' Joanna continued. She could not rush this interview. It must be taken at Alice's pace and that was slow. But at least in this high hollow they were out of the blast of the wind. She glanced at Mike, perched on a projection, watching the old woman with disbelieving eyes.

Alice was staring down the hill where the police were walking the forensic line. 'At least they be in the right place this time,' she said, chuckling.

Behind her Joanna could hear Mike shuffling his

feet impatiently and knew he was thinking of wasted police hours, of forensic evidence blown away in the wind. But this would not help them now.

'What did you see?'

'The boy was already dead,' Alice said, her eyes misted and sad. 'I would have stopped him burnin' him if he had moved.' She stopped for a while and pursed her lips up. 'I knew he was dead when they got out of the car. Swung him over his shoulder, he did, like a dead sheep. Then he walked–'

'The car,' Mike interrupted. 'What make was it?'

She looked at him without understanding. 'How the 'ell should I know? It were barely dawn and I don't know different shapes of a car.'

'Colour?' Joanna asked gently.

'I think it were pale,' Alice said slowly.

'White?' Mike asked.

But Alice shook her head. 'I couldn't say,' she said. 'Maybe.'

'Then what?'

'Brought him up the bank. I was hid behind the rock, watching him.'

'You're sure it was a man?'

But again Alice shook her head. 'Had one of them hats on what covers your face,' she said. 'Something to do with the Crimea.'

They both stared at her puzzled, then it dawned on Joanna. 'Balaclava?' she asked.

Alice nodded. 'That's it,' she said. 'I couldn't see no face. And he was wearin' one of them thick, thorn-proof coats, trousers and Wellington boots. So it might have not bin a man. I can't swear and I can't say who it was but I did see.'

'Then what?' Joanna was finding it hard to

swallow her disappointment.

'The person dropped the body,' Alice said. 'There.'

'That wasn't where it was found.' Mike sounded sceptical.

'Wait for me,' Alice said slowly. 'I haven't finished.'

'So?'

'The stupid fool. He tried to fire the body along the gully, but the wind was howlin' up. It burned then blew out. But I can prove it.' She nodded down towards the police chain. 'They'll see burnin' there.'

'Then what?'

'He picks the child up,' Alice said. 'The early sun caught his hair. It was like gold.' She closed her eyes. 'Like golden seaweed swaying and blown in the wind. He carried him down the side of the bank, and when he tried to fire the child again he burned bright for a while and the person ran. I heard the car move. Like an old 'orse it was. Coughin' and noise-makin'.'

Joanna gave a loud sigh. 'Please, Alice. Can you tell me anything – anything at all about the car?'

Alice screwed up her face in tight thought. 'It were a long one,' she said eventually. 'Long.'

Mike gave a short curse and Joanna knew exactly what he was thinking. So near and yet no nearer. She had seen it – and could tell them nothing except that it was a long, pale, noisy car.

'Then what?' she suddenly asked. 'Alice, why didn't you try to put the fire out?'

'For three reasons,' Alice said, holding up three filthy fingers. 'One, I got no water. Two, I knowed that child were dead. I went and looked at 'im.'

'And put the posy of flowers there?'

'I sells them sometimes in the market,' Alice said

shyly. ''Twas all I 'ad for the child.'

'And what was the third reason?' Mike asked.

'The soldiers came,' Alice said, looking at him. 'With their noise and their painted faces and their creepin'. And they found 'im.'

'Did you know him?'

Alice shook her head. 'No,' she said, 'I did not. He were a pretty one but I never seen 'im before.'

The wind howled through the short curling bracken and Joanna found herself staring at another face so filthy it reminded her of the soldiers wearing their camouflage paint. In a wild setting this man looked even more wild – and mad – with his straggly hair and thick, black beard. And he too was wearing a huge greatcoat, tied around his middle with string. It could only be Jonathan Rutter.

The man stared at her woodenly.

Alice made a few deft gestures before turning back to Joanna. 'He can't tell you anythin',' she said. ''E slept right through.'

Jonathan glanced at his wife and gave a slow, toothy grin that gave him an idiot look.

Joanna shrugged her shoulders. She was inclined to believe Alice. There was nothing to be gained from him.

'Why do you live here?' she asked. 'It's cold and exposed and dangerous. You could die in the snow.'

Alice nodded sagely. 'People do,' she agreed. 'Four people one year, but they weren't in a cave else they would have lived. They was in a car.' She stopped speaking for a moment and stared out over the huge basin of the valley – all the time a slow, affectionate grin moving across her face. 'This is our kingdom,' she said. 'Our country. They try and make us ordinary and live down there.' She looked contemptuously at the toy-town of Leek. 'Social workers said we could 'ave a flat down there.' She spat sharply on the ground. ''Ow would we live in a flat?' she asked the wide panorama. 'After livin' 'ere all our lives. We got no 'lectricity. We got no 'ot water. But we got the silence and I'd rather 'ave that any day. While we can, Mrs Policeman, we'll stay 'ere.'

Joanna sighed. She was unsure of the legal position of the Rutters choosing to live here but she would lay a bet it was giving some virtuous social worker sleepless nights.

She touched Alice's shoulder. 'Thank you,' she said. 'If you do remember anything else, please get in touch with me.' She laid a white card on the woman's hand and Alice stared at it with a wry smile.

'Apart from decoration,' she said, 'there ain't no point me 'avin' this. I never learned readin'.'

'So what have we got?' Mike said scornfully as they dropped back down the hill. 'A couple of loons and no information.'

'Not quite.'

'A long car,' Mike said.

'An estate car?' Joanna queried. 'I'll take Alice into town and ask her to point out similar vehicles. It was a noisy car. Remember the barmaid at the Winking Man said she thought it was Herbert's Land Rover. Also, Mike, we know what the killer was wearing and even more important the route he or she took over the moors and why. I don't think we've done too badly. We are getting somewhere.' She smiled. 'It might not be quite fast enough for you but I'm more interested in final results and a conviction than in speed.'

He grinned at her. 'So I've noticed.' Then he paused at the foot of the hill. 'What are the odds on Private Swinton?'

She looked at him. 'They would be high,' she said, 'except that we both know it's impossible. Army security. He can't have been in two places at once. And there is no way he got out of the barracks, came back and got into his bunk. He didn't do it. Him finding the body was pure coincidence.'

'Why didn't he tell us he knew Dean then?'

'Come on, Mike,' she said, 'you know that type. Help the police? Not on your life. He knew we'd get the boy's identity sooner or later. However, I still want to question him.'

Eloise was sitting in the café bar, drinking Coca-Cola. Jane and Matthew were watching. Suddenly the child looked up self-consciously. Why had they stopped arguing? For two days now there had been peace – almost a truce between them. She sucked noisily through her straw and was quickly reprimanded by her mother.

'Manners,' Jane said, but mildly.

She swivelled her glance up to her father. He was staring out to sea as though he were a hundred miles from there. And he was far away, dreaming.

'I want to sit on your lap, Daddy.'

Matthew gave a shudder, quickly disguising it as a jerky laugh. 'You're far too big a girl to be sitting on your daddy's lap.'

Eloise's lower lip hung down. 'I want to.'

And Matthew gave in, held his arms out and Eloise struggled to tuck her long legs around him.

Jane's face grew hard. 'Just one more whole day of

the holiday,' she said. 'Then we fly on the next day.'

Eloise clapped her hands like a toddler. 'Goodee,' she said. 'And I can soon be riding Sparky.'

'Yes,' Jane said firmly.

They were holding tin bowls, lined up in the mess. Withers started first – on cue – prompted by a wink from Private Holt. He jostled Swinton. 'They know who the kid is, Swinton.'

Swinton felt his anger rise as quickly as he felt Tom-boy shrink beside him. 'Fuck off,' he said.

Holt and Withers were either side of him now. 'Some poor bastard from a home,' Withers said. 'A local home for bastards whose mothers can't be bothered to care for them.'

'What was the name of the place again?'

'Tweet Tweet Tweet Tweet.'

Holt was inane but the jibe was enough to tip Swinton into pure fury. He lashed out a punch at him, but Holt ducked and Swinton lost his balance and fell into the table.

Withers grinned. 'Careful ... careful.'

'Why don't you leave off?' Surprisingly it was Tom-boy – sensitive to his comrade's lack of a family home. Rare courage found from somewhere. But as quickly as it had erupted it subsided again and Tom-boy flushed and fell silent.

As usual, Swinton failed to appreciate the risk Tom-boy had taken. 'Piss off, blubber-face,' he said, then turned back to Withers. 'So the dead kid came from a home,' he snarled. 'So bloody what?'

'He came from the same place as you did, Swinton.' Another voice had joined the pack of jackals.

'And you were the one what found the body.'

'Don't tell me it was all a big coincidence.'

'Sure it was a body when you got there?'

Tom-boy blinked and moved forward. 'It was nothin' to do with Gary. The kid was dead. I saw he was dead. Gary had nothin' to do with it.'

Swinton turned on him again. 'I said piss off. I don't need Tom-soft-boy to fight my battles.' He faced Holt squarely. 'If you want to say something, soldier, come right out with it.' He leered and clenched his fist. The others sensed his great wish was to use those fists. 'Come on,' he said, beckoning with his hand. 'Come on ... don't be scared.'

The soldiers backed off. They were no match for Swinton. He didn't feel pain and when the wild look was in his eyes he positively welcomed it ... almost needed it. Swinton looked from one face to the other, grinning, the gap in his teeth giving him a crooked, evil expression.

Tom-boy saw the knife and gulped, uncertain whether to warn the others, but they had half expected it. This gave their planned beating a justification. Swinton had been armed. They pummelled him then, trying to make him scream, but they didn't understand him.

When he stood up, his face was already beginning to swell and the pain in his back told him one or two ribs had cracked. Stiffly he walked to the door, turning round when he reached it. 'I didn't kill the bloody kid, you morons,' he said. 'If you had any sense at all you'd know that. He was dead when we were all asleep here in our beds.'

'Gary ...' Tom-boy appealed to him, and Gary resigned himself. As he tottered through the door, Tom-boy held him up.

The soldiers carried on filling up their tin dishes. 'We can have extra,' Holt said cheerfully. 'Two missing.'

As Joanna and Mike reached the black police van they sensed an atmosphere of excitement. More had been found. There was a buzz in the air, quick activity, and instead of the unbroken line of uniforms a clump of officers were busy stringing off a round area, connected with a long corridor of red and white plastic ribbon.

Joanna nodded towards the spot. 'The first burning,' she said, and they walked until they reached the group of officers.

'It wasn't in the original search area, Inspector.' The SOC officer, Sergeant Barraclough, greeted them with a note of apology.

Joanna waved it aside.

'That's all right,' she said. 'What have you got?'

Triumphantly the sergeant held up a scorched black glove safely in its plastic bag.

Joanna grinned. 'Well done. Forensics could make a whole case out of that one glove. Tell me, Barra,' she said, feeling, at last, pleased, 'I've read they can get fingerprints from the inside of gloves. Any chance here, do you think?'

He shook his head dubiously. 'I doubt it,' he said. 'Wool's a terrible material for fingerprints. And it's been out here for three days now – damp and cold. Still if I remember rightly at PM I cut off some of Dean's clothing. I've got the feeling forensics said there were strands of black wool.' He looked at her. 'I didn't have a clue then where they'd come from.' He paused. 'Funny, isn't it, how all the little bits and pieces make up one big picture?'

'Over here, Sarge.' Joanna could never rid herself of the excitement the phrase evoked in her.

Armed with plastic bags the SOC officer moved to the spot. The constable pointed down. Caught on a sharp bramble was a tiny fragment of material. Tiny, but not too tiny to see, was a piece of coat-lining in the bright red Royal Stuart tartan.

Barraclough picked it up with a pair of tweezers. 'Well done, my lad,' he said. 'Sharp eyes.' He grinned. 'This is better. This is much better.'

Joanna thought for a minute. 'We want maps of the area,' she said, 'and plot the finds. I want to know the exact route.' She looked at Barraclough. 'Well done, we're getting somewhere now. Keep at it, Barra. Remind the men not to miss anything. A fragment such as this might be the piece we need to nail our killer. I don't want him getting away. He could kill again.'

It was the one horror that haunted any police officer in charge of a murder investigation. Fail to find the killer – as they had done for a long time with the Yorkshire Ripper – and you pay with another innocent life. If someone had to die, let it not be through the failure to pick up a strand of thread or interpret a clue. On the other hand, an arrest made with insufficient evidence would mean an acquittal and a killer still on the loose.

Joanna's mobile phone crackled and the voice informed her Private Gary Swinton was waiting in the station, ready to talk to her.

DC King met her as she walked into the station. He shook his head. 'I can't see how he could have done it,' he said. 'He was at the disco till two then came back with all the other blokes. He was seen back in by the soldier on duty.' He looked at Joanna. 'He definitely saw him. There's no way he could have got out and killed the boy. It's impossible.'

She nodded. 'I know,' she said. 'The firing was at about four. At that time we know Gary Swinton was in the bunkhouse with about 30 other soldiers. Thank you.' She smiled. 'He can be excluded from the inquiry. But I still have some questions I want to put to him.'

Swinton was sitting alone, looking ill-at-ease, still dressed in heavy black army boots and green camouflage fatigues. But his beret was tucked in an epaulette and he looked less menacing without the camouflage paint on his face. And his neck looked bony and thin sticking out from the thick collar. His bright hair was cut so short Joanna could see pink scalp beneath. He was younger than she had thought – barely 17 – and he looked frightened. The ugly swelling on his eye, the cut lip and the undisguised wincing as he moved did not escape her either. Summary justice? One thing she knew without doubt, life would never be easy for Gary Swinton. She felt it was important they put him at his ease.

'Thank you for coming in, Gary,' she said.

He mumbled his reply.

'Detective Sergeant Korpanski' – Gary shot an apprehensive look at the DS – 'and I really asked you to come in to go over a few details about the morning you found Dean's body.'

His shoulders stiffened at the sound of the boy's name, but she would ask him simple questions first. The difficult ones could come later. She looked at one of the uniformed police officers. 'Is there an interview room free?'

He nodded towards a green door on the left of the corridor and the three of them moved into it. Joanna switched on the tape recorder while Gary gave her a look like a frightened rabbit.

'Am I under arrest?' he asked.

Joanna shook her head. 'No, Gary,' she said, 'but I want you to clear up a few things.'

The look of apprehension remained on his face.

'Why didn't you tell us you knew Dean?' she asked.

His face paled. He licked his lips, fumbled in his pocket. 'Mind if I smoke?'

'Go ahead.' Mike slid an ashtray across the table.

'You and Dean were together at The Nest, weren't you? Both in care. You knew Dean very well, didn't you?'

He dragged deeply on his cigarette and nodded.

'Did it not occur to you that the first thing we needed to do to help us catch Dean's killer was find out his name?'

'I knew you'd pin it on me.'

Joanna leaned forward. 'Don't be so bloody silly, Gary,' she said. 'You didn't do it. There isn't a force in the country would try and pretend you did.'

He took another deep drag from his cigarette and blew it straight in her face.

'But I believe you can help us over another matter,' she went on.

'What's that then?' He scowled.

'Who was being cruel to Dean?' She picked up his packet of cigarettes. 'Someone was burning him, with cigarettes, just like these.' She looked the soldier straight in the face. 'Was it you?'

'It were a laugh,' he said. 'There weren't no harm

in it. They did it to me when I was a kid. It never hurt me.'

'And were you fucking him as well?'

Gary Swinton looked insulted. 'Don't be daft,' he said. 'I don't fancy little boys.' He drew an exaggerated female shape in the air. 'Curvy. That's how I like 'em.' He shot Joanna a cocky look. 'Like you.'

Mike stepped forward. 'Watch yourself,' he said.

Joanna waited before speaking again. 'So, Gary, if you weren't molesting Dean – who was?'

'I don't know,' he said. 'How should I know?'

'And where did he go when he absconded?'

'To his family I always thought.'

Joanna stared at him. 'But he didn't have a family.'

'Well, that's where I thought he went. I never bloody well asked him.'

The surly attitude finally began to irritate her. 'Well, I wish you had,' she said. 'We might have some idea who it was murdered your little friend.'

Gary Swinton blinked and Joanna spoke again to him, quietly. 'Just go over that morning, will you?'

Carefully he repeated what he had said before ... A platoon, B platoon ... the slow creep on his belly up the bank ...

She stopped him.

'How is it you didn't notice the fire?'

'We wasn't looking that way.'

'You didn't smell anything?'

'Wind must 'ave bin in the wrong direction.' He paused. 'It weren't until we got to nearly the top that me and Tom-boy smelt it.'

Mike moved behind him. 'You knew that smell, didn't you? Flesh burning.'

Gary Swinton half turned. 'It weren't like you're

saying,' he said. 'It weren't cruel. It were more of an endurance test. See?'

Mike gave a loud expression of disgust.

Gary was sweating now – in fear – shaking as though he was an alcoholic.

Mike moved closer to the table. 'What did you do to that poor kid?' he asked. When the soldier didn't answer he spoke again in a soft, dangerous voice. 'Who did the tattoos for you?'

'It were Jason. Bugger. He said he'd do 'em neat.'

'And he did Dean's as well?'

Gary seemed to crumple. Slowly he nodded and went silent.

Joanna looked at Mike. 'May I have a word?' she asked.

Outside, Joanna said, 'We have to let him go now. We both know we aren't going to charge him with anything.'

'I'd like to wring his bloody neck,' Mike said viciously.

She smiled at him. 'Really, Detective Sergeant?'

He gave a wry look and together they entered the interview room again. 'All right, Gary,' she said. 'Thank you. You're free to leave.'

For a moment he sat, quite frozen, as though he did not trust what he'd heard. Then without another word he stood up and bolted through the door.

11

The time when she missed Matthew most was when she was away from work – at home, alone and in the middle of the night when all was quiet and deeper thoughts intruded. What were his true feelings towards her? Had their love been based on warm ice? On deceit, excitement and furtive meetings that had blessed her, the 'other woman', with an illusion of glamour.

And if she was brutally honest with herself there were other thoughts too. Matthew had been the world's most exciting and intelligent lover – now and then. Their meetings had been infrequent and treasured, each second lived twice over. The sick thought that pervaded her now was, did she honestly want a full-time lover? A husband? Someone always there? Demanding? Or had one of the magic reasons she had been so magnetised by Matthew Levin been his intermittence?

And now the worry had woken her. She climbed out of bed and stepped under the shower. It was time to face Monday and her mood was not improved by knowing she had set most of this day aside to speak to the children from The Nest. Maree's presence had been arranged and it was thought better that she, Mike and a policewoman (she had chosen PC Cheryl Smith for her acuteness) should interview the children one at a time in familiar surroundings – in the living room of the children's home. However, as she sat at her breakfast bar, drinking the first coffee of the day, the telephone rang. It was the Chief Superintendent and he sounded irritable.

'Good morning, sir.'

'I hope you haven't bitten off more than you can chew, Piercy,' he said sharply, 'because I've got Ashford Leech's son here breathing fire. Says you've been harassing his aged mother. And', he said ominously, 'for some reason you've decided to make public the ring connection.'

She thought how Wagnerian the phrase sounded ... 'She isn't aged, sir,' Joanna protested, but the Chief was definitely not interested in discussing the relationship of *anno domini* to Gilly Leech.

'You'd better come down here, Piercy,' he said. 'He wants to speak to the officer in charge. And he's brought his solicitor.'

'Suits me,' she said. 'I needed to speak to him anyway.'

'Use the car. It's quicker. And I don't want you turning up in those bloody black shiny cycling shorts.'

She agreed to use the car and felt decidedly resentful towards Robin Leech for upsetting her routine. She left a message for Mike then – at the station. Would he arrange for the ring to be released from forensics, and also would he delay the children's interviews for an hour.

She finished dressing, applied two-minute make-up and headed for the station, giving her bike a reluctant glance as she got into her car.

She picked out Robin Leech's car easily enough in the car park, a rather battered cream Range Rover slewed across two parking spaces. He had obviously arrived in a hurry or a temper – or both.

He stood up as she walked in, a tall, thin man with wide nostrils and thinning hair. The man seated at his side was presumably his solicitor.

Joanna introduced herself and Robin Leech slapped the desk with the newspaper. 'Are you responsible for this?'

She glanced at the headline. *Dead MP's Ring Found on Murdered Boy's Finger* ... Caroline had surpassed herself.

Joanna sighed and looked at the solicitor. 'I don't think there's any problem with this, is there?'

Robin Leech snorted. 'No problem?' he said. 'Blackening the family name? This little squirt burgles our house – steals our property – then goes and gets himself murdered. And you have the effrontery to drag our family into it?'

'Mr Leech,' she said severely, 'I didn't drag you into this. The ring on Dean's finger was your father's.' She unfolded the paper and scanned the article. 'As far as I can see there isn't anything here to which you can object.'

He opened his mouth then shut it again.

'If you object to certain facts being made public I suggest you take it up with the Press Complaints Authority – not the police.'

'Harassment then,' the solicitor said. He was about the same age as Leech. Perhaps an old school friend. He was dark-eyed, dark-suited, with slicked-back hair and a cocksure manner, balancing a large black briefcase on bony knees.

These two, Joanna decided, looked down on the rest of the world as humans do ants. She ignored him. 'Shall we go into my office now the introductions are over?'

She sat down behind her desk, opposite both men. 'You want to make an official complaint about harassment?' she asked

The solicitor drew out a wired notepad and pencil, rested it on the desk and leaned back. 'My client wants to know the purpose of your questions,' he said.

'Just a minute,' Joanna said quickly, 'who exactly is your client – Mr Robin Leech or Mrs Gilly Leech?'

'I act for the family,' the solicitor said haughtily.

'And what exactly is your complaint against the police?'

'My client – Mr Robin Leech –' the solicitor spoke clearly, 'is anxious. He has volunteered to come here today to make a statement. He wants to make that statement and then for the police to leave him and his family alone. He does not want further police visits to Rock House. They upset his mother.'

'Well, hang on a minute.' Joanna's hackles were beginning to rise. She could feel a slow prickle at the back of her neck. 'A ring believed to belong to your father, Mr Leech, was found on the dead boy's finger. We know also that your father and this boy were acquainted.'

'Lies ...' Robin Leech was really breathing fire now. 'Damned bloody lies.'

Joanna stared hard at him. 'Mr Leech,' she said, 'the dead boy was from the children's home – The Nest. We know that your father entertained these children from time to time at your family home. We know this. Your mother has told us. So has Mr Riversdale, warden of the home. This is not conjecture – this is fact. Now, we are not suggesting there was anything improper about this association, Mr Leech. We believe it was through your father's role as a local benefactor.'

The flattery had its desired effect. Robin Leech visibly relaxed. His solicitor smirked. Fool police, the look said.

'That's right,' Robin burbled. 'That's right. As an MP he took his duties very seriously ... Father was a benefactor.'

'However,' Joanna said, knowing this was more boggy ground, 'we are slightly curious about the burglary following which the ring was noted to be missing.'

The solicitor cleared his throat. 'What do you mean, "slightly curious"?' he asked.

'We're not prepared to say at the moment,' Joanna said, 'but we will need to speak to Mrs Leech again at some point.'

'About the burglary?' Robin demanded.

'Yes,' she said.

'Then I must insist ...' the solicitor puffed out his chest, 'that I be present during all interviews with either Mrs Gilly Leech or Mr Robin Leech.'

Joanna gave him one of her most winning smiles. 'Certainly,' she said. 'Now, Mr Leech, could you just tell me ...' She pushed across the desk the photograph of Dean Tunstall.

Robin Leech visibly winced.

'Do you know this boy?' she asked.

He found it difficult to look at and she had to ask him again. Then he stuttered – no, he didn't think so.

'And where were you on Sunday night?'

'At home.'

'Alone?'

'Yes,' he said angrily, 'I was bloody well alone – watching the telly, if you must know ...' He was blustering. 'I watched the damned film. Stupid thing – New York ... murder ... the usual sort of rubbish.'

'Then why watch it?' she asked conversationally.

He glowered at her.

'You live with your mother?' she asked.

He nodded. 'Yes – and no. When my marriage broke up I ... we had the stables converted into a two-bedroom flat. I live there – alone.

She nodded. 'Lucky you had some stables.'

The sarcasm was not wasted on him. 'Yes, it is,' he said defiantly.

'No cardboard city for you.'

The solicitor fidgeted.

'Just one more thing,' she said, knowing the answer. 'What car do you drive?'

'It's outside,' he said. 'A cream Range Rover.'

The solicitor moved again. 'May I ask why you want to know this?'

She looked coolly at him. 'Just routine,' she said.

Robin Leech shot her a furious look.

Joanna stood up. 'Well, that's all for now.' Again she gave both men a broad smile, shook hands with them in turn. 'Thank you very, very much for calling in.' She could have been a successful society hostess thanking them for coming to dinner. And it made both men, she noticed, quickly discount her as a force to be reckoned with.

She spoke then to the solicitor. 'I will want to speak to both the Leeches again,' she said, still in the same 'society' tone. 'But I will certainly let you know.'

The two men filed out and minutes later she

heard the splutter of a broken silencer.

Mike looked curiously at her as she walked out of her office. 'So?' he said.

She chewed her lip. 'I can't see a motive,' she said, 'not even a connection at the moment. He denies knowing Dean.' She clapped him on the shoulder. 'But I'd love to get forensics on to that Range Rover.' She sighed. 'Why does the law protect the guilty so completely? Surely one would think if he is innocent he'd be only too delighted to help the police with their enquiries. But oh no ...'

Mike grinned at her. 'Police training video,' he mocked.

'Sod you,' she said. 'I feel like breaking rules today.'

'Not today. Not with minors. The Super would blow your brains out.'

She gave a long, shuddering yawn.

'No sleep again?' he asked.

She shook her head. 'I keep thinking. Cases are always like this. They prey on your mind until they're solved. Come on. Time to get to The Nest.'

As they drove along the Ashbourne road they discussed the recent developments. 'I suppose Leech is a suspect,' said Mike.

She nodded. 'I'd just love to get him dancing on hot coals. There are a few things that bring him to mind. He was the son of his father. That might have given him reason to wish Dean Tunstall out of the way. I daresay exposure – especially posthumous exposure – of unsavoury exploits might have been a potent threat to the Leech family. People like that care more about position and a pure reputation than they do about money or morals. Also the Leeches knew that there was a risk Dean might have contracted Aids if he had been abused by Ashford Leech deceased. Also ...' she glanced at the DS, 'he drives a cream Range Rover.'

He nodded.

'Do you think we could get Alice Rutter to identify it?'

He met her eyes. 'It's worth a try.'

'That's what I thought. I'll pick her up tomorrow.' She laughed suddenly. 'At the cave.'

Mike looked at her curiously. 'You seem very relaxed, Jo.'

'Yes,' she said. 'Because we're getting there, Mike. We're closing in.' She met his eyes and felt herself flush. 'I'm sorry. I must sound overconfident.'

He shook his head. 'No.'

'By the way ... I've applied for a warrant to search Keith Latos's flat and shop. I'm not very happy about him.' She frowned. 'I'm sure he's been lying.'

Mike looked up. 'What about?'

'The shoes. They weren't quite as new as they looked. Clean – yes. New – no. I know it's a stab in the dark, but I don't think Dean stole them. I think they might have belonged to someone. If he stole them it was not from a shop but from another person.'

'Doesn't that take the heat off Latos?'

'No. He stays on the list.'

Mike nodded.

'The one thing we do know,' she said, 'is that Dean almost certainly didn't buy them. He didn't have the money.' She looked over at him. 'Either someone bought them for him – the same person who fed, clothed, cared for him on his mysterious disappearances – or he stole them from someone.'

'Have we anyone else in the inquiry?'

She shook her head. 'The uniformed boys have worked really hard, but I can't say they've come up with anything.'

As they neared the large Victorian house, she said, 'Just fill me in on the children here.'

'There should be eight,' he said, 'but as we know two left earlier on this year. They haven't, as yet, been replaced.' He paused. 'Three of the children are quite young. I think we might find it tricky to get accepted statements from them.'

'Their names?'

'The youngest is a little girl called Sonya. She's four years old, mixed race. Next is Shirley and she's five. Then comes Timmy, who's eight, but he's retarded with a mental age of five.'

'And the older children?'

'Jason and Kirsty,' he said. 'Fourteen and 13 and a half respectively. Unfortunately, from what Eve heard, they aren't exactly the police force's greatest fans.'

She sighed. 'Well, if Dean had access to drugs,' she said, 'it's likely they do too.'

They pulled into the gravelled drive of the children's home and knocked on the front door. It was flung open by Maree, who looked very angry. 'Where the bloody hell have you been?' she demanded. 'I've been here nearly an hour. I've a load of work to do.'

'I'm sorry,' Joanna said. 'I did send a message. I was involved with a possible witness.'

'Yeah, well ...' the young woman said grudgingly, 'the kids were getting upset. You know what they're like.'

'Not as well as you do,' Joanna said.

Maree grinned and swept her fingers through her hair. 'Sorry,' she said. 'Sorry. Always was a bit fiery.

Bark, as you might say. No bite – I assure you.'

'Good,' Mike said.

'I really came to find out a little more about the children,' said Joanna.

'There isn't a lot of point you talking to the little ones,' Maree replied. 'Sonya, Shirley and Timmy won't know anything. You'll get far more out of Jason and Kirsty. They were pretty thick with Dean.'

'And Mr Riversdale?'

'You want to speak to him too? Again?'

Joanna nodded.

'He's out at the moment. I think he'll be back though. Soon.' She gave a rueful smile. 'Shopping.'

The three youngest were peeping at them through the banisters ... Wide-eyed and innocent, they scuttled up the stairs, giggling, as soon as Mike looked up at them.

They saw Kirsty first. 'Thirteen and a half,' she said defiantly when Joanna asked her age. She was a small girl with a tight, mean mouth, a heart-shaped face and the green, intelligent eyes of a cat. That day she was wearing thick mascara and a smudge of bright lipstick. The lipstick seemed to add a touch of bravado to the childish face.

'You were Dean's friend?'

'Course.' Kirsty leaned back on the sofa, her arm extended along the back. 'We all was. I liked little Dean. He was cute.'

'Was anybody hurting him?'

'What do you mean?'

Joanna glanced at the social worker. Maree filled the gap. 'Was anybody ever cruel to him?'

'To Dean – no.' The girl was indignant.

'We know,' Joanna said cautiously, 'that someone

was. There were marks.'

The girl looked less defiant. 'You don't mean the tattoos, do you? Jason does the tattoos.' She held her hands out proudly. 'He did mine.' She grinned. 'Professional, aren't they?'

Joanna raised her eyebrows. 'Very, but I don't mean those. I mean the cigarette burns.'

Kirsty looked at the floor. 'I don't know about those,' she said. She gave a helpless glance at Maree. 'I can't really say.'

'Was it Gary?' Joanna asked. 'Gary Swinton?'

The girl tightened her lips. 'It made us brave. Brave so we could stand bein' hurt.' She blinked. 'Dean was brave, you know – really brave. He never shouted out – not once. Not like me. I didn't like it,' she said slowly, then closed her eyes. 'The smell, you know.' Her gaze fixed on Joanna. 'Burnin'.' She shrugged her shoulders. 'Anyway, he's gone now.'

Maree gave a quiet sound of protest. 'Why didn't you say anything?'

Kirsty gave her a disconcertingly clear stare. 'What could you do? It'd only 'ave made things worse. Where else was we goin' to go? Enquiries,' she muttered. 'People askin'. No way.

'Anyway ... He's gone. Last year some time. He's in the army now,' she said proudly. 'I've seen him. Round the town. So it does work, don't it? It does make you brave.' And with a curious attempt at logic she said, 'They wouldn't have 'im in the army, would they, if he weren't brave.'

No-one in the room had an answer to that. 'Kirsty.' Joanna spoke gently. 'Somebody killed Dean. They murdered him and then tried to burn his body. We want very badly to find out who it was. When we ask you all these questions it's only to find out who it was. Do you understand?'

'Course,' the girl said.

'Kirsty,' Joanna tried again, 'when Dean used to disappear, someone looked after him, didn't they?'

The girl blinked. 'I don't know.'

Maree tried next. 'Kirsty,' she said, 'someone must have looked after Dean. He was always clean when he came back. He had money in his pocket. Sometimes he had new clothes. Who bought them for him?'

The girl looked from one to the other. 'You don't understand, do you? Dean was close with his secrets. He never told no-one. All we knew was he went to his family.'

'But he had no family,' Maree replied. 'His mother abandoned him when he was two.'

'That's what you think. She weren't 'is real mother. If she had have been she wouldn't have abandoned him. Would she? And another thing ... she can't have been his real mother. Elsewhere is she now?'

Maree looked helplessly at Joanna.

'Do you know who killed him?'

'No.' The girl's eyelids fluttered. 'We all loved Dean. He was a funny little bugger.'

Joanna tried another avenue of questioning. 'Was it Gary who gave him the drugs?'

Kirsty looked towards Maree. 'I don't know a thing about no drugs,' she said firmly. 'Not here.'

Again a blank.

'Were any of the older boys intimate with him?' Joanna was floundering. The words were old-fashioned – inappropriate. Maree came to the rescue.

'Interfering,' she said. 'You know, like on the

telly, that Esther Rantzen thing ... Sexy?'

Kirsty stared at the floor. 'I don't know. I don't know ...' She looked helplessly at Maree. 'Please, make her stop. I've had enough now,' she said.

When she had left the room Joanna and Mike looked at Maree. 'He didn't have a family,' Maree said. 'His mother abandoned him when he was two. There isn't a father on his birth certificate. It doesn't make sense.'

'Well, he was going somewhere,' Mike pointed out.

Maree sighed. 'It was in the nature of an imagined friend. He made it up.' She hesitated. 'He had to have done. All the kids here have fantasies about wonderful, TV-advert families who are just dying to take them back to the stately home and spend thousands of pounds indulging their every whim.' She was upset. 'It's one of the things I find most pathetic here. They lie.' She glanced at Joanna. 'They lie.'

'And was Dean lying?' Mike sounded angry. 'Someone strangled the little blighter – probably a few hours after giving him a £50 pair of Reebok trainers.'

Maree looked away. 'Adults use the children's dreams,' she said, 'for their own ends.'

Jason was a pale boy, thin with sad eyes and an uncomfortable habit of shaking his head intermittently. He looked younger than the 14 Maree assured Joanna he was. But before she could ask one question he blinked tightly. 'I can't help you.' He spoke in a low, pleading voice. 'I haven't a clue who killed Dean. Honest,' he said, 'I don't know anything.'

He looked terrified.

Joanna tried to put him at his ease. 'You're the artist, Jason?'

'No ... please – leave me alone. I don't know anything. I haven't done anything. Don't ask me.'

Joanna smiled at the boy. 'Don't worry,' she said. 'It's the job of the police to find out all about Dean. Just tell me a little bit about him. Maree says you three were best friends.'

'He was clever.' Jason stared out of the window. 'Really clever. He knew loads of things. He could get things too.'

'What sort of things?'

Jason shook his head vaguely. 'You know, all sorts of things – money, sweets ...'

'Drugs?' Joanna asked.

Maree shot her a warning look, then turned to reassure the boy. 'It's all right, Jason, we don't want to cause trouble, but we know Dean had had some drugs. Where did they come from?'

His whole head bounced rapidly from side to side. 'Don't know,' he said. 'They'd bloody kill me ...'

Joanna touched his arm. 'Was it the big boys?' she asked.

Maree cleared her throat. 'Inspector ... I must ask you. Don't put words into his mouth.'

Joanna tried another tack. 'The two boys who left last year, Swinton and ...' she glanced through her notebook, 'and Jim Pullen. Was Dean very good friends with them?'

Jason looked wary. 'Yes,' he said casually.

'Good,' she said. 'And now, Jason, why don't you tell me where Dean used to go when he disappeared?'

'To his family,' he said.

Both Mike and Joanna moved forward.

'What family?' she asked.

'I don't know.'

'Do you mean his mother?' Now Joanna was puzzled. If a mother, then where was she? The child was due to be buried soon and she hadn't turned up.

She looked at Maree who nodded thoughtfully.

'I don't think it was his mother,' Jason said slowly, frowning in concentration. 'He always called it his real family. And they was rich,' he added defiantly.

Maree glanced at Joanna. I told you so.

'How long had he been in contact with this family?'

'Ever since 'e was about seven,' Jason said. 'That's when 'e started runnin' off. 'E might have been seven. 'E bogged off one day when he didn't fancy goin' to school. Said he was going to find his ma. It was about a day or two later he came back and he had things. You know – clothes and a new pair of trainers, and he had a £10 note.'

Joanna felt her pulse quickening. 'Jason,' she said softly, 'this is very important. Where was it? Was it somewhere near or was it far away? How did he find out about it? How did he know they were his real family?'

The boy shrugged his shoulders. 'Dunno,' he said, then he stopped. 'Hang on a minute, I remember now. I told him the police had been all over looking for him and he said 'e'd been right under our noses all the time.'

'Did he come back in a car?'

Jason shook his head slowly.

'Please, Jason. This could help us very much. Can you remember if Dean said anything about the place or the people he'd been with?'

The boy shook his head again. 'He told me it was a secret when I asked him ...' He turned to Maree. 'Can

I go now?'

She nodded, and he hurried from the room.

Mike stared after him. 'He knows who it is,' he said. 'We'd better watch these kids.'

'You think so?'

'I know so, Joanna,' he said.

'I have a suggestion.' Maree spoke. 'Let me talk to them. I've known them for years. They trust me. Besides,' she pointed out, 'they're far more likely to confide in me than they are in you.'

They had to agree.

Mike sat down and looked at the two women. 'The question is,' he said, 'is he telling the truth?'

'Well?' Joanna spoke to Maree.

The social worker thought for a moment. 'I've known Jason for about ten years,' she said. 'As you probably gathered, he isn't very bright. But neither is he imaginative ... Of the two, Dean would have been far more likely to fabricate a story. But ...' she held one finger up to give the words emphasis, 'if ... if any part of this story is to be believed, and just assuming that it is true ...'

'What?' Mike asked angrily. 'That some raving paedo took a little kid home, buggered him and then bought him clothes, gave him money and sent him packing?'

'What I'm saying is,' Maree spoke patiently, 'if it did happen, I very much doubt that it was Dean's father. There is no father.'

'There has to be one,' Mike said. 'Biologically.'

'It's a space on the birth certificate.'

'He never said where he got to on his "excursions",' Joanna reminded them. 'So,' she frowned, 'assuming that it was this "father" who killed

Dean – possibly because things were getting too dangerous if Dean did talk to Jason – Jason himself could be in danger.'

'He could still have thieved the stuff,' Mike said.

'I don't think he did.' Joanna was thoughtful. 'He was a very pretty child – easy prey to someone with predatory instincts. I believe someone was conning him.'

'All right then,' Mike said. 'Who? The person had to have somewhere to keep him. He was sometimes gone for days on end. It had to be somewhere they wouldn't be disturbed.'

'My money goes on Latos,' Joanna said. 'The sooner we poke around his premises the better.' She looked at Mike. 'I want pictures of Dean to saturate the town. All I want is one sighting of them together by a witness who will stand up in court. That's all I ask.' She turned to the other two in the room. 'Not a lot, is it?'

She crossed the room towards the window and caught sight of Mark Riversdale's battered white Vauxhall spin to a halt at the top of the drive. 'And this is where we get more facts from.'

The three of them watched silently as Riversdale opened the door of the Cavalier and climbed out. He stood for a moment, staring at the police car, his hands in his pockets. Then he lifted the tail door and struggled with a cardboard box. A minute later they heard him open the front door and footsteps along the passage. There were voices in the kitchen, then he entered the living room.

He held out his hand. 'Sorry I wasn't here when you arrived. We ran out of a few things.'

He was sweating profusely and nervously wiped the sweat from his brow with his sleeve. 'Hot, isn't it?'

'I don't find it so.' Mike was at his most stolid.

Mark Riversdale chose to ignore the remark. He sat down heavily on the sofa and glanced at Maree. 'Any problems?'

'They weren't terribly helpful,' she said, 'but we didn't try too hard – didn't want to upset them.'

He nodded.

Joanna spoke then. 'I'm sure they know something, but they're not telling. Please – can you impress on them they are in danger if they don't tell us all they know. Someone killed Dean. I believe they could strike again. Until the killer is caught they are in danger.' She paused as Mark Riversdale's eyes flickered over her. 'You've worked here for how long?'

'Eighteen months,' he said cautiously.

'So you were here when Gary Swinton lived here?'

He nodded. 'And glad when he left.'

'Were you aware he was bullying some of the younger children?'

'Look,' he said, 'it happens in these sorts of places. There isn't a lot you can do about it.'

'Couldn't you have tackled him about it?'

He grimaced. 'It makes things worse for the kids,' he said. 'They would have been picked on more than ever.'

'And you find drugs acceptable too?'

He shrugged his shoulders. 'What do you expect me to do? Bring the police in?'

'It might seem a good idea.' Mike's tone was hostile, his dislike shining through his words. 'It's what we're here for.'

'It wasn't a big problem,' he said defensively.

'Dean was given intravenous drugs on more than

one occasion,' Joanna said.

Mark Riversdale blinked. 'Not here he wasn't. I'd have known ... A few tablets at the most.'

'Tablets you don't mind?' she said sharply.

'I do mind.' He glared at her. 'But I am realistic. In a place like this you don't get choirboys, you know. What you get is problems. Problems no-one else wants to take on. If I keep them alive and get 50 percent school attendance, and keep them out of the Young Offenders Institution until they're 16, I consider I'm doing pretty well. I don't even look for such things as GCSEs or university entrance, Inspector.'

Joanna could almost feel Mike Korpanski's hackles rise and the heat increase in the room. She cleared her throat and tried a new tack. 'What did you do before you came here?'

'I worked in local government,' he said.

'Which department?'

'Inland Revenue,' he said ruefully, and gave a slight, tentative smile.

She met his eyes. 'Why did you leave?'

He looked paralysed by the question. 'I ... I ... I wanted a change.' It sounded lame.

'What made you come here?' she asked.

'I'm fond of children,' he said.

'But you have none of your own?'

'I'm not married,' he said.

She smiled. 'A girlfriend, perhaps?'

'Not at the moment.'

'I see.' She paused for a moment to regroup her questions. 'When you came here, Mr Riversdale, what did you think of Dean?'

He thought for a minute. 'Confident, prone to telling stories–'

She interrupted. 'What sort of stories?'

'The usual ones, having a family, money, they were coming to claim him one day ... All rather pathetic really.'

She looked enquiringly.

'They haven't a family,' he said, 'so they invent one.'

'There is no family?'

'No,' he replied. 'His mother has shown no interest at all in him since he was a baby. A brief visit when he was two, since then – nothing. You can look at his case file if you like.'

'Thank you ... Mr Riversdale ...' She paused. 'Let me just get this right. Are you saying that although Dean had been badly treated – on PM it was noted he had been physically and sexually abused – you can shed no light on this?'

'Not since I've been here,' he said, glancing angrily at Maree. 'You've looked after him longer than I have. Why aren't they asking you all the questions?'

'Calm down, Mark,' she said quietly. 'They've already asked me all this. I couldn't help them any more than you could. But you lived with him.'

He looked ashamed. 'Yes,' he said, 'I lived with him.'

Joanna was suddenly angry. She looked at Riversdale and then at the social worker. 'You two were in charge of this boy,' she said. 'He was a child in your care. I want to know. What was going on?' Her eyes, Mike noted, had changed colour to a steely grey-blue. At the station this was the sign they all dreaded, this cold grey anger. The angry gypsy. 'I warn you both,' she said. 'A police enquiry will be intrusive and merciless. It would be better if one of you told me the full truth. Who was sexually abusing Dean?'

They looked at one another.

Joanna spoke again. 'All right.' She stared at Mark. 'Was it you?'

He began to bluster then – to deny it hotly. He had been in charge of the boy ... in *loco parentis* ... definitely not.

And all the time Joanna watched him and wondered.

'Let me put it another way ... did you suspect he was being abused?'

They both nodded.

'Right,' she said. 'Who did you think it was?'

It was Maree who spoke. 'We thought it was Leech,' she said. 'But we didn't dare do anything about it. He was a powerful man, and a vocal one too. Besides, Dean was really fond of him.'

'And to your knowledge,' she asked, 'did he know Keith Latos?'

They looked at one another again, this time in puzzlement.

'He has the sports shop on the High Street,' Joanna explained.

Both shook their heads. 'Not as far as we know,' Maree said.

'And where did you think Dean disappeared to when he absconded?'

'We just didn't know,' Riversdale said. 'We couldn't get to the bottom of it. We noticed he seemed ill once or twice when he came home. We were going to do something about it. Then it stopped. He had been much better. He even stayed here for two months at a time.' He looked at her. 'That's why I didn't think he'd gone this time.'

'Well, he had,' she said brutally. 'But you can stop worrying about Dean. He's out of your hands now. Just start worrying about the two we spoke to this morning. Now – let's start again. Where did he go?'

They were both silent.

Maree spoke first. 'We honestly don't know, Inspector.'

She turned to Mark. 'All right then, Mr Riversdale, where did you think he went?'

'I don't know.' His voice was shaking, his hands were too.

Joanna knew she could have continued further, broken him. But time and the law had taught her other ways. She stood up and stared at him for a moment. 'We will want to question you further,' she said, 'at the station.'

'When?' The panic in his voice made him squeak the word.

'I don't know.'

'Will you be pressing charges?' he asked timidly.

'I don't know,' she said. 'But if I were you I would be prepared to face an internal inquiry at the very least – if not criminal charges.'

As she walked to the police car Joanna glanced back into the room. Mark Riversdale was sat on the sofa, his face in his hands. Maree was standing over him, shouting. As Joanna's eyes travelled up to the bedroom window she saw Kirsty and Jason staring down at her. As soon as they realised they had been seen they disappeared from view.

'Honestly,' she said to Mike as they turned out into the main road, 'I thought the days of the workhouse and Oliver Twist were over and done with. Christ,' she exploded, 'he's worse than the bloody beadle.'

'Yes, but what else?' Mike asked. 'How much of that poor kid's troubles came from Riversdale himself?'

'What do you think?'

Mike considered for a moment before he spoke. 'Not sure,' he said.

It was quiet in the cottage as Joanna let herself in through the front door, and after the bustle of the station working to capacity over the murder hunt she felt enveloped by loneliness. She sat in the dark for a long while, trying to ponder the case. She forced herself to picture the child – alive ... analyse his life and relationships. And the more she thought, the stronger became the conviction that Jason and Kirsty held the answers to many questions she would like to put to them. She chewed her lip and decided she would pay another visit to The Nest in the morning.

And then slowly would follow the exposures ... uncomfortable ones. Unpleasant and dirty secrets would be dug up. Questions would be asked. And the whisperings would start. She was only now beginning to understand the basics of this case. She closed her eyes and dreamed.

The telephone woke her much later. She picked it up and yawned into the receiver. 'Hello?'

'Joanna.'

She didn't know whether to be glad or sad it was Caro. But she did feel a snag of apprehension.

'I said I'd help you find Dean's mother,' she said. 'Get the paper tomorrow. If it doesn't bring results I'll munch my way through a morning copy. I promise. You can watch.'

Joanna laughed, lifted by the tone of mischief in her friend's voice. 'Thanks,' she said.

'Scratch my back,' Caro said gaily, 'and I'll scratch yours.'

'Your headline on the ring brought results.'

'Really?'

'Brought Robin Leech down on me like a ton of bricks.'

'Power of the pen,' Caro said lightly, then added, 'When's Matthew back?'

'I don't know – a couple of days.'

'Mmm,' she said. 'And I wonder what will happen then.'

'I don't know,' Joanna said shortly.

'I'll be in touch.' And the line went dead.

12

Joanna rose early to read the newspaper over breakfast, and propped it up against a carton of fresh orange juice. It was wonderful. A huge headline splashed over Tuesday's front page: *Mother – Where Are You?*. Dean's mother could not fail to see it. She scanned the first column. 'We are anxious to contact you ... Would be willing to pay for your story ...'

Joanna grimaced into her bowl of muesli. It would bring the mother out of the woodwork – if she was alive. Not for the first time she pondered the value of the press – not often acknowledged. Usually the law and the media clashed. But surely they could sometimes work to each other's advantage?

She decided, as she parked her bicycle at the police station and padlocked it, that she might as well speak to the Super before he asked to speak to her. He tended to view the media with a less enlightened attitude. She took a deep breath, knocked on his door and walked in. He was holding the paper flat on the desk.

'Tell me, Piercy,' he said. 'Do you think this sort of thing is a good idea?'

In the few years she had worked as a DI in this force

she had come to respect Arthur Colclough. A man in his fifties, he had been instrumental in her appointment; and for that she owed him gratitude, acknowledgement and loyalty. There were not many senior officers who would have stuck their necks out and appointed a woman as a detective inspector when there were excellent male candidates. But the knowledge that he had favoured her made her even more responsible towards him. She could not let him down. She sat opposite him, took another glance at the photo of Dean's smiling face that they knew now had hidden fear and loneliness. This was the worst aspect of the case. What hell had this child been through – with no-one to help him? Maree and Mark Riversdale should have but they, like this mother and society, had failed him.

She looked up to meet the Super's tiny, intelligent eyes, set in the plump face. 'Yes,' she said. 'We've tried hard to find Dean's mother. Two policemen have worked solidly to find her ever since we knew who he was. They've got nowhere. She wasn't ever going to come to us. We need help, sir. And if it takes this to find her, then yes, sir, I do think it's a good idea.'

He nodded gravely, frowning and scratching his bald patch. 'Okay Piercy,' he said. 'Just be careful. Cleverer people than you have had the illusion they can use the press to advantage. Some of them were wrong.'

'I'll be careful, sir.'

There was an uneasy silence and she was glad when the telephone rang. He answered it and handed it to her. It was Mike.

'Joanna,' he said, his voice tight, 'we've just had a phone call from The Nest. Jason Fogg and Kirsty. They've both left – gone missing. Nobody's seen them since we were there. Their beds weren't slept in.'

It was rare during a case to feel the cold clamp of panic. She looked up at Arthur Colclough. 'Two children missing, sir, from the home.'

His face sagged. 'God, Piercy,' he said, 'God.'

Professional pride seemed irrelevant now. 'Do you want to call in help, sir?' she asked.

He shook his head, gave her a brief, preoccupied smile. 'No,' he said. 'Extra men, but you remain in charge. You will get results.'

She wished she felt as confident. As she stood up to leave he walked with her to the door and touched her shoulder. 'I trust you, Piercy,' he said.

Mike drove her to The Nest. Already the driveway was blocked with police cars. She and Mike threaded their way through them and walked up the steps to the front door. A uniformed officer was standing at the top. He said good morning and gave her a quick glance of sympathy. She knew that look. It said, 'I wouldn't be in your shoes for status, for salary, for stripes.' Once or twice she had given a senior officer exactly the same look.

Maree and Mark were talking to Scottie.

'I think it's my fault,' Maree said. She had been crying. Her face was streaked with tears. She looked like an unhappy little elf in her black leggings, scarlet, baggy jumper and flat ankle boots. She sniffed.

'I was pretty harsh with them yesterday ... Told them they must tell me what was going on – who Dean had been with when he'd run away.' She sniffed again and wiped her nose inelegantly on her sleeve. 'I know they knew,' she said, 'all the time. And they wouldn't tell me anything.' She dropped onto the sofa. 'I thought those kids trusted me.'

'It wasn't their secret,' Joanna said. 'It was Dean's. Perhaps misguided loyalty.'

'And perhaps they were shit scared,' Mike said harshly. 'They knew what had happened to Dean.'

'What time did you speak to them?'

'As soon as you'd left,' Maree said. 'I was with them until seven – maybe eight – trying to gain their confidence.'

'That's the way you lot bloody well work,' Mike exploded. 'Don't you ever realise? It's no good with these sorts of kids. They just laugh at you.'

Maree looked angry. 'I think I know Jason and Kirsty a damned sight better than you do.'

'Did they tell you anything?'

'A cock-and-bull story ... They were making it up as they went along. A fairy story.'

'What fairy story?' Joanna felt cold.

Maree looked at her. 'The usual rubbish,' she said angrily. 'If you must know, it was the same old story that's trotted out to most of these kids. And they want to believe it so much that however pathetic we might find it they swallow it whole. Dean believed – because it was fed to him – that part of his family had turned up. Whoever it was was obviously abusing him. But he was given money and things, expensive things. To him this was love – the love of a family – something he had never known. But it gave him confidence and that certain swagger.'

'Leech?' Joanna's voice was low. The disgust she felt for the cruel trick made her feel sick.

Joanna turned to Mark Riversdale, who was stood staring out of the window, a dreamy, vague expression on his face.

'When did you last see Kirsty and Jason?' Joanna asked.

He came to abruptly, shuddered. Joanna noticed his hands were shaking, he swayed slightly as though blown by an invisible breeze.

'Tennish,' he said. 'They were watching TV together, sitting on the sofa. They went upstairs around ten.'

'That was the last you saw of them?'

He nodded.

'When did you notice they were missing, Mr Riversdale?'

He blinked. 'This morning,' he said. They were late down for breakfast. I went up to their rooms.' He paused, wriggled his glasses up his nose. 'Their beds were neat. They must have gone last night.' He gave a quiet hiccup and it was then that Joanna realised he was drunk.

As they watched, he slowly sank down on to the floor, his plump face bemused, a crumpled heap, clutching at the curtains.

Joanna turned her attention back to Maree O'Rourke. 'Did they say anything else – anything at all?'

She frowned and her face moved forwards a little as though propelled by the concentration, then she looked up. 'They said the person claimed to be his grandfather,' she said. 'He said he was his real mother's father. That the woman who claimed to be his mother was a foster parent – that his real mother was unable to look after him because she had to travel a lot with her job. That Ms Tunstall had been asked to look after him but was no good. So it was decided he should go into council care and that this so-called grandfather should visit him.' She looked apologetic. 'I'm sorry. It's all lies. It's a measure of how gullible Dean was and how very much he wanted to believe he had a family who loved him.'

'What if it's true?' Joanna said softly. 'What if it's all true?'

The four people in the room were silent. It was

Joanna who broke the silence. She crossed the room and found DC Alan King, who was leading the SOC team.

'I want this place searched,' she said, 'from top to bottom. Especially any places where Jason and Kirsty or Dean might have hidden something. And while you're at it, don't forget Riversdale's room and car. If there is anything to be found I want it bagged. Fingerprint any good surfaces.' She glanced at the slumped figure in the corner.

'Get his to exclude them – and everyone else here. We should be able to find the two missing teenagers' prints.'

She was silent all the way back to the station. And this time there was an air of tension at the briefing. The casual camaraderie was gone. The strain showed on all their faces. Two more children were missing. An arrest was vital. There was an urgency now. Not a corpse to be dealt with but two children they had met and questioned.

'The first point is that these two children are missing. They went last night. It is possible they knew the identity of the murderer. We can assume they have absconded, hidden in a safe place or approached the killer. We are sure that the person who abused Dean sexually was a man. We also believe that the person who burned and supplied Dean with drugs was Gary Swinton. We want to talk to Private Swinton. I want him brought in for questioning later on this afternoon.

'We have a list of suspects. We know someone claimed to be Dean's grandfather.' She stopped. 'Unless, of course, he was lying. But I believe more of Dean's so-called "stories" were the truth than people around him credited. I also believe this person was Ashford Leech. If so, the regular abuser cannot have been the killer.

'I have spoken to the criminal psychologist.' A

ripple ran around the room. 'Listen, you lot,' she said crisply, 'we need all the help we can get. Two children are out there. We don't even know whether they are alive or dead. Understand? We are looking for a man – probably between 25 and 50. He is physically fit, lives alone, is a homosexual, probably ashamed of his leanings. He might have been married. He is a local person – someone the boy trusted – with evidence that he was comfortably off, probably without children of his own.'

She glanced at Roger Farthing. 'Keith Latos,' she said, 'the man who owns the sports shop.' She perched herself on the edge of the desk. 'There are a number of points that make him a likely suspect. First, he lives alone. He would have been able to tempt Dean with expensive sports goods from his shop. Secondly, he is a homosexual with a documented penchant for young boys.' She met each person's eyes. 'We search there this afternoon. And I want two of you to speak to Martin Shane, Keith's boyfriend, the man he claims he was with the night of the murder.'

She paused. 'However, he is not the only fish in the bowl.' Again she paused to lend her words weight. 'I'm very curious about the connection with Ashford Leech. Why should he have spent time with the children from The Nest? It wasn't publicised. If anything, he kept this particular light well under a bushel. Dean was wearing Leech's ring. And although we have absolutely no evidence that Leech was a homosexual, we believe he might have died of Aids. Drug addict or homosexual ... whichever he was, he kept it well hidden. Apart from a minor traffic offence he has no record. He can't be the killer. He's been dead for months, but it seems likely that he is the "grandfather" Dean boasted of. Dean has absconded, according to Mark Riversdale, five times in the last 18 months, each time for longer and longer periods. The last time he was missing for over a week.' She stopped, convinced of something. 'Ashford Leech might have been the abuser. But it wasn't a dead man who strangled that kid and set his body alight. If it wasn't Ashford Leech – who was it – and why? The abuse had stopped – both physical and mental. He was free. But still he kept wandering, staying somewhere. So who was looking after him, buying him expensive shoes, caring for him for long periods? Who and why?' She glanced around the room. 'Anyone got any ideas?'

There was a silence, then Mike frowned. 'Was he blackmailing someone?'

She met his eyes. 'Maybe,' she said.

'What about Robin Leech?'

She shook her head. 'We know of no connection between them. In fact, as far as we know, he never even met Dean.'

'Pity,' Mike muttered.

'It *is* a pity. I would have loved to have nailed him to the tree. However,' she said reluctantly, 'this is a personal indulgence. And I can't afford it.' She looked back around the room.

'Please note,' she said, raising her voice now, 'we've had reports from forensics about the samples we found on the moor. The piece of green cotton was waxed. It came from a waxed jacket, olive green. But even better the red wool also came from the jacket, from the lining. The only time the two materials are matched together is in a very expensive coat – the Wilderness Collection, it's called. They aren't sold anywhere in Leek except at one outfitter – Grunwelds. Two of you get a list of customers who have bought a Wilderness coat from there in the last few years. Cheryl ...,' she looked at the young WPC, 'I think it's time to get "Queen Alice" down from the moors. Show her a few cars. Let's see if we can narrow the field a bit from the long, pale car. I want a couple of you to speak to Herbert Machin, the farmer. The murderer used that road. It goes right past the farm and ends at Flash. Please see if he saw or heard anything – anything at all that would pin down the time the car went along that road. Tyre tracks, any markings.'

She looked at Mike. 'I think we should call on the Leech household. Can you give them a ring?' She made a face. 'They'll probably want their solicitor. We'll go round the minute we've sorted out Keith Latos's flat. Above all,' she said soberly, 'find those children. We want them back safe and sound. My instinct is that they've done a runner. I don't think they've been abducted. The trouble is that we don't know where they are. The person who killed Dean obviously knows a great deal more than we do about these children's habits. He may know where their hiding places are. I don't want him finding them before we do. So look everywhere.' She stopped, frowning. 'And good luck.'

As the force clattered out of the room Phil Scott stepped forward. 'What time do you want Private Swinton down?'

'Late,' she said. 'After lunch.' She licked her lips. 'I get the feeling this morning will be rather busy.'

She picked up the telephone and dialled.

Cathy Parker answered at the other end. 'Yes,' she said quietly in response to Joanna's question. 'Of course – once we'd found the signs we did test. Dean was HIV positive.'

Joanna put the phone back on the cradle with a cold feeling of outrage. Murder in two ways.

'Lucky for you, Leech,' she said furiously, 'lucky for

you you're dead.' She knew that otherwise she would have used every single power – every single dirty trick – to have him exposed. But he hadn't killed Dean ...

Six officers had been assigned to the search of Keith Latos's shop, and by the time Joanna arrived they were well into the task. Boxes and boxes of shoes had been opened, all the cupboards emptied.

DC Greg Stanway held up a pile of magazines. 'Take a look at these,' he said. 'Under the counter.'

They were filthy, degrading gay porn magazines, mostly printed in Dutch or German. But words were not the reason Keith had bought them. It was the pictures; and many depicted young boys under the age of consent in graphic sexual poses.

'Well, we've got him on these at least,' she said, putting them down in disgust. 'Have you found anything else?'

'Not here,' he said. 'Just shoes and other sports stuff.'

'Where is he?' she asked grimly.

She found the owner of the shop upstairs, in his flat, watching the proceedings with his arms tightly folded.

He looked angrily at her when she walked in. 'What in sod's name is going on?'

She sighed. 'Mr Latos,' she said, 'we are trying to find two children who are missing. We have reason to believe their disappearance might be connected with the murder of Dean Tunstall.'

'I didn't even know the boy.' He was close to tears. 'I told you. I didn't recognise his picture–' He stopped. 'It's always the same. One slip up – that's all. Then you've got the cops on your tail all your bloody life.' He took a step nearer Joanna. 'I told you. I didn't know him.'

She met his gaze steadily. 'Then you have nothing to worry about, Mr Latos.'

His eyes narrowed and he sneered at her. 'Oh yes, I do. If you lot don't find anything you'll plant it here. Don't think I'm naive ... I know what you do. You plant it.'

It was a statement she met almost every time now ... Planting of evidence. She wearied of the accusation.

'Mr Latos,' she said crisply, 'I never planted anything in my life except primroses, daffodils and tulips. If you have nothing here to connect you with the murder of Dean and the disappearance of the other two children you have absolutely nothing to fear. Understand?'

He looked sulky and sat down on the sofa, watching the police work through the room. 'Put everything back tidy,' he said nastily. 'The way you found it.'

But apart from a quantity of pornographic videos, magazines, one or two books and some extremely unhealthy 'sex aids' nothing was found in the search of the flat, and an hour later they were almost finished.

'I told you,' Latos sneered as Joanna walked down the stairs, back into the shop, 'there's nothing to find.'

'We can charge you under the Criminal Justices Act 1988,' she said. 'In case you aren't terribly well informed, the law covers the possession of an indecent photograph of a child. And if you didn't know, Mr Latos, that means someone under the age of 16. Understand?'

'Yeah, but not exactly murder, is it?' His eyes were

bright with malice and dislike.

'Charge him,' she said to Mike.

Unfortunately, Latos was right. It wasn't exactly murder. Motive – yes. But no proof. There was nothing to connect Dean with this place. And if his truant holidays had been spent here they would have found some sign – clothes, hair – someone would have seen him. She crossed the shop and caught one of the top piles of shoe boxes with her foot. A pair spilled out onto the floor. She picked one up. New, unlaced, the skein of laces pushed into the toe of the shoe. She stared at it.

Joanna tried to telephone Caro when she arrived back at the station, to find out if she had received any response to that morning's headline. But the secretary told her she had received a phone call first thing and had gone out. She did not know when Caro would be back.

'Was it anything to do with child murder?'

The secretary didn't know. 'Would you like me to ask Miss Penn to telephone you when she returns?'

Joanna said yes and put the phone down.

The Leeches' house looked deserted apart from a black Mercedes estate car parked in the drive. Joanna glanced through the car's tinted window. The keys were still swinging. Whoever had driven it had only just arrived. She looked at Mike.

'Do you think our legal beagle?' she asked.

A plump domestic in a plastic apron over ski pants and slippers showed them into the living room, where Gilly and Robin Leech sat together with the sombre-suited solicitor.

The solicitor nodded at them curtly. 'May I ask why you need to speak to my clients yet again?'

His voice was formal and Joanna knew he was just waiting for the police to make one mistake. Then all the weight of the British legal system, which protected innocent and guilty so effectively, would drop down on her head like a ton of bricks.

So she played the game and addressed her answer to him. 'We are curious as to the nature of the relationship between Mr Ashford Leech and the dead boy,' she said.

Gilly Leech leaned forward. She looked old and tired in a floral brown dress of some silky material that reached almost down to her ankles. It rustled as she moved, giving her an effect of tired elegance. 'What exactly are you implying, Inspector?' Even her voice sounded old and defeated. Most of the fight had melted out of it.

'All right then,' Joanna said. 'What did your husband die of, Mrs Leech?'

'Is this relevant to your case, Inspector?' The solicitor was determined to make his presence felt.

But Gilly Leech put a hand up as though to hold him back. 'It's all right, Don,' she said. She bit her lip and stared at Joanna, then abruptly stood up.

'Mother ...' Robin Leech's low voice sounded a warning. But Gilly Leech shot him a frosty look and he sat back in his chair.

Joanna stared at Robin. In sharp contrast to his mother he seemed to have gained confidence – whether from the presence of the solicitor or some other fact Joanna could not work out, but he was sure of himself, cocksure. He pressed his lips together and gave Joanna a smug smile.

Gilly Leech was taking a framed photograph from the top of a polished antique bureau. She handed it to Joanna. 'This was my husband,' she said.

Joanna stared at the weak chin, the balding head so reminiscent of his son's, and the long, bony nose. 'What was the nature of the relationship between your husband and the dead boy?' she asked bluntly.

Robin Leech stood up. 'Bloody typical,' he said. 'Father – out of sheer goodness and charity – looks after some filthy little tykes and you come round here, sniffing for scandal.'

Joanna ignored him. 'Well?' She addressed Mrs Leech.

But the lady of the house retained her dignity. 'He was fond of the boy.'

'How fond?' Mike asked.

'Just a minute.' The solicitor bounced up in his seat. 'What are you getting at?'

'We want the truth,' Joanna said. 'Your husband was friendly with Dean Tunstall. Dean is dead. Now two more children from The Nest are missing. Mrs Leech, I want to find those children before something happens to them.'

She looked angry. 'This can't have anything to do with my husband,' she said. 'He's dead. You and your mob can't touch him now.'

'Exactly,' the solicitor said smartly. 'This can have no connection with Mr Leech.'

'Two more children are missing?' Robin Leech's eyes were bright with curiosity.

'Two other teenagers,' Joanna said. 'Police are searching for them now but we are very worried. If either of you know anything ...'

The three people sat dumbly.

'Let's go back to the things Dean stole, shall we?' said Joanna.

Immediately Gilly Leech looked wary. 'Why?'

'Don't play games with me.'

The solicitor gave a squeak. 'This constitutes threatening behaviour.'

Joanna ignored him. 'There was another reason you wanted to play down the connection between your husband and Dean Tunstall, wasn't there?'

Gilly was in a panic and gaped at Joanna.

'He was buggering him, wasn't he?'

The solicitor chipped in. 'My client reserves the right to remain silent.'

'Dean stole the things, didn't he?'

Then Gilly Leech surprised her. She held her head up high. 'It was my belief,' she said, 'that Ashford gave those things to Dean.' She stopped. 'For what reason, I could never work out.'

'That wasn't all he gave, was it?'

Even the solicitor could hardly fail to miss the aggression in Mike's voice.

'I don't know what you mean.'

'Ever heard of the Aids virus, Mrs Leech?'

She blinked at him.

Joanna walked towards the grand piano and picked up the picture of a smiling young woman in a university cap and gown. 'Your daughter, I believe.'

Now Gilly Leech really was dumbfounded. She gaped at Joanna, and it was her son who stepped forward. 'Fleur is in America,' he said sharply.

'Did your daughter have a son?'

'No ...' Gilly Leech looked shocked. 'Fleur – no. Never.'

'But we believe your husband made out to Dean

that he was Fleur's son.'

The solicitor stood up. 'Prove it,' he said, 'or defend your allegation in a court of law.'

'The jewellery that was stolen,' Joanna said softly. 'Cheap stuff. Your daughter's?'

'Possibly.' Gilly Leech spoke through stiff lips.

'Well, thank you, Mrs Leech.' Joanna stood up to leave. 'You've been a great help.'

Herbert Machin stared at the two police officers from underneath his navy bobble hat. 'What night did you say?'

Detective Sergeant Hannah Beardmore had a gentle, patient voice. Brought up on the moorlands, she found their slow pace natural. 'It was Sunday night,' she said, 'the night before Newcastle market day. I think you usually go there.'

He looked aggressively at her. 'Who says?' he asked.

'The landlady from the Winking Man.'

'Nosy old tart, she is,' the farmer said fiercely.

'But is it true?'

'What we want to know is' – Alan King was a native of Birmingham and less patient than his moorland colleague – 'did you hear anything on Sunday night?'

'Night afore market,' the old farmer said. 'Aye, I think I did.'

'Think carefully,' Hannah said. 'What did you hear, exactly?'

He was silent for a few moments, screwing up his eyes to aid concentration. 'It were about three or four,' he said at last. 'I heard a car headin' for Flash but–' He stopped. 'It turned round. It didn't come past the farm. It turned.'

'Where did it turn?'

'In my driveway.'

'Did you look out of the window?'

Herbert Machin chuckled and shook his head. 'It were bloody cold that time of mornin' I tucked me 'ead under blankets.'

The disappointment was acute. Neither of the police officers was old enough or experienced enough to have learned not to depend too much on witnesses seeing things, remembering them or being sure. And if every witness who had looked the other way had, instead, looked the right way and remembered exactly who and what they had seen, then could swear to it in the witness box, the crime solution rate would have doubled.

They all went outside to study the drive, but it was sloppy with cow dung and many cars and tractors had passed that way. There was nothing to be gained there.

Herbert Machin stared around the yard. 'What's the 'urry anyway?'

'Two more children are missing from the children's home,' Hannah said. 'We're concerned for their safety.'

Herbert Machin made a face. 'I don't blame these kids for runnin' off,' he said. 'Them places – isn't much of an 'ome, is it?'

And this, the police found, was the prevailing view of the moorlands people.

13

In the army they believed in summary punishment. Somehow someone had got wind of the way Swinton had treated the children at The Nest. First came the humiliation. They stripped him naked. Then they tied him, spread-eagled, to his bunk and dragged on their cigarettes until they glowed – bright red.

Swinton screwed his head round and watched them disdainfully. It was only when they turned him over and sizzled the cigarette against the tip of his penis that he uttered a low moan. Tom-boy clutched on to the doorpost, terrified they would notice him, yet not quite able to bring himself to abandon his only friend. But if he went for the officers he knew that they would delay their arrival – both out of dislike for Swinton and also because they believed in this 'justice'.

'Jesus Christ,' he muttered, 'oh, Jesus Christ.'

When the officer arrived to deliver Swinton to the police station he found Tom-boy crying and Swinton, still tied up, alone in the bunkhouse.

He threw some clothes towards the rigidly angry Swinton and loosened the knots around his wrists and ankles. Swinton's chest was heaving with fury.

'Bastards,' he muttered over and over again.

'We want you down the nick.' PC Farthing could muster up not a scrap of sympathy for the soldier.

Joanna decided Swinton looked even more surly than usual, grim-faced, eyes stuck on the floor. She switched the tape recorder on.

'Gary, we already know that you assaulted Dean on more than one occasion.'

He nodded, chewing slowly on his gum.

'Did you kill him?'

For a moment Gary Swinton stopped chewing his gum, then he gave a few, rapid bites and looked up. 'You can't be trying to pin this on me,' he said. 'You bloody can't. I was with people all night when that kid was murdered.'

Mike leaned over him. 'What time was Dean murdered?'

Gary gave a few fast open-mouthed chews. 'You can't catch me like that,' he said. 'I don't bloody know. All I do know is that the fire was still burning. But it hadn't got to him all ...' He thought for a moment. 'His hand was cold,' he remembered.

'You'd been fond of burning Dean.'

Swinton looked worried. 'That was different,' he protested.

'Yes it was, wasn't it?' Mike stared at him. 'Dean was alive then. He would have felt the pain. You recognised the scent of burning flesh, didn't you?'

Swinton whipped round. 'You can't bloody well prove it,' he said.

'Other kids will act as witnesses.'

Then Joanna glanced at Mike, the same thought

hitting them both at the same time.

Swinton was still nonchalantly chewing his gum, cow-like, slow and rhythmic. Like Chinese water torture, it was beginning to irritate Joanna.

'The other kids,' Swinton said slowly, 'they wouldn't grass on me. We're all in it together.'

Joanna felt angry then but knew to display that anger towards Swinton would not touch him. He was too used to it. Instead she checked her dislike of him.

'So you made this child's life a misery,' she said. Swinton chewed his gum. 'Were you buggering him too?'

He leered at her. 'I ain't queer,' he said. 'Ask any of the birds at the disco.' He grinned. She could see the gum through his teeth. 'They should know.' He leaned right back in his chair. 'Quite a reputation I got with the ladies.'

'Really,' she said coolly, 'I'd never have guessed it.'

'Want me to prove it?'

'I don't think so,' she said.

Mike chipped in. 'Dean wasn't touched in the last year, Swinton,' he said. 'I think you left The Nest about six months ago.'

Swinton swivelled round and stared at Mike. 'You accusing me, copper?'

And there the law protected him, but they needed to threaten him – to use a lever ...

Joanna took over. 'Well, if it wasn't you, Gary,' she said sweetly, 'who was it?'

He stared at her and she knew he was rattled. And his mind began working fast.

''Is grandfather,' he said. 'This bloke what used to come for 'im.'

Mike touched the table with his fist. 'Are you

lying, Swinton?'

The soldier boy shook his head slowly, stopped chewing his gum, stared hard at Mike. Eyeball to eyeball, it was a battle.

'I ain't lyin',' he said disdainfully.

'Did you see the man?' Joanna asked.

Swinton turned his stare on her. 'Yes,' he said, 'I did.'

The description he gave matched Ashford Leech perfectly and the photograph they had dug up from an old newspaper drew the same response.

''E drove some great white estate car,' Swinton said – strangely anxious to please. 'I think I saw him a couple of months ago.'

Joanna looked at Mike. Both felt a distinct shiver. Dead men don't drive cars, but Swinton obviously did not know Leech was dead.

'What sort of car?' Mike asked.

Swinton shrugged his shoulders. 'Don't know,' he said.

Joanna decided to try to rope him in on the investigation. She leaned across the table and offered Swinton a cigarette.

He stared at it with distaste. 'No thanks. I'll have one later.' Then, taking advantage of this new-found comradeship, he leaned back in his chair and grinned, the gap between his front teeth giving him an oddly wicked air. 'Any chance of a coffee?'

Gritting his teeth Mike stood up.

While he was gone Joanna tried her luck.

'Gary,' she said, smiling, 'we've had a bit of bad luck.'

His gaze swivelled round to her.

'We probably won't press charges, you know – not

over the cigarette burns,' she said smoothly. 'After all, the children are safe now, aren't they?'

He looked suspiciously at her.

'I mean, you've left the home.'

He nodded.

'But – unfortunately ...' Mike returned with the coffee. 'Unfortunately, Jason and Kirsty are missing.'

Swinton actually looked concerned. 'Since when?' he asked sharply.

'They went yesterday morning.' Joanna stopped. 'We're very worried about them, Gary. Do you have any idea where they might be?'

He drank his coffee, frowning into the cup.

Joanna tried again. 'Do you know any of their hideouts?'

'Only the moors,' he said. 'That's all I know.'

Mike bent over him. 'In this weather?' he said. 'Have they got some shelter?'

'Not as I know of.'

Joanna sighed. She had been sure Swinton would be able to help them.

'Okay,' she said. 'Thanks.'

'Can I go now?'

Wearily she nodded.

When he had gone Joanna turned to Mike. 'Where are they, Mike? Have we been barking up the wrong tree? Is something happening to them? Is there someone we've let go who is guilty? Are we about to find two more bodies like Dean's?'

'Hey, don't let it get to you, Jo,' he said roughly. 'It's a job. You're human. I'm human. We all are.'

'The press don't quite see it like that,' she said.

'Talking of the press, what's happened to your blonde friend from London? The one with the eye-catching headlines?'

'Seems to have disappeared,' she said, then she touched him lightly on the shoulder. 'Come on. We're booked for a briefing. And, Mike,' she added, 'thanks.'

He gave a sheepish grin.

She stood at the front of the briefing room, facing her team – Phil Scott, Roger Farthing, Cheryl Smith, Alan King, Mike and the other uniformed officers lent for the investigation. 'I think we're getting close to four suspects – all of them male. I'll just run over them. Please remember the legal phrases – *mens rea, actus rea*. The guilty mind, the guilty act. If any of you have anything to add, don't hesitate. Jason Fogg and Kirsty are both missing. We presume they are together. It's possible they have absconded from the children's home – both have done this before. We've alerted police forces countrywide, faxed descriptions to all of them. They may have absconded to escape questioning from both the police and Maree, their social worker. However, bear in mind it is also possible they might know something we don't. They may well know the identity of the murderer. They might even have approached him. So they could come to harm. I am very, very anxious that they are found and brought back as quickly as possible. The Super's offered me an extra ten uniformed help. They'll be doing the house-to-house searches and helping collate some of the information on the computer. But we are the original team and I want us to be clear what we are doing. As yet we have dug up quite a bit of dirt and circumstantial evidence but nothing conclusive. But we are getting there. Ashford Leech was the person who posed as his grandfather, regularly abused him and incidentally infected him with Aids. Leech died and the abuse stopped. But Dean continued a friendship. A platonic friendship. This might have been because the "friend" suspected Dean was HIV positive. The person may have been a woman, a homosexual man or even a heterosexual man.

'I want you to bear in mind Cathy Parker's opinion. He might have been killed accidentally. However, the attempted destruction of the body was a deliberate act and we must view the case from that angle. The courts will hold judgement when we have gathered all of the facts.' There was a muttering in the room and she held up her hand. 'I know,' she said. 'Our top priority must now be to find the two missing children.' She paused. 'And obviously I am worried that Dean confided something to Jason and Kirsty. My one big fear is that for God knows what reason they not only know the identity of Dean's killer but have made some contact with him.' She stopped. 'That does frighten me.' And from the silence in the room she knew she was not alone.

She turned back to the board. 'So for now we will run over the possible suspects. Keith Latos. He owns the sportswear shop at the top of the High Street. We believe that the shoes Dean was wearing when he died came from there. He is the only stockist in Leek and they were nearly new shoes. It does not seem that Dean left Leek in the few days before he died. Remember they were the wrong size, cross-laced. We are working on the assumption that they were shoplifted, possibly some time on Saturday from the basket outside the shop.'

She frowned. There was something not quite right there. She let it go. She would have to ponder it later – after the briefing.

'We've been through Latos's books and it does seem

that a pair of Reebok Reformers the same size as the pair Dean was wearing are missing from his shop. The shoes were almost new so we are keeping the option open that Latos is implicated in Dean's last 24 hours. On the other hand, he could have stolen them. We know Dean was in the habit of shoplifting. He was charged on more than one occasion. Alternatively, he could have been given them, and you can all draw your own conclusions from that particular scenario. We are still looking for Dean's old trainers, black and red and very well worn. Size fives. I don't need to remind you they are vital evidence. Latos is a known paedophile. He's been brought in a few times for soliciting near the men's public toilets, trying to invite young boys back to his flat, etc. He says he was at the opera on Sunday night with a friend called Martin Shane, who he claims spent the night with him.' She broke off to consult DC Greg Stanway. 'Over to you, Greg.'

Greg stood up and shook his head. 'Not much joy here, I'm afraid, ma'am. Shane claims he was at the opera with Latos until late Sunday night.' He made an expression of disgust. 'Started singing some of the bloody songs.'

'And later?'

'Says they had a skinful and he decided to stay the night at Latos's flat.' He pulled a notebook from his pocket. 'I've got a witness statement to verify it,' he said. 'Man opposite couldn't sleep. Got up at three and saw Shane's car parked outside.'

Mike interrupted. 'What sort of car?'

'White Lada estate.'

Joanna and Mike looked at one another.

Joanna turned back to the board, to the second name on the list. 'Next is Mark Riversdale. In charge of the children's home, The Nest. No known paedophile connection. But we know he has an alcohol problem and has been under psychiatric care. A bit of a dark horse. Says he was out of the country before taking up this post. He could easily have taken Dean's body to the moors – has no alibi for Sunday night. Kids heard his television on all night but didn't see him. He can't remember the programmes – says he fell asleep. I think he probably drinks all evening. We found a number of cans of Carlsberg Special Brew in his room. Did Dean disturb him? Did he threaten him with exposure about his drinking? Did Riversdale lose his rag – throttle the child?' She looked around the room. 'It's possible. I certainly think we should speak to him again. He also drives a white Vauxhall Cavalier estate, which fits in with the witness's sighting of a long, pale car.'

A few police officers nodded.

'I think we know where Dean used to go on his disappearances. He used to go to Leech's place – probably to the stable flat. But the real question is – where did he go after Leech's death? Where was his bolthole?'

'Excuse me, ma'am?' Roger Farthing spoke. 'Couldn't he just have thieved all the things – the new clothes ... the shoes ...'

'It's possible,' she said, 'but Maree and the other kids at the home all say he arrived back clean, washed, fed. Someone was looking after him. You know as well as I do, Roger, kids who have slept rough look rough.'

'His mother?'

She frowned, tugged at a piece of stray hair, nibbled at her fingernail. 'So where is she?'

No-one had any answer to that.

'We have absolutely no evidence that there was any contact between Dean and his mother from the age of two. If there had been I'm sure she would have come forward by now. Unless ...' She paused, released the lock of hair. 'Unless she's a woman so paranoid about the police she's frightened to come forward.'

Mike cleared his throat. 'No,' he said decisively. 'That's going a bit far. Her kid's dead. No-one's blaming her.'

Joanna bit her lip. 'I wonder,' she said. 'If she had been the one who had been looking after him periodically ...' She looked around the room. 'She might have thought the social services would have pressured her to look after him.'

Mike agreed. 'We could do with talking to her. Any luck with the papers?'

She shook her head. 'Not so far, but I'll try and get hold of Caro later on today. You see,' she added, 'the mother might even think we'd charge her with neglect or something similar.'

'I doubt it.' he said.

'But you have to admit, Mike, people like her who have abandoned their children are naturally mistrustful of the police.'

'True.' He nodded.

'Next in line is our "boy soldier". We are sure that he was cruel to Dean – from an early age. He burned him with cigarettes. And yes ...' she smiled, 'our psychologist does make a connection with the attempted destruction of Dean's body. He also, we believe, forcibly injected him with some drugs. He has certainly displayed psychopathic but not paedophile tendencies. However, again according to the criminal psychologist ...' Someone spoke in the back and she glared. 'Listen to me, laddie,' she said. 'Catching criminals is a serious business. Forensics and psychologists are the way forward. They are the smart way to know your criminal. It isn't all physical – car chases up the High Street at 90 miles an hour, scattering old ladies and prams like chickens before a tractor. Understand?'

The muttering softened and she carried on. 'The psychologist is of the opinion that Dean's murderer was not a psychopath but a paedophile. I know he had not been abused immediately prior to his murder – possibly not for some time before his death, maybe months according to the pathologist.' She stopped. 'The forensic psychologist had the idea the killing might even have had something to do with Dean's HIV status ... sexual frustration.'

Mike looked at her. 'Why does he think he was a paedophile,' he asked, 'rather than a psychopath?'

'Because there was no mutilation. No damage. I don't like the phrase myself but it was a gentle murder – not done in hatred or temper. Again we have the pathologist's opinion,' she said. 'It could have been an accident.'

There was another mutter at the back and she knew what they were saying – that a woman pathologist was being soft; a man would not have been so benevolent. She tightened her lips.

Mike was speaking. 'A gentle murder ...' He spoke in disgust. 'Of a ten-year-old? Then burn the body?'

Again the team were muttering, and in a way Joanna shared their abhorrence of the particular phrase Cathy Parker had used. But the experts who analysed the victims of homicide knew what hatred and temper could do to the human body. And Dean's had been unmarked – apart from the livid hand marks around his neck.

She continued. 'The psychologist's profile of the killer is a man who killed, then in horror at what he had done tried to eradicate it from his mind and from the earth by destroying it with fire. Purging it, if you want to be fanciful. It fits in with a paedophile but not – I repeat not – with a psychopath. It was, if you like, more of an execution. So Gary, the boy soldier, is in the clear. He didn't do it. Don't waste your energies there. He doesn't even fit in–'

'With the psychological profile,' Mike chimed in. 'Aren't we taking too much notice of this psychological profile?'

'I believe in them,' she said defiantly. 'I do. And remember the evidence of the officer on duty at the gate on Sunday night. He was alert and guarding the entrance. The rest of the camp, as you know, is bordered by a high electric fence. Swinton was in the camp all night from 3 am. So ...' She gazed around the room, ending at Mike's taut features. 'I know how you all feel. We'd love to get Swinton. But he didn't do it.'

'Sure?' It was Mike.

She nodded. 'Sure. He didn't do it.' She sighed. 'Don't worry,' she said. 'Swinton's sort – we'll get him in the end for something or other. He won't stay clear of the law.'

'Bash an old lady over the head?'

Again she sighed. 'He'll do something. Now let's get on. We're supposed to be going over this case together – swapping ideas.

'Lastly is Robin Leech.' She frowned. 'My opinion is it was either Leech or Latos. One or the other – although I really don't know what their motive might have been.' She sighed then grinned. 'Too deep for me, just an ordinary copper. There's more here too than meets the eye. A lot of cloud and questions. Unfortunately, Leech is one of those people who arm themselves with a solicitor who advises them of their right to silence. There are a number of lies being put across our path by this entire family, who are blessed with the comfortable illusion that they are above the common law of the land. Thank goodness the daughter's abroad. At least one of them is safely out of it. Mother and son have admitted lying about the supposed burglary and about Ashford Leech's HIV. I think it is more than likely that he caught it through homosexuality, although there's nothing on record. But I'm curious. If Leech gave Dean the ring, what about the other things? Did Dean steal the photograph album to peep at and further the illusion of a family? Let's just think.' She sat down to talk to Mike for a moment.

'We know Dean went to Rock House on a number of occasions. Robin Leech said he lived in Chester over those years and they never actually met. Quite honestly, I'm sceptical, Mike. I think we might consider driving there and speaking to Mrs Leech Junior about her husband. I'm curious about the breakdown of their marriage.'

Mike looked at her. 'I can't really see what that might have to do with it.'

She shrugged her shoulder. 'I know,' she said. 'But unless you follow up all the leads you never quite know where one might have led.' She touched his arm. 'I'm sure we will eventually find out which one of them did it. But that isn't enough for me, Mike. I want to know why. What drove someone to kill this boy?'

He grinned at her. 'Sort of police analyst.'

She laughed and he joined her, and the warmth of their shared humour reached the rest of the room.

Alan King nudged Cheryl Smith. 'They're getting on all right these days ...' He grinned. 'Bit different from a couple of months ago.'

She nodded. 'Better make sure Mrs Korpanski

doesn't get wind of it.' She laughed and drew her finger across her throat. 'She suffers with the green-eyed monsters.'

Joanna cleared her throat. 'And remember,' she said, 'Robin Leech drives a cream Range Rover. Also he lives alone and has no alibi.'

She paused to think for a moment. 'Then there is Gilly, Mrs Leech. I think she has some more answers for us.' She scanned the roomful of faces. 'How much was she a party to Dean's abduction and abuse?' She met Cheryl Smith's eyes. 'Yes,' she said, 'unpleasant, isn't it? But she wouldn't be the first woman to be party to such exploitation, would she? Was the burglary story concocted for just such an occasion?

'The last point I want to impress on you is the two children missing from the home. Jason and Kirsty.' She gave a brief description of the two children and handed round copies of their photographs. 'Obviously it's vital we find them – the sooner the better.' Heads nodded in agreement.

'Now then – before we go out there I want to remind you all what we're looking for. Clothes with petrol splashed on them – maybe scorch marks, boxes of matches, lighters ... Hair ... Remember Dean's was cut quite close – and recently. It was golden in colour.' She smiled. 'Then there is the coat ... Wilderness Collection, expensive, green oilskin with a scarlet, tartan lining. A black, woollen glove – twin to the one we found scorched on the moor. Also Dean's old shoes, the ones he was wearing when he left The Nest, cheap trainers, well-worn, size fives, black and red with the word Bronx written on the side.'

When the police officers had filed out, Joanna spoke to Mike. 'What do you think, Mike?' she asked. 'Should I apply for a warrant to search Rock House, and Robin Leech's stable flat?'

'He'll make it very difficult,' he said. 'Why not wait a day or two – see what crops up?'

'I don't like it,' she said. 'We're only holding back because of who he is and because he's articulate enough to make a fuss – write to the papers, make a formal complaint.' She sighed and stared out of the window. 'What if the two children are there?'

This time it was PC Roger Farthing who struck gold, at the traditional gent's outfitters halfway along the High Street. Positioned in the centre of the shop window, artistically draped with its scarlet, tartan lining displayed bright as a beacon, was an olive green, waxed jacket, and even before he stepped closer to the window PC Farthing could see the logo – the three mountain peaks and the name, Wilderness. Smiling he pushed open the glass door.

'Good morning,' he said.

The owner was a small man with pale eyes and a tape measure draped around his neck. He looked warily at the six-and-a-half-foot tall policeman.

'Morning,' he said.

'The coat in the window?' Roger Farthing asked casually. 'Sell many, do you?'

'Not so many of those,' the owner replied carefully. 'They're a bit expensive. And they can get one for half the price at the market. Not as good quality,' he added quickly, 'but most people don't recognise quality.'

'How many have you sold in the past year?'

The man thought for a minute, then crossed to the

rack, counted the coats swinging on the rail, scratched his head. 'Five,' he said. 'I ordered eight – two of each size. I've three left.'

'Do you remember who you sold the five to?' Farthing asked.

The man met his eyes. 'Why?'

'I can't say exactly at the moment,' Farthing explained. 'But all I can tell you is it's part of a serious investigation.'

'Not to do with that kid, is it?'

'It might be.'

The man leafed through his book, pulled a notepad towards him, wrote five names. 'I've a good memory,' he said. 'Leek is a small town. It's an expensive coat and I don't hold with murdering kids ...'

Farthing glanced down at the list of names. Top of the list was Robin Leech.

Alice Rutter walked into the police station at five o'clock in the afternoon, ignored the officer at the entrance and demanded to see 'the lady officer in charge.' She flatly refused to speak to anyone else.

She seemed even more out of place here in the small, tidy office with its brick-wall view than she did up on the moors with a background of storms and weather, light and shade, dawn, dusk and the rocks. There she looked a wild woman, a troglodyte woman of nature, a throwback to the man who surely must have been half-ape, half-human. Here, in the small modern office, she looked merely dirty, scruffy and unhygienic. And as she walked in through the door, Joanna felt a wave of nausea at the unwashed scent.

'I've come because I know I must help you,' Alice

said slowly. ''E didna want me to come. Said I would not be able to 'elp you. I dunna know. But the child is dead.'

Joanna waited and Alice sat down stiffly in one of the armchairs, fingering the imitation plastic.

Joanna faced her. 'We want you to help us identify the car,' she said clearly. 'Do you remember? You recalled it was a long, white car.'

Alice shook her head slowly. 'Light, I said. I did not remember it as bein' white.' She looked at Joanna. 'If I 'elp, you must promise me. No tryin' to get us out of the Rock.'

'It isn't up to me,' Joanna said. 'We won't evict you. It would be social workers, worried you might not be safe up there.'

'Pah.' For a short moment Joanna thought Alice might spit. Instead she sat silent, chewing her lips. Then she sighed and stared out of the window at the wall. 'Why do they put a window where there is nothing to see?'

'There was something to see once,' Joanna replied, looking in the same direction. 'They had to build some more cells. There was nowhere else to put people. I've lost my view,' she said ruefully, 'but I still have ventilation.'

Alice shook her head slowly. 'That isn't ventilation. Ventilation's air. Clean air. Not dust and filth from cars.' She looked again at Joanna. 'I can't breathe down here,' she said. 'It would be cruel to take us away from the moor. We belong there.'

Joanna nodded. 'I know, Alice.'

There was a moment of empathy between them, then Alice licked her lips. 'It might come again,' she said.

'What?'

'The car.'

'How would you know if it was the same car?'

Alice Rutter blinked. 'I know sounds,' she said. 'The lapwing pretending to have a broken wing to protect its young, fox cubs lonely and frightened for their mother. Kestrel hungry for food. Sounds tell me all. And the car is loud and broken.'

Joanna stood up, the embryo of an idea taking shape. 'Would you let me drive you around Leek?' she asked. 'Tell me if you see a car like the one ... or hear something similar?'

Alice stood up heavily then lumbered out of the door.

They drove around Leek, then five miles towards Macclesfield, looking at cars, the windows open to listen to engine noises. Alice gave each vehicle slow consideration.

'Long,' Joanna soon found out, was any car at all – except possibly a Mini. Alice picked out hatchbacks and estates, saloons and fastbacks. Similarly, a light colour covered 50 percent of cars on the road; pale, metallic greens and greys, whites and creams, yellows and pale blues. So they stood on a street corner and Joanna asked Alice to close her eyes and identify a car that sounded right. But when Alice was convinced she had 'heard the car,' it turned out to be a motor bike.

Alice looked close to tears. 'Jonathan was right,' she said. 'I'm a silly old fool. I aren't familiar with cars. I never 'ad one.' Then she stopped. 'I don't know nothin'. I can't 'elp. And I was near. I saw. I didn't do nothin'. I was scared. But I could 'ave saved the burnin'.'

Joanna tried to comfort the old woman and

offered to drive her back to her home.

Alice looked at her. 'You have a car?'

Joanna grinned. 'I usually use my bike,' she said. 'But I have had to use the car lately.' She smiled ruefully. 'There's been so much haring around.'

It was a fine evening but September was turning cool. Joanna slipped her coat on and walked slowly up the grey slope of the moor, towards the Winking Man, outlined in black against the grey sky.

At the top Alice called out, 'Jonathan ... Jonathan. I 'ave the police lady with me.'

His head appeared through the gloom from behind the rock, hostile and suspicious. He glared at Joanna. 'What are you 'ere for?' he demanded.

'She brought me home.'

He looked from one to the other. 'You find the car then?' he mocked.

Alice shook her head, iron-grey dreadlocks bouncing off her cheeks.

'I knew she wouldn't.' It was Joanna he addressed.

'Sit down a minute,' said Alice.

Joanna sat on the rock and gazed across the wide view, lake and town, mountains and valleys.

Alice watched her face like a hawk. 'That is a view,' she said proudly. 'Not bricks. Not dirty air. Not even people at all. Just the hills and the land and God.' She glanced at Joanna. 'You married, then?'

Joanna shook her head.

'You want to be married?'

And suddenly the anguish of Matthew flooded back – the old confusion and uncertainty. She shrugged her shoulders while Alice watched her, puzzled.

Alice touched her arm with a gnarled, wrinkled hand. ''Ard world, isn't it?'

Joanna laughed. 'But our worlds are different, Alice.'

Alice Rutter gave a slow chuckle. 'Don't be daft,' she said. 'It's the same world. We all has different ways of livin' in it, but it's the same world all right.'

Joanna stared down at the hollow where the town sat. 'How do you live up here, Alice?'

The old woman blinked. 'The animals does. Why shouldn't we? We can survive too. It's just that people like you have bred too fine. You forgets you has legs for walkin'. Because you use cars. You never learn how to catch food and store it through the winter. There's things you knows, I dare say,' she said, winking at Jonathan, 'but there's an awful lot of things you don't know.'

Joanna looked at the woman's face and read something there – something wise, a hidden, superior knowledge – something she didn't understand but could respect. 'Two children are missing,' she said, 'from the same house that the boy was from.'

Alice was watching her steadily.

'I'm worried about them.'

Alice stood up, Jonathan too, towering over her, bulky in their layers of clothes.

'You'll find them,' Alice said. 'Soon enough and ...' she wagged her finger at Joanna, 'when they wants to be found. You'll find them when they lets you.' There was a stern hostility in her face and Joanna felt unnerved, lonely. She was standing on alien territory.

'I have to go now,' she said, 'but I'll come back.' Joanna ran down the side of the blackening mountain, conscious all the way of the woman's powerful presence behind her. When she reached the car the phone was crackling. She answered it and heard Mike's voice. They had found another body.

14

Flashing blue lights lit the front of the sports shop, which was already sealed off with tape. Mike met Joanna as she drew to a halt.

'A customer alerted us.' His voice was shaking. However many murders they investigated, violent death was always a shock.

She stared at him. 'How was he killed?'

'Slit throat, Jo. God, there's blood everywhere.' He stopped for a moment. 'I never saw such a messy murder,' he said softly.

She walked inside. She had steeled herself for a gruesome spectacle but nothing could have prepared her for this. The knife had slit an artery. The heart had pumped out blood. It had spurted and hit the ceiling in a great splash. Joanna stared at it, then at the small body of Keith Latos, his neck a gaping pulp, his T-shirt drenched.

'Yet who would have thought the old man to have had so much blood in him,' she said softly.

'Sorry?' One of the SOC officers looked up.

'Never mind,' she said. 'Another murder.'

'I don't think there was a struggle,' he said. 'For a small chap he was pretty muscular. But he never had a chance. Quick slash ... Phhht.' He whistled through his teeth. 'Bloody quick end.'

'I don't suppose it was a burglary gone wrong?'

The SOC officer shook his head. 'Not a chance,' he said.

'Pathologist sent for?'

'I'm here.' Cathy was standing behind her with her small black scene-of-crimes case in her hand. She smiled at Joanna. 'Leek's getting pretty ghastly,' she said with a thin smile. 'Matthew promised me it would be a complete holiday.' She looked down at the bloodied corpse. 'I don't call this much of a holiday, Joanna.' She knelt down beside the corpse and slipped on some surgeon's gloves. 'I suppose you've heard the good news. Matthew should be home in a couple of days.'

Joanna stared at her. 'He rang?'

'Yes ... He had to let the hospital know when he'd be back.' She touched Latos's face. 'Cold,' she said, then looked up at Joanna. 'Didn't you know?'

Joanna couldn't tell if her voice contained a hint of malice. 'No,' she said shortly. 'I didn't.' So Matthew was coming home and he hadn't even had the courtesy to ring her. He had contacted colleagues – made sure they would expect him back. And he hadn't lifted the telephone to let her know. She gritted her teeth, feeling as though she had been punched. Fortunately Cathy did not notice.

'Been dead around two hours,' she said. 'One very sure slice to the neck. Probably with a carving knife. The sort you carve the joint with. Strong too. Gone right through the carotid artery, jugular vein, trachea ... Look.'

She tilted the head just a little. 'See that. Spinal column. One hell of a blow.'

One of the police officers ran out of the room

rather quickly.

Cathy looked up at her. 'I'll be able to tell you more about the knife when I get him to the mortuary. Just tell me one thing, Joanna,' she asked curiously, 'was he connected with the boy?'

'One of the chief suspects,' Joanna said gloomily.

Cathy looked at her. 'Well, he didn't do this,' she said.

Joanna found DC Alan King with the police photographer.

'Turned up anything?'

He shook his head. 'Must have been close to closing time,' he said. 'Whoever it was was in and out quickly.'

'Any useful prints?'

King shook his head again. 'Not a bloody thing to go on,' he said. 'If it wasn't connected with the Tunstall case, I'd think it was done by a homicidal maniac.'

Joanna looked at the blood-drenched corpse and came to a decision. 'Mike,' she said. 'I'm going to ask the Super for some extra men. We have to find the two children. I think we should return to The Nest. I want to speak to Mark Riversdale and make another search of their rooms. We must have missed something.' She stared down at the white face. 'I didn't expect this,' she said through her teeth.

Mike touched her shoulder. 'None of us did.'

Outside she sat in the car and looked at him. 'Why was Latos killed?' It was a simple question. She felt she should know the answer, but no brainwaves, no inspiration came, only the ugly vision of the opened neck. She sat for a while, pondering as pictures moved in front of her eyes. Neatly boxed shoelaces unthreaded, knotted in skeins as they arrived from the manufacturer.

Pairs of trainers tossed together in the basket outside the shop, neatly laced, tied together in pairs ... A photograph album, a ring ... She put the car into gear and headed towards the Ashbourne road.

To Joanna's surprise, Maree O'Rourke opened the door to The Nest. She seemed confused at the appearance of the two police officers. And embarrassed too. 'Hello,' she said, dragging her fingers through her spiky hair. 'Have you heard anything about Jason and Kirsty?'

'I'm sorry,' Joanna said.

Maree looked close to tears. 'God,' she said, 'what the hell's happened to them?'

Joanna said nothing. Mike merely stared.

Maree gave him a glance then quickly looked away. 'Was there anything ...?'

'We wanted to speak to Mark,' Joanna said. 'And we would like to search Jason and Kirsty's rooms.'

'Again?' She paused then nodded. 'Of course – fine.' Now she was over-friendly, almost effusive ... 'Come in ...' She stood back against the door. 'Mark isn't exactly available at the moment.'

'Is he in or not?' Mike pushed forwards.

Maree flushed. 'He isn't terribly well,' she said. 'He's upset. Look, why don't you search the rooms first? Then you can speak to him.'

The boys' room seemed empty now. Dean and Jason both gone. Twin beds, neatly made up, clothes out of sight. Even the posters seemed characterless – *Terminator*, *Edward Scissorhands* ... an unknown character with blood dripping from his nose, and strangely a soft poster of a bright blue bird flapping its wings over water. It looked out of place amongst the aggression portrayed around it. Joanna studied it for a while. 'I wonder which of them put this one up.'

She opened the wardrobe. School uniform, school shoes, shirts, T-shirts, jeans. Some were probably Dean's – the rest Jason's. She stared at them and wondered if he would ever wear them again. Damn it, she thought, where was the boy?

She turned to Mike. 'There's nothing here, Mike,' she said.

He nodded. 'The lads have been through it,' he said.

'It's so ...' she grappled for a word, 'typical...'

Kirsty's room was different in that she did not share it. The posters were of Take That, East 17 ... The clothes were less dissimilar, baggy jeans, baggy T-shirts, the school uniform skirt, cardigan, Doc Martens shoes. Joanna pulled open a drawer, fumbled through underwear. Again there was nothing there. She looked around in desperation. There must be something ... some clue as to the girl's whereabouts. A photograph was stuck onto the wall, of three children. It was fuzzy and blurred but she could just make out Kirsty, Jason and Dean, stood on the top of some rock, fists clenched as though they had conquered Everest. Dean's hair was blown in the wind, bright yellow, his clenched fist raised towards the sky. Jason had his arm crooked around the younger boy's neck while Kirsty was wiping her hair out of her eyes, squinting up at the sun. Joanna stared at the print and wondered who had taken the photograph. None of the children, as far as she knew, possessed a camera. She took a last glance around the room and went downstairs.

Mark Riversdale was in the corner of the sitting room, his head in his hands, looking as pale as death. He glanced up as they entered. 'Haven't you found them yet?' His voice was pleading and he was drunk. 'I could lose my job over this, you know.' He screwed up his face. 'Haven't you any idea where they are?'

Maree met their eyes, shook her head very slightly and handed Mark a cup of black coffee. 'Would you like one?'

They both shook their heads. Joanna sat down while Mike watched.

'What were they like when you last saw them?' Joanna asked.

He thought for a while as though confused by the question. Then he shrugged his shoulders. 'Just normal,' he said.

'Were they very upset by Dean's death?'

'Inspector,' he said, 'these kids have a lot of things happen to them. They're pretty hard. They learn not to let their feelings show.'

'But you're by way of being a parent,' Joanna said. 'Surely you know what their feelings are?'

Riversdale shook his head. 'No,' he said simply, 'I don't. If they were upset they didn't show it. They were good kids,' he added.

'Did they mention anything about Dean?'

'Not really.'

'Mr Riversdale,' Joanna said quietly, 'where were you at five o'clock this evening?'

He looked in genuine puzzlement. 'Why?'

'Just answer the question.' Mike stepped forward. His voice was sharp. He too had been affected by what he had witnessed.

Mark looked helplessly at Maree, and when she shook her head again slightly her earrings moved like wind chimes. The negative movement said it. I can't help you. You're on your own.

'I was here,' he said, 'thinking.'

'Alone?' Mike could not keep the note of aggression out of his voice.

Riversdale heard it and looked puzzled. 'I was thinking,' he said. 'Wondering where they are.' His face changed then, became paler and seemed to shrink. 'Why?' he asked. 'Why are you asking me all this?' Then his voice changed too. 'What's happened?'

Maree stood up, gripped the back of the chair. 'Oh my God,' she said. 'Not Jason and Kirsty too?'

Joanna had learned to use fear and confusion as a weapon. So for a moment she said nothing but watched their faces silently. They showed upset and apprehension but no foreknowledge or guilt. So she told them. No ... the children had not been found but Latos had – with his throat sliced through to the spine.

Riversdale frowned. 'I'm sorry,' he said. 'I don't understand. What has all this to do with Dean?'

Mike cleared his throat. 'We don't know,' he said. 'Yet.'

Maree looked angry. 'Why can't you bloody well find them?'

'Could you ever, when they absconded before? When Dean went, you never found out where he was.'

'That was different.' She looked even more angry. 'They could have been kidnapped.'

'We know all that,' Mike said woodenly. 'We are trying, Maree.'

She sighed and sank back down on the sofa.

'This case ...' she said.

When Joanna returned to the station she was met by a triumphant Caro, who produced a pale, thin woman dressed in long, dangly earrings, a short skirt and bent stilettos.

'This is Dean's mother,' Caro said. Her triumph was complete – the magician had brought a live white rabbit out of a seemingly empty top hat. 'She answered our plea for the missing mother.'

'You'd better come into one of the interview rooms,' Joanna said. Caro didn't even ask. She knew the rules by now.

So Mike and Joanna faced the woman who claimed to be Dean's mother, and Joanna felt uneasy. She didn't know whether or not to say she was sorry. In the end she decided she should – however inappropriate it might be.

Joanna smiled. 'I'm – sorry about Dean,' she said, 'Mrs ... Miss ...?'

But the woman didn't look interested – let alone perturbed. 'Ms'll do me nicely,' she said. 'Gaynor's me name – Gaynor Tunstall. I actually was married – just the once. But it sort of fell through. Ever since then I've gone back to usin' me unmarried name.'

'Were you married to Dean's father?'

Gaynor Tunstall looked uneasy. 'Not exactly,' she said. She glanced around at Mike. 'Does he have to stay here?'

'Look, Gaynor ...' Joanna spoke frankly. 'We aren't pressing charges. The tape recorder is off. You came here of your own free will. We hope you might be able to help us find your son's killer. Gaynor,' she said softly, 'we need your help.'

She nodded sagely. ''Avin' trouble, are you?'

'It isn't proving an easy case,' Joanna said, 'but I rely on Detective Sergeant Korpanski. He is simply here because he might pick up something I miss. You understand?'

Gaynor nodded. 'Seems funny,' she said. 'I don't really think of him as my son.'

'Was he your son?'

She sighed. 'Deany ...? Yeah. He was mine all right.'

Joanna and Mike exchanged glances. 'Who was his father?'

Gaynor was like a sharp little bird. She put her head on one side. 'Who wants to know?' she demanded.

Joanna leaned forwards. 'Please,' she said.

She bit her lip. 'I can't really say,' she said. 'I was sort of – busy at the time. I suppose blood tests. But... I never bothered. It wasn't as if I was bringing him up anyway.' She looked at Joanna. 'I'm an 'opeless mum,' she said without apology. 'Just not born for it.' Then she glowered at Mike. 'Dean was my only mistake,' she said with dignity. 'And I did try with him. I tried 'ard. By the time 'e'd got to two I knew it was a waste of time. He was better off where he was. Home ... looked after ... clothes – schooling. Bloody social workers. They were always on at me. "'E's yours ..." You know the sort of thing. Mother love – something called bonding.' She gave a sharp cackle. 'Always reminded me of bondage.' She paused. 'It was a bloody waste of time. I couldn't cope. I never did Dean no good. I did the best for him.'

'You didn't think of having him adopted?'

Now Gaynor Tunstall looked indignant. 'What do you take me for? Give 'im away?'

Joanna leaned forward. 'Please, Gaynor,' she said. 'Can you think of any reason why anyone might have wanted to kill Dean?'

The woman frowned, thought for a moment, then

shook her head slowly. 'No,' she said. 'Kill Deany – no.' She blinked away a couple of tears. ''Ad the funeral yet?'

Joanna's face grew tight with dislike. 'No,' she said. 'We were missing the chief mourner.'

It was the photograph that led her there, early the following morning. Reluctantly leaving her bike in the garage, Joanna backed the car along the narrow lane and turned towards the moors.

She'd had a sleepless night pondering the picture of the three children. In the end, at half-past three, after tossing and turning and being denied sleep from every angle, she'd risen, slipped on a towelling dressing-gown and made herself a cup of blackcurrant tea, the picture in her hand. She had suddenly realised then why it had struck a lost chord. Behind the children was a rock – the crag of a hooked nose. She knew where they had been standing. And someone had taken the photograph.

That morning the moors seemed clothed in gold. No creeping soldiers, no burning corpses. Only the lone call of a curlew and the shriek of a fox cub. Looking around at the wide expanse of moors Joanna shivered and thought she knew no lonelier place on God's earth. It seemed cut off from civilisation, towns and streets. And yet there was a raw beauty up there – a sense of truth and purity. And she began to understand why Alice and Jonathan Rutter chose to live there in the dark and cold, through the northerly and easterly winds that had carved a man out of rock.

She began to climb. Thank God for strong legs.

She knew they were there before she reached the top. She could recognise the silhouette of tangled hair and Jason's thin shoulders. Tears moved into her eyes. Thank God, she thought. No more corpses ... dead children. The evil had not penetrated here.

The four of them were sitting round a small fire. Not one of them looked surprised to see her.

'Cup of tea,' Alice said comfortably.

Joanna cradled the filthy cup in her hands while the wind bit around her. 'Why didn't you tell me they were safe?'

'They told me not to.' Alice didn't look guilty or apologetic. She was merely stating facts. They had asked her not to tell.

'Thank God you're safe.'

Kirsty was shivering and pale. Jason doggedly determined.

'We knew we'd be safer up here.' Jason stared defiantly at Joanna. 'Trouble is,' he said, 'sometimes you don't know who your friends are. We knew her was all right.' He put his arm around Alice Rutter's shoulders. 'Her knows what it's like to be different, to be laughed at and have people on to you all the time. She aren't like them in the towns. You can trust 'er.'

'Yeah ...' Kirsty joined in. 'Trust 'er. You know where you are with 'er. We knew she weren't goin' to let us down.' She touched the old woman's cheek and Alice glared at Joanna.

'See,' she said, 'there aren't no harm up here. The boy were laid to rest 'ere. But he weren't killed 'ere. The evil happened in the town.' Her piece said, Alice shrugged her shoulders. But it deceived none of them. They knew she was pleased. 'We's clear people,' she said, 'Kids – they knows that.'

Kirsty was looking at her sharply and Alice nodded. 'Go get it, girl,' she said.

Kirsty rose, light as a little gazelle, hair streaming behind her as she dodged between the crags and disappeared into a narrow fissure. When she returned she was holding a bulky book. She handed it to Joanna. 'Dean's,' she said simply... and Joanna knew she had reached the epicentre of the boy's murder. To her side the granite profile of the man gave a slow, solemn wink. Perhaps some ancient law allows certain rocks to possess their own energy source.

The ring of faces watched her apprehensively, waiting. Perhaps for her to open the book. But she needed to do that alone. Instead she turned her attention to Alice Rutter. 'I could charge you, you know.' The words seemed to have no effect. Alice simply stared at her defiantly.

Joanna tried again. 'Wasting police time ... obstructing the course of justice.'

'We was frightened.' Jason moved closer to protect the old woman. A timid lamb protecting a buffalo?

Joanna felt she must make some attempt to make them understand. 'Didn't you think we might be concerned about you?'

Kirsty's green eyes were fixed on hers. 'What's going to 'appen to them?' she demanded, and Joanna knew the child's sole concern was for the two cave-dwellers. In her own fate she showed no interest. 'Will they get into trouble – just for lookin' after us? It don't seem fair. They was only 'elping.'

Joanna clutched the album closer to her chest.

'I very much doubt we'll be pressing charges against them. But it does all have to go in the report. We wasted a great deal of time and effort searching for you both.'

They were still watching her.

'It isn't up to me.'

Alice stood up then, clutched her coat around her, moved closer to her husband. 'But we'll have to leave here?'

'It's nothing to do with the police, Alice. Social services will have to decide. And the people who own this land. They may evict you. They may allow you to stay.'

'Excuse me ...' Jason was touching her arm timidly. 'Where shall we stay tonight?'

There was something resigned about the way he asked it. Something in the thin face that spoke of many decisions made in which he had played no part except to comply.

'You'll be safe back at The Nest,' Joanna said finally.

'And Alice and Jonathan?'

'Can remain here – for now.'

As she led the two children down the track she saw the silhouettes of the two rock-dwellers side by side with the profile of the Winking Man. And she could almost imagine that if the social workers did climb the rocks to evict Alice and Jonathan Rutter, they would find no people, only three stone statues.

15

Joanna sat in her office, poring over each page of the photograph album, a part of her crying at the pathetic, childish scrawl, arrows pointing to 'my mother', 'my father', 'my uncle and auntie', 'my grandpa and grandma' ... Little footnotes. 'This is my mum when she was a little girl.' 'Me and my grandpa.' Dean's handwriting. All lies.

And through the Leeches' missing photograph album the whole futile, tragic story began to emerge. She read it and felt angry.

Mike turned up at nine, yawning and ruffling both hands through his hair. Mid-yawn he stopped and stared at Joanna. 'I thought it was your bike outside,' he said. 'What's up?'

She opened the album, still feeling furious at the cheating and manipulation. 'I know exactly what happened,' she said. 'I know why. I know who. I've got a warrant to search Robin Leech's flat and car. I want him cautioned and brought in.'

He blinked. 'You've found something out?'

She gave a wry smile. 'The value of a sleepless night. And by the way, I've found the children.'

'Thank God,' he said. 'Where are they?'

'Safe.'

She stood up. 'We've got him, you know,' she said, tapping the photograph album. 'We've got him.'

'If you mean Leech,' Mike said, 'the SOC team are ready for the kill.'

Rock House looked dignified at 11 o'clock that morning, and as the cavalcade of police cars moved slowly up the drive Joanna found it difficult to connect the sordid, modern crime with this bastion of Victorian housing. The cars drove past the front door and round to the courtyard at the back, to the stable block. Robin Leech walked out right on cue.

'Robin Leech,' Joanna said formally, 'we have a warrant here to search your premises.'

His eyes flickered. 'Are you arresting me?'

'We would like you to come down to the station for questioning.'

'Are – you – arresting me?'

Joanna nodded. 'Robin Leech,' she said, 'we are arresting you in connection with the murder of Dean Tunstall and the murder of Keith Latos. You do not have to say anything. But it may harm your defence if you do not mention when questioned something that you later rely on in court. Anything you do say may be given in evidence.'

He blinked.

But it was as she cautioned him that the first, startling doubts were seeded. Something was wrong. Murderers were often shocked that they had been found out. Sometimes they were still confident their lawyers would get them off the hook and seemed nonchalant ... Some were frightened ... But Robin Leech looked genuinely astonished. He stood his ground, opening and closing his mouth like a fish.

'What did you say?'

Joanna cautioned him again just as Gilly Leech rounded the side of the house, crossing the courtyard.

Leech looked helplessly at her. 'They're accusing me,' he said.

She stared at him, lips pressed tightly together. For a long moment mother and son stood frozen, then Gilly Leech turned to Joanna and shot her a venomous glance. 'What's going on?'

Mike stepped forward. 'We're taking your son down to the station,' he said. 'Just for some questions.'

She stared at him, her face strained and taut. 'Questions?' she repeated stupidly. 'Questions?' She looked back at her son. 'Robin?'

'Mother ...' It was an appeal. 'Mother.'

She moved towards him, her face twisted in concern. Then she turned to Joanna. 'Have you charged him?'

Joanna nodded, the tension of the figures standing so still in the courtyard reaching her. Even the team of police officers preparing to strip the premises of all forensic evidence stood back – witnesses to the drama.

'Take the handcuffs off.' Gilly Leech's voice was so quiet Joanna could hardly hear her. She spoke again. 'I said take the handcuffs off him.' She looked at Joanna. 'He didn't do it,' she said. 'It wasn't him. Robin ...' She glanced at her son – half-contemptuous, half-pitying. 'Well, let's just say he doesn't really have the balls.'

When none of the police officers moved, she

spoke again. 'I killed the brat,' she said. 'For God's sake. I killed him. Now let Robin go. I killed him – took the body away from here – tried to get rid of it. I wish to God I had succeeded in wiping the little swine off the face of the earth.'

Mike caught Joanna's eye and raised his eyebrows. Neither would forget this day.

The SOCOs did their work. Forensic samples, numbered one to 51, provided the Crown Prosecution Service with enough to take the case to the Crown Court. Exhibit one – Wilderness coat, torn, scorched, matches in pocket, a positive test for petrol. Exhibits 14 to 19 – hairs with the same DNA as the hair taken from Dean Tunstall's scalp at post-mortem. Short, blond, recently cut. Exhibit 21 – found in dishwasher, unwashed ... knife, blood-stained, similar to the instrument used to sever Keith Latos's neck. The blood stains proved to match Keith Latos's blood group. Exhibit 30 – clothes spattered with blood ... the pattern on the arms proved by an expert witness to have been worn by the assailant at the time of the attack. Exhibit 34 – the saddest exhibit of all – one pair of shabby, worn red and black trainers under the bed, probably kicked there by Dean when he spied a new pair. Why should he have cared that they were the wrong size, someone else's. They were new.

'Wriggle out of this lot,' Joanna muttered.

As the car moved down the drive, Gilly Leech turned to Joanna and spoke with cold dislike. 'Inspector,' she said, 'I expect you're wondering why.' There was a certain conceit in her voice.

Joanna nodded.

Gilly Leech wriggled back in her seat, her eyes staring straight ahead. 'Did you ever read a story called the farmer and the snake?' Without waiting for a reply she spoke in a clear, harsh tone. 'A farmer found a snake stiff and frozen with the cold. He placed it in his bosom. But the snake – revived by the warmth – bit him and the farmer died. Dying he cried out, "I am rightly served for pitying a scoundrel".' Her voice was very clear. 'Dean was that snake. My husband,' she said haughtily, 'gave that child all the affection he ever received.'

Joanna was angry now. 'You may call it affection, Mrs Leech,' she said. 'I happen to call it perversion. Dean Tunstall was probably less than eight years old when your husband first abused him.'

Gilly Leech tossed her head. 'You police have no imagination,' she said.

'I do have an imagination,' Joanna retorted. 'I can only too well imagine what it was like for Dean, especially after he discovered he had contracted Aids – that is, if he ever realised he had.'

Ashford Leech's widow took absolutely no notice. 'So can you imagine, Inspector, what it was like for me? A boy my husband had befriended – claiming all sorts of heinous things against my husband.' She spread her thin hands out. 'Ashford was dead. He couldn't defend himself.'

'Neither could Dean,' Joanna said quietly. 'He was quite defenceless both emotionally and physically.'

They had arrived at the police station, Robin Leech protesting, Gilly Leech defiant. As they climbed out of the car, Joanna spoke. 'By the way, Mrs Leech,' she said, 'your solicitor will advise you of something. If you can't retain your silence and plead innocent convincingly it's far, far better to display some measure of remorse.'

Gilly Leech gave her a look of sweet poison.

While the custody officer was taking down the details of the Leech family, Joanna had a word with Mike.

'It was all in here,' she said, indicating the photograph album. 'The whole lot. We should have known – the photograph album and the ring. Two things to identify Dean with his family. Cheap jewellery he thought was his mother's.'

Mike stared. 'Come on, Jo,' he said. 'His family was Gaynor.'

'That's the tragedy,' she said. 'It is true. Gaynor Tunstall really was his mother. His father really was unknown. But what did Dean know? He only knew what he was told, Mike. People kept telling us that for all his streetwise ways he was quite naive. Naive and vulnerable.'

She opened the album on the first page. '"My mum when she was a little girl."' Tears threatened. 'Pathetic,' she said. 'Leech told Dean that he was his grandfather, and that he was the son of his daughter, Fleur. He gave the boy pictures.' She turned the page. '"Their house." "My grandmother."' Joanna paused. 'It allowed Leech to become close to the child. And in time he began abusing Dean. Dean probably thought this was a loving family. After all, compared with the treatment the likes of Gary Swinton was giving him, it was love. Leech gave him things – looked after him. Loved him.'

'Dead men don't kill, Jo,' Mike reminded her. 'It wasn't Ashford Leech. It was his widow.'

They could hear Gilly Leech's unmistakable haughty voice travelling up the corridor.

'The second clue was sitting there. We failed to

recognise it for what it was. The new shoe was cross-laced. It never came from the basket outside the shop. We thought it had been bought for or stolen by Dean. It was bought by Leech's son Robin – for himself. I expect Dean saw them and liked them, took them. Latos knew the shoes had been bought – and by whom. He probably tried to capitalise on the knowledge.

'I suppose after Ashford Leech's death Dean felt naturally he could appeal to the woman he believed was his grandmother. Damn it, Mike,' she said angrily, 'how can a kid have so little knowledge of true family relationships?'

Mike could find nothing to say and Joanna carried on, puzzled. 'For some reason, for a while she played along with it. Perhaps it seemed the most expedient thing to do. But it carried dangers. As long as Dean perceived her as a blood relative she could never shake him off. And unlike her husband she had no real gain – certainly no sexual advantage. Unfortunately, though Dean was naive in family relationships, he did understand some things.' She tapped the photograph album. 'Just think what the tabloids would make of this.'

There was an ominous silence along the corridor of the police station.

Mike spoke first. 'Solicitor speaking to client?'

'Let's go and have a chat to Gilly, shall we?'

As they approached the interview room she added, 'The solicitor may well persuade her to plead involuntary manslaughter, but I believe she intended to kill him, and we'll work together on the case for premeditated murder. Mike, if she bought the petrol can before she killed him we have a strong case. If not ...' She stopped. 'Well, it's up to us and the CPS and that worm of a lawyer to work something out.' She stopped. 'I just regret Ashford Leech, the biggest shit of them all, is beyond the law.'

Mike chuckled. 'Depends what religion you are.' She laughed and put her hand on his shoulder.

It was early the next morning that Robin Leech was finally put into the picture and, as Joanna had half expected, he blustered for an hour or two, then supported his mother all the way.

Gilly Leech, meanwhile, whatever her lawyer advised, was unrepentant.

'He was a filthy, illiterate little sod,' she said.

'Do you mean the deceased?' Joanna was determined to make heavy mileage out of this prosecution.

'Dean – the little sod.'

'Who made the boy into a sod?' Joanna asked sharply.

'He didn't even count,' Gilly Leech said slowly. 'People like my husband. They count. Look at what he achieved. MP for more than 30 years. Well respected, and he had a hand in laws on many topics ... Field-planning and city policies. Defence and industry. Important things. He was an important man. If he happened to want something personal that was unusual, well ... he was an unusual man. What harm did it do?'

'An enormous amount.'

'The boy was a nothing,' she said contemptuously. 'A nothing. Latos too – sleazy little piece of crap.'

Mike had to say something. 'Funny,' he said

softly. 'In police college they never taught us anyone was a nothing. To them, murder is murder ... never mind who the dead person was.'

She shot him a fleeting glance.

The solicitor gave a swift peep at his watch. His face reddened. He was not enjoying himself.

'Unfortunately, my husband was struck down in his prime by disease.' She looked down her nose at Joanna. 'Do you know how he acquired Aids? Far Eastern fleshpots. He was forced there. Scandal, you see, in this country, would have been disastrous.'

'Disastrous?' Joanna didn't even try to keep the sarcasm out of her voice.

Mrs Leech shrugged her shoulders. 'And this filthy little tyke was threatening to take his story to some tabloid – get some money. Posed as one of the family. One of the family ... Imagine. I gave him money,' she said casually. 'I let him stay in the flat. I wanted him to get out, leave me alone. I gave him the chance.' She made a desperate pulling action on her clothes as though trying to free herself from hidden bonds. 'He kept insisting he was part of the family. My family.'

Then she looked at Joanna with an intelligent sharpness. 'I shall say it was an accident,' she said calmly, 'not murder. I shall say there was no premeditation, but there was provocation. I warn you, Inspector. You're not dealing with some plebeian half-wit here. I'm a clever woman and I can afford a good lawyer.'

Mike leaned across the table. 'You can have bloody Marshall Hall,' he said. 'I don't think you'll get off.'

Again Gilly Leech chose to ignore the remark

until Mike goaded her again. 'And what about Latos?'

'I shall say I panicked,' she said. 'I shall say he threatened me.' She held out thin arms. 'I'm not a big woman. I shall say I picked up the first thing that came into my hand.' She glared at Joanna. 'Prove otherwise,' she challenged.

Joanna knew the work was not over yet. The familiar battle of wits and lies, of stories and angles, of deals and burdens of proof, was just beginning.

Hours of work still lay ahead of her, and if the whole case was not carried out perfectly, even the hard-baked Gilly Leech could go free, with a clever solicitor. Joanna smiled to herself. The one the Leeches had landed themselves with so far was not clever enough. They would need better than him. Joanna rolled her pencil between her fingers and pondered what Gilly's plea would be ... Diminished responsibility? Provocation?

Mike walked in and dropped down on the chair opposite. 'I always feel like this,' he complained, 'when a case finishes. Flat – really flat.'

'I know,' she agreed. 'It's all I can do to put pen to paper.' She met his eyes. 'Mike,' she said, 'I'm glad we got her.'

He nodded then gave a huge yawn, stretching his arms above his head. 'Want a drink?'

She shook her head. 'You', she said laughing, 'should get back home to your wife.'

He looked at her curiously. 'What about you?'

She shuffled the sheaf of papers tidy and flipped an elastic band around them. 'First of all,' she said, 'I'm going to finish this case and watch it through the courts, see her sentenced. Then ... then I think I'm going to take a holiday.' Now she stretched and yawned too. 'After I've had a long, hot bath.'

'Then what?'

She stood up. 'Who knows?'

Eloise sat between her parents on the flight home. She glanced from one to the other and seemed satisfied with what she saw. Then she slipped her small hand into her father's.

'Home,' she said, and gave a happy smile.

ABOUT THE AUTHOR

Priscilla Masters was born in 1952 in Halifax, Yorkshire and adopted at six weeks old by an orthopaedic surgeon and his Classics graduate wife – number three of seven multi-racial adopted children! She moved to Birmingham at the age of 16, and qualified as a registered nurse at the Queen Elizabeth Hospital in 1973.

A lifelong fan of crime novels, she began writing in the mid 1980s in response to a challenge made by an aunt asking her what she intended doing with the rest of her life. She borrowed a typewriter the next day. In 1995 the first of her DI Joanna Piercy novels, *Winding up the Serpent*, was published by Pan Macmillan. She has now written 11 Joanna Piercy novels in total and is currently working on the twelfth. She has also written five novels set in Shropshire featuring Shrewsbury Coroner Martha Gunn, and a number of medical stand-alones dealing with such issues as the blurred line between sanity and insanity, the arrogance of a surgeon and the difficulties faced by a female GP.

She is married to a doctor, now retired and running a successful antiques business in Leek, Staffordshire, which is where her Joanna Piercy novels are set. They have two sons and two grandsons.

ALSO AVAILABLE FROM TELOS PUBLISHING

CRIME

PRISCILLA MASTERS
WINDING UP THE SERPENT
A WREATH FOR MY SISTER
AND NONE SHALL SLEEP
EMBROIDERING SHROUDS
SCARING CROWS

MIKE RIPLEY
JUST ANOTHER ANGEL
ANGEL TOUCH
ANGEL HUNT
ANGEL ON THE INSIDE
ANGEL CONFIDENTIAL
ANGEL CITY
ANGELS IN ARMS
FAMILY OF ANGELS
BOOTLEGGED ANGEL
THAT ANGEL LOOK

HELEN MCCABE
PIPER
THE PIERCING

ANDREW HOOK
THE IMMORTALISTS
CHURCH OF WIRE

HANK JANSON

TORMENT
WOMEN HATE TILL DEATH
SOME LOOK BETTER DEAD
SKIRTS BRING ME SORROW
WHEN DAMES GET TOUGH
ACCUSED
KILLER
FRAILS CAN BE SO TOUGH
BROADS DON'T SCARE EASY
KILL HER IF YOU CAN
LILIES FOR MY LOVELY
BLONDE ON THE SPOT
THIS WOMAN IS DEATH
THE LADY HAS A SCAR

OTHER CRIME

THE LONG, BIG KISS GOODBYE
by SCOTT MONTGOMERY

NON-FICTION

THE TRIALS OF HANK JANSON
by STEVE HOLLAND

TELOS PUBLISHING LTD
Email: orders@telos.co.uk
Web: www.telos.co.uk

To order copies of any Telos books, please visit our
website where there are full details of all titles and
facilities for worldwide credit card online ordering, as
well as occasional special offers.

CPSIA information can be obtained
at www.ICGtesting.com
Printed in the USA
LVHW041535151118
597260LV00012B/924/P